# WANTED BOYS

# WANTED BOYS

**A NOVEL**

## S.E. McPHERSON

Cover illustration and design by S.E. McPherson

ISBN 979-8-9922543-7-2

TO THE ONES WHO NEEDED TO HEAR
THERE WAS NOTHING WRONG WITH THEM

For a full list of content warnings
and ending spoilers for anxious readers, visit
**semcpherson.com/books/wanted-boys**

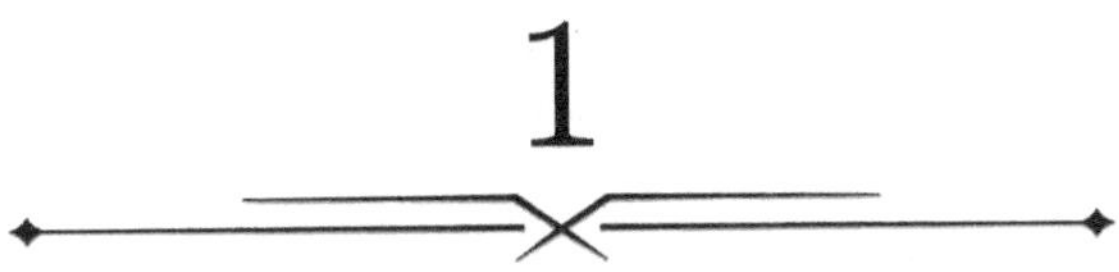

## A CHANGE OF EXISTENCE

Because he technically did not exist, Logan dropped to his belly the second the knock sounded at the door. Heart pumping ice, hands palsied with fear, he crawled on knees and elbows to the basement stairs, then lurched down in four bounding steps. Above, he heard his mother's quick jerky steps, the shush of the wheels on his father's chair as they both reacted more slowly to the sound than Logan did.

*Knock–knock–knock.* Three sharp raps from glove-muffled knuckles came again.

Logan scrambled through the darkness before crouching between the weight set and the storage boxes of old toys. Although folding his tall body under the stairs was harder than it had been when he was a kid, he did it silently, knowing those at the door could hear everything that went on in the basement, just as he heard them. Knees pressed to the cold, concrete floor, he took shallow gasps of the musty air. He stared fixedly at the sun-and-sky-painted canvas hung over the narrow window in front of him years ago by his mother to make the unfinished basement feel more like home.

Heavily his mother's steps moved toward the door as though she fought a great weight to drag herself toward it. "Hello. Can I help you?" Her voice held a noticeable quaver, which meant no neighbor or friend had knocked.

Logan's heart galloped harder, and he tried keeping his breathing quiet as his lungs crammed themselves into his windpipe. Three sets of steel-lined boots thumped onto the creaking boards of the entry hall—oh, *God*, it was the Black Lapels. Logan swallowed hard, past the ball of panic wedged in his throat. If they were here, they already knew.

He scanned the basement for an escape route—anywhere— but the windows down here didn't open, and running up the stairs would mean heading straight into their arms. Like a beetle under a glass, he was trapped, and so were his parents.

"Where's your son, Mrs. Cardot?" The question was so cold, so casual in a stranger's deep, unfeeling voice.

Logan's mother laughed nervously, frantic as a bird beating wings against a closed window. "My...son? I'm afraid I don't have a son, Officer. You must be mistaken."

The floor squealed ominously as someone shifted their weight. "Mrs. Cardot, we don't have the time or patience for denial. We wouldn't be here if you didn't have a son. Now where is he?"

"We don't—ah!" Even through the floor, Logan heard the panicked noises his mother tried to suppress. "Please don't shoot. Please, please. We don't have—"

Something thudded, a merciless strike on flesh; Logan's mom cried out. The hardwood planks groaned as everyone overhead moved at once. His dad bellowed something, but fear and helplessness strained his voice, not anger. Not fighting back.

Logan squeezed his eyes shut, hands shaking in fists curled against his stomach. *No, no, no. How could they have found me? How could they have found my family?*

"Cardot boy?" a man shouted. "You're going to step out here quietly. Your unauthorized caregivers are already under arrest. If we're not able to take you into protective custody, we'll have to assume you've come to harm under their care. We'd hate to see anyone die over a misunderstanding. Wouldn't you? It'd be better for everyone if you came with us."

His mother wept with small, defeated bleats, a sound he'd never heard her make. Logan could picture the scene above: the Black Lapels would have their pistols out, pointed at his mother, pointed at his father in his wheelchair. The Hallsburg Special Police had no reputation for mercy. What good would it do him to hide if they killed his parents? He had nothing without them. The idea of a world without his mother's warmth, his father's steady patience was unconscionable. He'd do anything not to lose that.

Even if he could hole up until his mom and dad were hauled away to prison, what then? He couldn't show his face outside the house until he turned eighteen, which was four months away—he *was not* supposed to exist.

As he unfolded himself and stood, his knees threatened to give way, but he gripped the handrail and hauled himself up one monumental step at a time. Although he knew they heard his every step, no one called down or made a move until he emerged at the top of the stairs, his view of his parents framed through the bars of the stair rail.

Logan's mother leaned against his father's chair, her hands behind her back and one side of her gray-tinseled black hair shaken over her face. She stared at her husband's lap, where his cuffed hands lay palm up. It was the only way to avoid staring into the muzzle of the squared black pistol pointed inches from her head. Logan's dad looked at him, though, with so much written on his face that Logan could make nothing of his expression at all. His warm, gray eyes, usually crinkled with laughter, shone with tears. Logan had never seen him cry.

A meaty-fingered hand gripped Logan's upper arm, drawing him back from his parents so sharply that he tripped over his feet. In a fleeting moment of hope, he wondered if he could bluff, pretend he was a neighbor kid or a student of his mother's that had dropped by for a visit. But he wasn't a good liar, and he was wearing his mother's dark hair and naturally upturned lips, his father's gray eyes and straight brows.

"Unregistered Cardot, the state of Hallsburg has authorized me to take you into protective custody under section 634.12 of the Juvenile Custody and Parental Privileges Act. Will I need to cuff you or will you cooperate?"

The Black Lapel held Logan so he couldn't turn to see his face. What had the officer asked him? He couldn't think; he nodded, hoping it was an appropriate answer. His mom still didn't look at him; instead she sank to the floor an inch at a time, as though gravity had become too much for her.

"Good," the Black Lapel said crisply. Then he resumed his dry, clearly oft-repeated speech. "You'll be held in protective custody for no more than twenty-four hours before an officer delivers you to Child Rehoming Services, which will appoint a caseworker to find an appropriate rehoming situation for you."

With a small, desperate moan, Logan's mother collapsed, sobs shaking her body.

"Mom!" With the officer holding his arms so tightly, he couldn't step forward to help her up—not without starting a fight he was ill-equipped for—and his father couldn't reach her, especially with his hands cuffed, so she remained in a heap, ignored by the two other Black Lapels, who watched Logan with bored, hooded eyes.

"Why are you doing this?" Logan demanded. "We haven't done anything wrong. I'm almost an adult, for God's sake!"

"Yes," the officer holding him said acidly. "You *are* almost an adult. You're probably unsalvageable now, full of their radical poison. If I had my way, we'd put you in Shalecrest right along with them. But seventeen is still *technically* a child, so—"

They marched Logan out separately from his parents before putting him in the back of a black car, followed by his parents in another. Through the back window he watched as they hefted his father into the backseat next to his mom, leaving the wheelchair on the sidewalk. They'd left the front door of the little brick house wide-open. Logan must have left some internal organs back there as well, because his chest was altogether too hollow.

The next few days passed in a gray-and-beige blur during which Logan felt barely conscious: long, silent periods of waiting on benches and office chairs and hard mattresses and the backseats of government vehicles. Some folks were kind to him; others were angry; still others treated him like he was furniture. He gave them all the same empty stare.

No matter what they offered—even pot roast like his father made—he couldn't bear to eat, but they didn't care enough to force the issue. He couldn't recall if he had slept. Everything was a nightmare, whether he was asleep or awake. His parents were gone. After that last glimpse of them being hauled into the Black Lapel vehicle, he hadn't seen them. For all he knew, they'd been shot and rolled back out of the squad car onto the road, though more likely they'd been delivered to one of the Shalecrest work camps.

The headlines said Shalecrest was a "triumph of reeducation and industry," with the women's camp producing medical supplies and the men's camp producing weapons and vehicles. Logan's father said Shalecrest was best at producing corpses.

He became more conscious of his surroundings as he was loaded into a government sedan and driven to Childers Coast, which he was told was a home for kids like him, born illegally to unlicensed parents with whom they couldn't be left. His overly cheerful CRS caseworker chirpily declared this his "new home and chance for a better life." He wanted to sock her in the face.

They pulled up a long, narrow road through woods that grew sparser until a sprawling brick and stone building appeared through the trees: a massive central block that reached a dozen octopoid halls to smaller brick towers.

The blonde woman with her permanent, ghoulish smile sat him on a wooden bench outside the director's office, where he tried not to fidget. Across from him hung a poster with the silhouette of a Black Lapel posed like a superhero, along with PROTECT OUR WAY OF LIFE in heavy block letters. Logan's eyes skittered away from it and traced the pale green walls and white trim; the speckled linoleum; the rows and rows of doors lining the long, wide hallway.

Childers Coast was a dismal place, smelling of pink, institutional hand soap and echoing with the distant phantom calls of children. He contemplated fleeing out the front doors, sprinting until he was so far away no one had ever heard of the Black Lapels. There'd been no fence around this place, no walls trapping the children into the wooded grounds.

But running would mean death. He had no money, no ID, no prospects. As much as he hated it, he needed this place.

On the other side of the wall, the adults' discussion reached a low, intense murmur. During the ride over, his caseworker had assured him there was no chance he'd be turned away, but as the conversation stretched longer, he wasn't certain. Everything else had already gone wrong. At any moment, they might decide he deserved to be pounding sheet metal in a cramped cell at Shalecrest instead.

To stop the irritating clenching and unclenching of his hands, Logan plucked a brochure from the clear plastic stand on the end table. They were dusty, like no one had read them in ages. But why would they need to? According to the CRS lady, "everyone" had heard of Childers Coast.

He flipped open the trifold and settled back to read the section titled "Our History."

*Childers Coast Home has stood at the northmost corner of the Lenning Sea for nearly fifty years, since General McGregor's Great Division fractured the nation into city-states and created a flood of orphaned and displaced children.*

*His rival General Reeves not only provided the funds to build larger dormitories, hire more nurses, and bring private schooling within Childers Coasts' walls, but as part of his glorious restructuring of Hallsburg following his victory, he also established our current system of strict licensing requirements for parents, requiring genetic, physical, and IQ testing; proof of income that meets required levels; establishment of permanent residence; reliable work history; and a stable parental relationship.*

*Prospective parents who meet all requirements are issued a license for one, two, or three children, depending on their creditworthiness. Existing parents who fail in one or more areas and are not able to remedy it within six months are required to surrender their children to the state.*

*Although children who can be are rehomed with approved couples without children of their own, unauthorized children who cannot be properly placed require a safe and structured environment in which to develop. General Reeves, First Chancellor of Hallsburg, established Childers Coast as one of the official homes of boys who cannot be placed with a family and our sister school, Ambrosia Hall, for girls.*

*Today, Childers Coast houses, feeds, clothes, schools, and cares for nearly four thousand boys ranging in age from newborns to eighteen. We have—*

The director's door opened with a thud, rattling its pane of frosted glass. Logan's head shot up, and the brochure fell from suddenly sweaty fingers.

A paunchy, red-faced man with a genial light in his eyes, the director stepped out first and shook Logan's hand with a smile. "Welcome to Childers Coast, Mr. Cardot. I'm Director Rollins."

A pallid sense of relief rose somewhere beneath the bleak, blank layers of shock Logan had been wrapped in since the Black Lapels had darkened his door.

"So…I'm accepted? I can stay? The CRS rep said because my parents didn't surrender me and I didn't turn myself in—"

"I assure you, Mr. Cardot," Director Rollins said, squeezing Logan's shoulder companionably, "you are most welcome here. If you'll follow Ms. Lee, she'll show you to your dormitory. You're lucky—a bed just opened up with the older boys in Eagle Hold."

The names were nonsense to Logan, but he followed obediently, leaving his caseworker to make arrangements and fill out the paperwork. He supposed he was officially an orphan now. He wished he could feel…anything about it, but he was so desperately empty.

Ms. Lee, the director's secretary, was a slender woman with mouse-brown hair and a breathy voice that made it difficult to understand her as she talked over her shoulder at him. She said something unintelligible as Logan half jogged to catch up with her.

"Sorry, what?"

She glanced back at him with a patient sort of exasperation, then repeated herself. "I said, you'll be rooming with one of our more notorious residents. You seem like a nice, quiet boy. I hope you won't let Mr. Evans be a bad influence on you."

"I'll…do my best." He didn't expect he'd be talking to anyone enough for them to influence him.

He received a stack of linens, two spare uniforms to wear until his custom order came in, and a small bag of toiletries. "Oh, I brought the toothbrush and the stuff CRS gave me," he said, but Ms. Lee pushed the bag into his hands anyway.

"Everyone gets one. At some point, you'll run out of what you brought. Just let Ms. Lowell know—she's the dean of Eagle Hold— if you need anything. She'll make sure you get it."

Ms. Lee trotted down a set of stairs and opened a polished wood door. She and Logan passed through a common room. Boys of all ages sprawled over couches and chairs, reading, talking, snacking, and killing time. All stopped to stare as Logan walked past.

"He looks old enough to be gettin' the boot already!" someone said in a whisper that carried to every corner of the room.

Logan flushed, avoiding the eyes on him. Because of his life in hiding as an unauthorized child, he'd never been around many people. Aside from the very occasional trusted family friend, he'd interacted with no one but his parents. The attention of so many at once was nauseatingly claustrophobic.

Up another set of stairs and into a corridor they went, walking past a series of doors until the hall dead-ended in another staircase. Up, up, up to another corridor and another long set of doors on the left wall. Finally, they reached the last door on the left, and Ms. Lee rapped sharply on the wood frame. "Staff call," she said loudly.

A rustle of hurried movement was audible on the other side of the wall as Ms. Lee smiled to herself and counted to three under her breath. Then she opened the door, revealing a narrow room with eight twin-size beds draped in pinned-back green curtains, four on each wall, with heavy trunks at the foot and a small bookshelf at the head of each. Seven teenage boys sat, lay, or stood around the room, curiosity on every face.

"Oi, a newbie, at our age?" said one of the boys incredulously. By far the smallest in the room, the boy had dark hair cut too short so it stood up in the back.

"Yes, Mr. Bailey. Give him a proper Childers Coast welcome. This is Logan Cardot, and he'll be taking Mr. Dodd's old bed." Ms. Lee gestured toward the second bunk from the door on the right, and Logan plodded over uncomfortably, dropping his pile of linens and clothing on the mattress. To Logan, she said, "Ms. Lowell will have your class and chores schedule sorted in the morning."

She left, shutting the door behind her, her absence leaving silent stares in its wake. Logan surveyed the boys he'd be sharing a room with and tried not to cringe from the curious gawping.

The boy in the bed directly across from Logan's slid down and padded across the room in his bare feet. He was tall, certainly over six feet, and probably about Logan's height, and when he grinned at the newcomer, his uneven smile made one blue eye crinkle more than the other.

"Hey, Logan. I'm Jace Evans. Welcome to ChilCo Eagle."

Jace extended a hand to shake, and Logan took it. When the boy's strong grip nearly crushed his hand, Logan fought down the competitive urge to tighten his own with difficulty. "Evans? You're the bad influence I've been warned about then."

Jace laughed, releasing Logan's hand. The other boys snickered along with him, though all of it seemed good-natured. "That's me. Voted 'Most likely to get arrested before I'm old enough to get the boot' ten years running. If you believe the administration, these boys here are my 'gang' of unruly youths." The other boys laughed harder.

"So…you're not a gang or you're not unruly?" Logan asked, trying to get a feel for the room. He'd never had to do this kind of thing before, make friends out of nothing. He'd been homeschooled and hidden his entire life. He wasn't sure he was up for this now, but it had been thrust upon him whether or not he was ready.

"Logan, buddy, we're both." Jace clapped Logan on the shoulder, then draped a friendly arm around him and led him from one end of the room to the other to meet the rest.

There was Larry Quintz, a small boy with wide, friendly brown eyes, called "Squints" because of his bad eyesight, even with glasses. Randall Halls, called Randy, had straight red hair and a smattering of freckles, and was the only other boy close to the same height as Jace and Logan. Todd Bailey—nicknamed "Bails"—had a big mouth, both literally and figuratively; he continued to express his amazement that someone would be brought to ChilCo so late until Jace lightly advised him to shut the fuck up. The other three were the Bens: Ben Perrey, Ben Witemeyer, and Ben Mitchell barely bothered to identify themselves individually. Each had dirty blond hair, brown eyes, and gangly limbs.

All the boys had been at ChilCo for at least a decade, bunked together; they were clearly close, and Logan felt a small twinge of regret that he'd never have a chance to break into their close-knit circle before he came of age and was asked to leave.

"So, Squints, Randy, Bails, and the Bens," Logan said, gesturing to each boy in turn.

"And Jace!" Jace reminded him.

The boys had formed a circle around Logan, and he turned to face Jace as the other boy spoke. "And Jace," he agreed. There was something nice about the crinkling around Jace's blue eyes. Logan and his parents all had gray eyes; that bright blue was something of a pleasant shock.

He shook himself and turned away before he was caught staring; even a homeschooled kid knew better than to announce to his brand-new roommates just *how* different he was.

"So what *are* you doing here at this age?" Bails said, sitting at the foot of Logan's bed. All the boys seemed to take this as a cue, plopping down on the beds on either side of Logan's. Logan sat against his headboard, knees drawn up to his chest.

The thought of recounting the events of the week made him so nauseous that he felt the vomit in his throat, tasted its acrid tang. But they were all looking at him, waiting for him to say something.

"Bails," Squints said irritably, "not everyone wants to talk about how they got here." Squints gave Logan a very warm look, and the small kindness buoyed Logan up.

"No, it's okay," Logan said. He had to swallow twice to clear the frogginess from his voice. He peered up at the faces around him, taking in the boys' rapt attention. If his stories of the outside world were the only currency he had with which to buy friendships at the moment, he supposed he could find it in himself to spend it. "I was born unauthorized. My parents pretty much hid me in the basement for most of my life. Since I obviously couldn't go to school—"

"Holy shit, you've never learned anything? What's two plus two?" Bails interjected. Randy and Squints, seated on either side of him, elbowed him hard in the chest to shut him up.

"No, I did learn. My mom—" As he pictured his mother on the last day, crumpled and sobbing, his breath caught in his chest. Wrestling his mind back into the present moment took a monumental effort. "My mom's a teacher at the public school—uh, she was. She'd bring home some of her books and teach me at night."

Logan sighed. "I guess somebody figured it out. The Black Lapels showed up at my house a week ago. They took my parents to…to Shalecrest, and they put me in CRS." He shrugged, trying to make this sound like it wasn't the worst, most earth-shattering thing that could ever have happened. "No one wants to waste a rehoming credit on a seventeen-year-old, I guess, so my caseworker brought me here."

"Shalecrest," Squints muttered. "Dude, that's rough." The other boys murmured their assent and their sympathies. Unspoken, the stories of Shalecrest's murderous conditions—of people packed too tightly into rooms so they died standing up, unable to breathe; of people cutting themselves on tools and being allowed to die slowly of the infections that followed, pieces of their bodies dropping off as they continued to work; of the experiments that made the women's prison so prolific in its production of new medical supplies—were so heavy in their collective thoughts they made the air hard to breathe.

There was a moment of silence, and then one of the Bens asked, "So are you coming on the raid with us tonight?"

"Raid?" The abrupt change of subject baffled Logan.

Everyone turned to Jace, apparently expecting him to explain. Logan was glad for a reason to place his undivided attention on the curly-haired, blue-eyed boy.

Jace absorbed their attention smirkingly for a long moment, savoring it without speaking, before gesturing at one of the Bens. "Get the lockpick."

What the Ben pulled out of Jace's footlocker was most certainly not a lockpick. In fact, it looked like a—

"Is that a bomb?" Logan blurted.

Jace laughed, taking the "lockpick" and tossing it lightly from hand to hand. "A very small incendiary device," he corrected. "It's our key into the science labs."

"Why do you want to get into the labs?" Logan seized onto the curiosity that rose up in him like a raft in a sea of less pleasant thoughts and emotions. He supposed he ought to feel uneasy about whatever they were planning, but he'd lived most of his life illegally—what was a little mischief now that the worst had happened and he'd been discovered?

Jace grinned, delighted by the question. "These guys want to get into the chem lab and swipe some sodium and magnesium for base-level pranks." He rolled his eyes, but the rest of the boys laughed gleefully. "I've got my own plans for the electrical lab. But don't forget my potassium nitrate, guys."

"All right," Logan said, shrugging. Any distraction from the crumbling remnants of his life would do, at present. "I'm game." He thought about what Jace had said. "But if you're trying to make nitric acid, don't play around with potassium nitrate. Doing that process with whatever shit you can steal and carry up here will get your hands blown off."

Jace raised an eyebrow at Logan. "What makes you think I want nitric acid?"

Now it was Logan's turn to raise his eyebrow. "Maybe you don't. Maybe you want ammonium nitrate, but if they're smart enough to lock you out of the labs, they're smart enough not to keep that stuff here where bad influences can build bombs in their bunks."

Jace threw his head back and laughed, revealing perfect rows of white teeth except for a missing canine in the bottom row. "I think I'm gonna like you."

Logan paused, marveling at how much the unprompted acceptance from Jace warmed him. Was this what it was like, being around other boys his own age, having friends? This wasn't what he'd expected even ten minutes ago. It was...not as bad as he'd dreaded it would be.

Everything in the whole fucking world was terrible, but Jace, at least, was a bright spot in the swirling shit storm of that week.

Jace's judgment of the newcomer pronounced, the boys drifted back to whatever they'd been doing when Logan arrived, chatting idly. Logan stood to make his bed, dropping the uniforms and toiletries into his trunk, but Bails interrupted him. "You're gonna want to put one of those on before dinner," he said, pointing at the spare uniforms. "They won't let you eat like that, in your street clothes."

Logan looked down at himself, wearing the same outfit he had been when he was taken from his home. It had been washed once since then, but he hadn't been able to bear trading his own clothes for any of the spares CRS offered him. With a sigh, he scooped up the top uniform and looked around for somewhere private to change.

"No dressing rooms in here, Your Highness," Jace joked. "You'll have to strip to your skivvies in the open like the rest of us." A few of the boys laughed, and Logan hoped he wasn't blushing; he'd never undressed in front of anyone before.

To his relief, everyone mostly ignored him as he changed as quickly as possible, folding his street clothes in the bottom of the trunk next to the second uniform. The gray collared shirt, black vest, and black pants looked almost funereal, which fit his mood.

His mother had always said their family shouldn't wear dark-colored clothes because, with their dark hair, "it makes it look like we're mourning existence!" She'd worn bright colors, purples and pinks and oranges. His father had made his own loudly patterned, multicolored pants to wear—at first as a joke, but over time they became his signature. He'd have sewn bright orange patches over the knees of these uniform pants. Logan cleared his throat, shaking away thoughts of his parents.

He made his bed neatly, plumped his pillow, and spread out on his bunk, wondering how in the world he'd fill his empty hours in this place. He hadn't been permitted to bring any of his books from home; the Hallsburg government seized everything in the house.

As he stared at the ceiling, trying to make patterns out of the texture, Jace's crooked grin appeared above him and something heavy *thunked* onto his chest.

"You look bored. Here."

Logan sat up and examined the pair of books that were stacked on his chest as Jace returned to his own bunk. All the boys threw on jackets, shuffled into shoes, and shoved books into messenger bags. Like Pavlov's dogs, they glanced toward the door just in time to hear a jangling bell ring out.

"That's sixth bell," Jace said. "Logan, meet us at the Eagle Hold tables in two bells for dinner." He started to leave, then added, "Oh, we eat in Blue Hall. Ask anybody—they'll show you how to get there."

They swept out in a noisy swirl, bound for their different classes and chore assignments. Logan was left alone to look over the books Jace had given him. *The Immortal Kings* was a heavy, hardbound thing with gilt edges; *Guardians of Lead* was thick as well, but it was a paperback, and the middle section of pages appeared to have been glued back in several times. Both, Logan had read before.

They were good books, though, and the paperback, at least, was worth rereading. He settled back and flipped it open to the first page, smiling as he remembered the last time he'd read this one— he'd been perched fifteen feet off the ground in his backyard tree, peeling shells off pecans and eating them, though they weren't quite ripe. He was forever getting caught up there, and no amount of butt whipping or lost privileges could keep him from that tree for long.

The memories were piled over instantly with a scramble of thoughts: Was that what had gotten him discovered? God, he'd never see that tree again! Why had he given his parents so much trouble, always doing stupid shit like climbing the backyard tree when they'd told him not to?

He wanted to take back every moment of disobedience, every unkind word, every fit and frustration. His parents had done the best they could, and now they were…they were—

Tears pricked at his eyes, and he frantically submerged himself in the book before he started to cry in this unfamiliar place. He tried to think only of the young protagonist of the story, whose adventures Logan had imagined himself on a thousand times.

Again, the story was a great one, so he was able to lose himself in it, releasing his sense of the passing of time until someone exploded back through the door of the dorm room.

"Hey, glad I caught you before the bell." Jace slammed into the room before dropping his bag with a heavy *whump* on his trunk and leaning over the foot of Logan's bed. "After I left, I thought about it and realized most of the guys around here are gonna be dicks if you don't know where you're going. They're pretty good to the littles who turn up, but someone our age…" He laughed and shrugged. "Come on! Eighth bell's in about thirty seconds, and we're gonna be at the back of the line if we don't get a move on."

Logan folded the corner down to mark his page and tossed the other book, the hardback, to Jace. "That one's pretty good, but I've never been a huge fan of Tom's character."

"You've read it before?" Jace wasn't quite smiling, but his eyes crinkled in a lopsided, thoughtful way.

"I've read both, but I'm happy enough to reread Ketren's stuff."

"Here." Jace waved his hand over the entire height of his bookshelf, which was stacked two and three books deep. "You're welcome to anything in here. You don't have to reread." He tucked the hardback into his seemingly nonsensical organizational system.

When he turned back to Logan, Jace was pinching his lower lip between thumb and forefinger, like he was thinking hard. It was a weirdly self-conscious mannerism for a guy so obviously confident in himself. Logan wanted to pull Jace's hand away.

Instead, he dropped the paperback onto the blanket beside him and swung off the side of the bed, stuffing his feet into the too-small shoes the home had provided to match the uniform. "Thanks. Shall we?"

They each gestured for the other to go first, then hesitated, then tried to step into the aisle at the same time, nearly colliding. "Fine," Logan said with a laugh, "I'll go first." Jace didn't speak as he reached up to absentmindedly mess with his lip again.

Logan knew he could navigate back to the common room, at least, so he led the way until they'd weaved through the comfortably worn furniture populating the now-empty room and reached the door that led out of Eagle Hold.

"Don't get separated from me," Jace warned before he opened the door. "You can get lost forever in this place."

Logan didn't think the warning was warranted until the doors opened. Hundreds and hundreds of people—more people than he had ever seen together—made their ways through the halls to a dozen different places. Logan was so overwhelmed, he could only stand still and take in the whole spectacle, letting the flow of people break around him.

"What did I *just* tell you?" Jace called, annoyed, fighting his way backward through the stream of people and grabbing Logan by the arm. "You're lucky you're so tall or I'd already have lost you. Seriously, stay close, Homeschool."

Jace walked a few paces before he let go of Logan's arm, and immediately the babbling, lurching crowd tried to pull Logan away from his guide. He snaked through a gap between two younger boys and seized Jace's upper arm—which was surprisingly warm, even through the layers of both shirt and jacket—and didn't let go again until they emerged into a huge, low-ceilinged dining room Logan supposed must be the Blue Hall.

A blue band was painted around the center of the cinder-block walls and, above and below, hand-lettered sayings like MAKE IT A GREAT DAY OR NOT—THE CHOICE IS YOURS, and LISTEN AND OBEY, THE CHILDERS COAST WAY in black.

"Eagle and Wolf Holds eat in Blue Hall," Jace called over his shoulder. If possible, it was even louder in the cafeteria than it had been in the corridor. Every boy in the room, it seemed, was competing to be heard over the others. "Tiger and Hawk in Red, Panther and Mustang in Yellow, Lion and Bear in green."

After they stood at the back of the long line for food, Jace continued his explanation. "It used to be different, but we started forming some alliances that I think spooked the administration a bit, so now they rotate which groups eat where every six months."

Logan ran his eyes over the room. "Who were we…allied with? Eagle Hold, I mean." He wasn't sure if he should subscribe to the collective identity, but Jace seemed to take it in stride.

"We're in good with Bear. Good guys over there. Watch out for Wolf Hold guys. If they can figure out a way to fuck your day up, they will. When you're in here for meals, stick with your own kind." Jace gestured to the Eagle insignia embroidered on the left side of his chest.

Logan looked down at his own chest; in his generic, ill-fitting uniform, he had no insignia.

"I guess I don't have a kind for now," he said with half a laugh.

"Eh, stick with me and everyone will know you're one of us."

Jace turned his back on Logan to watch the movement of the line, and it gave Logan room to enjoy the burst of genuine warmth—*one of us*. He liked that. It didn't make up for what he'd lost, but it was something good. A lifeline.

The food looked awful, but Logan decided to reserve judgment until he could sit and taste it. The adults serving the food eyed him oddly, he supposed for the same reason everyone else did: he was too old to be surrendered by a parent. Were there really so few kids with stories like his? Or were the other unauthorized families just better at not getting caught?

Clearing his throat to chase the lump out of it, he followed Jace to seats at the end of a table, next to Squints and two Bens.

They nodded greetings while they shoveled food into their mouths. Jace leaned over so he could speak where only Logan could hear. "You'd better eat fast, or these locusts will take that food straight off your tray." He laughed, his hot breath on Logan's ear before he moved back and practically inhaled his dinner.

The smell and texture were gruesome compared to the homemade meals he'd eaten his whole life. Trying to keep his mind off his parents cooking side by side, his mother humming the same three lines of a Holly Garland song from thirty years ago and twirling around the kitchen while his father chopped vegetables with a slow, steady rhythm, Logan took a bite of each thing on his tray: canned peaches, unseasoned turkey, mashed potatoes, green peas. The taste was slightly better than the smell suggested, but after a few mouthfuls of the mushy fruit, he felt ill.

"You gonna finish that?" a Ben asked with mouth full, already stabbing one of Logan's slimy peaches onto his fork before Logan could answer. He crammed it into his mouth, then grinned revoltingly. "Thunks," he mumbled around the wad of half-chewed food.

"Told ya," Jace said with another laugh. His own tray was empty except for the roll he was using to mop up the various juices and gravies.

Logan pushed his tray toward the other boys. "You're welcome to it." They descended on it like beasts, forks beating forks out of the way. Jace ignored the tray, looking at Logan with the same thoughtful crinkle in his eyes.

He leaned over to speak again for Logan's ears only. "Tomorrow night I can show you where they keep the food worth eating, if you want."

Logan shot his new friend a puzzled look. "If there's better food, why eat this stuff?"

Jace laughed. "We've gotta pick our battles, Homeschool. The good stuff is constantly supervised and under lock and key—not as high security as the labs, but it's a much ballsier raid. Can't risk it all the time." He sat back and spoke up so he could be heard by anyone. "Who's ready for the great homework trade?"

The boys grumbled as they polished away the last food on Logan's tray, then rose and started toward the door. "What about the other guys? You don't eat with them?" Logan asked. Someone handed him his tray, and he put it on the stack next to the trash cans with the others.

Squints shrugged. "We eat with whoever's here. Some guys have other friends to see. Some probably beat us here. Some head straight back to the dorms. It's whatever."

Back in the hold—after passing through the, fortunately, much less crowded hall—the third Ben, Randy, and Bails were waiting for them, stacks of books and papers spread on the beds and floor. "Squints, got history for you. I'll take your economics if you didn't finish in class," Bails called out.

Then commenced a great trading frenzy, each boy taking the homework for which he was best suited. Jace, Logan noticed, took several others' papers but handed none out himself.

"Logan, you any good at languages? We're all shit at languages," Squints said. "Except Jace, but, you know…*Jace*." He rolled his warm brown eyes, but grinned, apparently without bitterness. Logan didn't point out that he did not, in fact, know Jace.

"I've told you over and over that I'll do your worksheets, Squints," Jace said, "but when Ms. Olare calls you out to speak in front of the class, you're gonna be glad I don't."

Logan sat on his own bed, the only one without a spread of homework. "I've done fairly well with the Thogran-based languages, but don't get me started on those tonal languages from the Eastern Continent. I'm a speaker, not a singer, right?" He laughed, but only Jace joined in.

After a moment of semi-awkward silence, Jace laughed even harder, a rolling, delighted sound. "Don't even know what you don't know!" he crowed at the boys who were staring at them with blank looks. "How do you expect to get by in the real world?"

"Who cares what kind of language they speak on the Eastern Continent? It's not like we'll ever see it," one of the Bens said. "Is Tychan a Thogran-based language? Because that's what's kicking my ass right now."

Logan spent the next hour peering over the other boys' shoulders, correcting their spelling and accent marks—and in some cases, whole sections of their writing.

When he asked them how they spoke the languages in class, he grimaced at their pronunciation. "Well, at least you've got Hallsburgian down pat," he said at last.

Jace, apparently done with his work, was sprawled on his bed when Logan finished his round of the room. He waved Logan over and pointed to the bookshelf. "I've got a couple books in Thogran and Old Dunisian, if you want to check them out."

"Sure. Thanks," Logan said. He caught the books Jace tossed up to him, then collapsed onto his own bed. The exhaustion of the week weighed him down. More than anything, he wanted to go to sleep and wake up to the realization that everything since that fateful knock had been a bad dream.

"It gets better, you know," Squints said. His bed was next to Logan's, and he smiled with a surprisingly compassionate expression, the single freckle just below his right eye rising as the apples of his cheeks rounded. He seemed to understand Logan's train of thought. "Doing the same thing day after day here kinda makes everything… numb, you know? If you need a minute to yourself, just close the curtains. Everyone'll leave you alone." Squints shrugged and went back to his work, leaving Logan to his own devices.

Logan opened his book and propped the base of the spine on his stomach, but instead of reading, he watched Jace read across from him. The other boy's loose blond curls fell into his eyes as he read, and he kept brushing them aside in distracted annoyance. Idly he ran his finger through the corners of the pages over and over, making a soft thrumming sound. He had a jokester's face, wry and lively, with full lips and long eyelashes made to charm.

Someone coughed, and Logan quickly looked away from Jace. It wouldn't do to be caught out. He didn't know what a place like ChilCo would do to someone like him, but whatever the school's official policy, he knew from the whispered conversations between his parents that the boys wouldn't be accepting.

He wasn't sure how long he'd be able to keep up the act here. Thank God there were no girls at ChilCo to pretend to chase.

Logan didn't realize he was staring at Jace again until Jace looked up and caught his eyes. The blond flashed him a crooked grin and went back to reading like nothing had happened. Hurriedly, Logan looked down at his book and started trying to read in earnest.

The book was a challenge. Written in Old Dunisian, it was a wild mixture of alien vocabulary, familiar everyday words, and roots that still made up the common tongue spoken in Hallsburg. But once he started concentrating on it, he was entranced; it was a collection of old folk tales, written in their original tongue and in the colorful narration of long-dead storytellers. As he read the tale of a witch being outsmarted by a baker and his pet frog, Logan found himself chuckling at the jokes and odd similes.

"Whatcha reading?" Bails popped his long nose over the edge of the book and tried to read upside down. He scanned for a moment, then furrowed his brow. "Uh, is it my imagination or is that total gibberish?"

Laughing, Logan laid the book spread open on his stomach. "It's Old Dunisian."

"And you're just...reading it?" Bails sounded both amazed and bored. His tremendously expressive eyebrows climbed his forehead. "Hell, I don't think even Jace can just read it like that. He's gotta translate like the rest of us."

Logan glanced up at Jace, who nodded thoughtfully. "Yeah, I figured you'd need that dictionary I gave you. Do you speak it too?"

"*Ay loqua juis om small,*" Logan replied: *I speak only a little.*

Jace squinted, his eyes rolling toward the ceiling as he struggled to remember something. "*Ay loqua een menus*," he said in a broken accent: *I speak even less.*

Bails blew a rude sound through loose lips. "Can we all quit speaking in tongues and get ready for the raid?"

For the first time in several hours, Logan looked around the room and saw many of the boys changing out of their uniforms and into dark pajamas and soft hooded jackets.

"Good point, Bails," Jace said, swinging off his bed and into action. "Logan, you can borrow some of my raid gear. Did they even give you pajamas? Administration!" He clucked his tongue and pulled two crumpled sets of pajamas out of his trunk.

Jace gestured for Logan to stand, then stood hip to hip with him for a moment, apparently measuring the length of their legs against each other. "These'll do," he said with finality, handing one of the one-piece outfits to Logan, who eyed it dubiously. "You'll have to get a hoodie from Randy. I've only got the one. Oi, Randy!"

Randall had fallen asleep under his calculus textbook. Two of the Bens shook him awake. "What? Raid time?" he asked drowsily.

"Yeah. You got a hoodie Logan can borrow?"

The room scrambled with hushed activity. Any voice that rose above the others was chased down by a chorus of shushing. Logan pulled on the borrowed clothes, which fit well, doing his best not to watch Jace button the front of his pajamas up over his abs and chest.

All the boys slipped out of the room in single file, Jace at the front with Logan right behind. In socked feet, they padded down the treacherously slick wooden steps and skidded into the common room. A couple of stragglers were seated at a table at one end of the room, bent over their homework, but they seemed to know what was going on and ignored the group after smirking glances at the black-garbed line of older boys.

Every hall was eerily silent as they passed through. They followed a bizarre, winding route, but Jace seemed to know exactly where he was going. When he stopped, they all stopped; when he crouched, they all crouched; when he ran, they slid and scrambled right behind him. Following him, Logan was not as nervous as he thought he ought to have been.

At length, they stood with backs pressed against a wall while Jace peered around the corner for the longest time. After perhaps two minutes, Logan leaned down to ask in a whisper, "What are we waiting for?"

He didn't get to finish the question, though. Jace snapped a hand over Logan's mouth and gestured desperately for him to be quiet. He waved for Logan to creep up and look around the corner as well. Acquiescing, Logan spotted two janitors seated on a bench outside the door that presumably led to the science labs.

With legs sprawled out in front of them and their heads leaned back against the wall, they seemed asleep, but there was no way they'd miss eight boys trotting past them and burning through the door's locking mechanism.

"Distraction?" Logan mouthed to Jace.

The curly-haired boy nodded, pointed at the Bens, and made a weird twisting motion with his hands, a hand signal that clearly meant something to the other boys. The Bens trotted around the corner, tiptoed past the sleeping janitors, then skittered farther down the hallway.

Moments later, sharp cracks resounded through the halls, and the janitors jolted up with a start. Logan and Jace ducked back around the corner just in time as the men searched blearily for the source of the noise. Another cracking report sounded from even farther away, and the janitors left their bench in search of the culprits.

Not waiting to see if the other boys would follow, Jace launched himself around the corner, sprinted the length of the hallway, and slid the last few feet to the door on his knees while he pulled the bulky, tape-and-wire-wrapped lockpick out of his waistband. He had it secured against the door and burning before Logan and the others had made it halfway up the hall. The white-hot light of magnesium burning lit Jace's face in sharp profile as he turned his head away from it.

With a clunk, the remnants of the lock fell out of the doorframe, and Jace used his sleeved elbow to push down on the door handle as the other boys were sliding up. "Hot," he said quietly as he slipped through into the darkness. "Don't touch it."

The boys obeyed, slipping through the dark space into the room beyond. Logan spared a moment to inspect the damage before he caught up with Jace in the labs' atrium. "Was that thermite?" he asked incredulously.

"*Nao muche*," Jace said with a cheeky grin: *Not much*. Little light entered through the slim gap of their entranceway, so darkness obscured the corridor as they moved deeper into the labs. Several boys, including Jace, pulled flashlights out of their waistbands to spotlight the rooms they were looking for. Everyone but Jace and Logan ducked into the chemistry lab and started filling the bag Randy had slung across his body with small glass jars of contraband.

Jace grabbed Logan's arm to haul him along with him as he moved toward the electrical lab. "Hold the light for me, will ya?"

Jace had a bag slung across his body as well, and he opened drawers and grabbed components faster than Logan could recognize them. Spools of wire, scrap metal, tiny motors and resistors, and a dozen other things went into the bag. Logan tried to keep the light pointed ahead of the fast-moving thief.

"It's time," Jace said abruptly. "Gotta get the boys out." He dashed past Logan and back out of the lab, snatching the flashlight out of his hands as he went. When he passed the chemistry lab, he pointed the light inside and switched it on and off several times, then darted for the door, peering out cautiously.

The way must have been clear, as he immediately waved for the boys to run past him and back to the dorms. They retraced their steps, ducking and dodging as they had on the way in, and when they arrived back at their common room, which was now empty, they were all flushed and breathless.

"What about the Bens?" Logan asked Jace as they trotted up the stairs to their bunks.

"Their job was over as soon as they set off those crackle packs," Jace said. "They probably beat us back." Sure enough, the three Bens were seated on Jace's bed, waiting for the rest of the crew to return.

The boys quietly rejoiced, splitting up their take and squirreling bottles and flasks away into a dozen different hiding places. Logan saw trunks with false bottoms, floor panels moved, and even sections of paneling around the ceiling taken down to reveal holes behind. In less than two minutes, all evidence of their stolen goods was gone, and the boys had pulled off their hoods and socks so the dorm looked like any roomful of boys preparing to sleep.

"Lights off," Jace commanded Squints, then tugged on Logan's hood. "Get that off. They'll be up here soon to blame us for what happened. You need to look like you've been asleep for hours. Do you sleep in PJs or your skivvies?"

"I...it depends," Logan said, thrown by the question.

"Whatever. Just get in it and get in bed." Jace dove into his own bed before pulling the sheet up to his chest and instantly adopting the lax-muscled face of the dead asleep. Logan looked around; the other boys were doing the same. Bails dropped the curtain on the side of his bed closest to the door to hide his face.

"Shit," Logan muttered, pulling the hooded sweater over his head and hurriedly shoving it into his trunk. Just as Jace had predicted, footsteps resounded in the hallway outside their room: the administration coming to find the delinquents.

Logan slid into bed and tried to emulate the boys around him, but he was a terrible actor; he knew he couldn't feign sleep like they were all doing effortlessly. Instead, he sat awake against the headboard, watching the door as it opened to reveal a very irritated-looking woman's head.

She glanced around the room, saw the apparently sleeping bodies sprawled in each bed, and sighed. Then she caught the glitter of Logan's open eyes. "You," she whisper-called. "The new boy? Come here."

Logan slid out of bed and headed to the doorway. On his way, he saw the slightest tension cross Jace's face as he ground his teeth, ruining the illusion of sleep.

The pale woman had layers and layers of faded freckles over her cheeks and chest, as if she'd spent years in the sun a long time ago. Logan guessed she was in her fifties, with deep smile lines around her mouth and eyes that made her seem always on the edge of creasing into a warm expression. It was not warm now, though.

"Sorry, ma'am," Logan said quietly. "I know it's lights out, but I couldn't sleep. Too many thoughts in my head." He swallowed hard and let memories of his parents swim up, knowing it would bring all the emotion he'd been temporarily distracted from to his face.

His expression must have struck something with her, as the woman's annoyance faded into a kind sort of understanding. The wrinkles around her eyes deepened as she softened. "It's always hard for the boys when they first get here, and the older they are, the worse it is. I reckon you have a good understanding of what's happened to your parents, don't you?"

Logan nodded, tears pricking at the backs of his eyes. They were standing in the doorway, and he desperately didn't want to shame himself by crying in front of all these boys he knew were awake. "Yeah. I've read about Shalecrest. I know I won't see them again." His voice broke on the last word, and he swallowed hard to clear his throat, looking at the ceiling so gravity could help him keep the tears contained.

The woman gently patted his cheek. It should have made him feel like a child being patronized, but he was so much taller that she had to fully extend her reach, which somewhat ruined the effect. "Try drinking some chamomile tea before bed. It always helps put my mind at ease. I'll get you some tomorrow. Oh, I'm Ms. Lowell, the dean of this hold."

"Logan Cardot," he said politely, if thickly, and shaking her hand. She had soft hands. "Pleased to meet you."

"Likewise. Come see me in the morning, Mr. Cardot, and we'll see if we can't get you sorted out," she said matter-of-factly. "My office is around the corner from the common room. One of the other boys can show you."

"Thanks, Ms. Lowell."

She turned to leave, then paused and spun back around. "Oh, Mr. Cardot, I have to ask: have these boys been having any adventures tonight?"

"Adventures?" Logan did his best impression of complete puzzlement. One of the tears brimmed over onto his cheek, which he brushed away as hastily as he could. "I mean, they did some homework, if that's what you mean?"

"No, no, I mean anything outside the dorms."

"Oh," Logan said. "I don't think anyone's left at all, except the one they call Bails. Apparently, he's got a bladder the size of a peanut, gets up to pee every other hour. Other than that, it's just been me and my thoughts."

She smiled at him, seeming genuinely reassured, and the expression looked so amiable and so natural that he trusted her immediately. "Thank you. Have a good evening, Mr. Cardot. And welcome to ChilCo!"

When Logan closed the door and slid back into his bed, several of the other boys sat up, grinning hugely. Jace bounded across the room. "Dude, that was awesome! You played that perfectly, with the choking up and everything. You're totally my hero. Probably the best alibi we've ever gotten. Of course, she'll never trust you that much again, but it was perfect this time." He ruffled Logan's hair roughly, then bounced back to his own bed.

The others added their own kudos before everyone settled down to sleep. It had been such a long day. Logan slept, and though his dreams weren't happy, they did at least hold a glimmer of hope that things might get better and despair might not consume him.

# 2

## THE CHAMELEON'S ATTENTION

"Come on in, Mr. Cardot. You can shut the door. Let's run through your schedule. The placement test they gave you at CRS put you on the advanced track, but if you have any concerns, we can make adjustments."

Ms. Lowell's office was small but neat, a thick-legged wooden desk taking up most of it. Every wall had bookshelves packed as full as Jace's. The woman herself looked more composed in the light of day, her heavily salted auburn hair pinned up in a severe bun and a pair of red-framed reading glasses perched on her nose. She smiled at him as he sat in one of her low leather chairs, tapping her nails idly on the desk. Though they were short, her nails were neatly painted a deep purple. The pops of color reminded him of his mother in a way that made him ache.

The sheet of paper she handed him was printed with a detailed schedule of his day. Calculus, literature, biology, physics, Thogran history, and Tychan language all seemed to be in order. He'd be about where he'd left off with his mom. "What's this? Library? And rugby?"

"That's your chore assignment in the library. As for the rugby, it's only a suggestion, but you'll need some sort of physical activity. The Eagle rugby team is looking for a new fullback, and you look like you'd fit the bill."

Logan looked down at himself. Housebound as he'd been, he'd never played a sport, but he'd spent many a lonely hour working out in his basement gym. He was in good shape, all lean muscle on a frame that could have supported more, if he'd ever eaten enough calories and lifted heavily enough to bulk up. "Someone will have to teach me the rules."

"You've got two players in your room: Mr. Halls is a flanker and Mr. Evans is the fly half. I'm sure either of them could give you a rundown of the game." Ms. Lowell shuffled a pile of papers into a neatly aligned stack and stapled it before shoving it into a folder and dropping it into one of her desk drawers. "We usually give new residents a buddy—an older student who can show them the ropes. I've partnered you with Mr. Evans for the time being. Your schedule fits his quite closely."

Logan's heart pounded, but he schooled his face into calmness. "Jace? That's a bit of a surprise."

Ms. Lowell raised her eyebrows, waiting for him to explain further. "Well," he said, "yesterday Ms. Lee warned me to stay away from him because he was a 'bad influence.' It didn't seem like the administration would be pairing up new kids with him."

A small voice in the back of Logan's mind wondered why he was arguing with this...intriguing turn of events.

The Eagle dean clucked her tongue in annoyance, tapping her purple nails on the desk's surface again. "Jace Evans is not a bad kid, whatever Katherine may think. In fact, I've made a habit of putting new students who might have a hard time close to him. He has a way of making their lives easier."

"How does he do that?"

Ms. Lowell shrugged slightly. "He's very popular among the residents. Well…that's not quite it. We have many students who are popular in their respective holds. Mr. Evans does well because he's a chameleon." She settled back, folding her hands over her stomach.

"You won't have seen it yet, as new as you are, but he has a gift for fitting whoever is around him. By day, he's an excellent, attentive student. By night, he's a thief and a saboteur." She said the harsh words almost fondly; she didn't seem angry at all. "With his friends, he's easygoing, but he's one of our more…frightening residents when he or his peers are threatened."

She fixed Logan with a thoughtful look and tapped her copy of his schedule. "I won't warn you away from Mr. Evans as a bad influence. But I will advise you that he's always showing exactly the face he *wants* to be showing. It's easy to get suckered in." She laughed, a brash, unladylike chuckle that made Logan want to laugh too. "God knows I've fallen for his acting a time or two. Everyone in ChilCo knows *of* Jace Evans, but I doubt there's a single person under this roof who actually *knows* him."

Logan had never seen anyone but his parents talk about someone with so much exasperated fondness. Seeming to realize she'd spent too much time discussing another resident to Logan, Ms. Lowell shook herself. "If you're happy with your schedule, all that's left is the orientation." There was something strange about the way she shaped the last word, like it tasted bitter. "I'm supposed to have you listen to it, but in the interest of time, perhaps I can just trust you to read the transcript?"

"Uh, sure?" Logan took the three sheets of paper she handed him, printed front and back with dense text.

"*Do* read it. Your circumstances are…well, you'll want to be on your best behavior while you're here, Mr. Cardot." Her gentle tone seemed to be tiptoeing around a chasm, and it sent a shiver up Logan's spine.

"That's all for now. There are a couple of spare bookbags in the closet just outside my door, and your classrooms will have the rest of the books and supplies you'll need. If you have any questions or concerns, you're welcome to stop by."

"Thanks." Clutching the papers to his chest, Logan backed out of her office and into the maelstrom of the hallways. He was surprised to see Jace waiting outside the door, the crowd splitting easily around him.

"Hey," Jace said, grinning. "Lowell sent a runner to lit to tell me I'm supposed to be your buddy. You get your schedule?"

Logan peeled his schedule off the top of the stack of papers and handed it to him before swimming up-current through the crowd to the closet door across the hall. There he found several bags hanging on hooks on the back of the door; he picked one at random and dropped it over his shoulder.

When he shut the door, a Black Lapel stared at him from a poster on the wall, a finger pointed toward Logan as if in accusation, Do Your Part written in block letters beneath his illustrated gaze. Logan shuddered.

"Sweet," Jace said, leaning against the wall in front of the poster. He hadn't realized the curly-haired boy had followed him. "Looks like we're mostly in the same classes. Oh, you play rugby?"

"Apparently I do now. You'll have to teach me the rules."

"Eh, it's easy. The hard part's getting in shape for it, but you look like you're covered there," Jace said without looking up from the schedule. He was remarkably good at dodging through the crowded halls blindly.

Logan felt a twinge of satisfaction. He'd never been grateful for the long, dull daytime hours he'd filled with lifting and running and calisthenics before, but he was now.

Classes were mostly a blur. He picked up books, took whatever seat was open, and listened to the lecture until he could figure out where in the curriculum the class was compared to him. He was ahead in everything except calculus—his mom had hated the subject and flat out refused to teach it, but he'd done a fair bit of studying on his own, reading the book and working through the problems, so he wasn't too desperately behind.

Only two things gave him pause.

The first was the moment at the beginning of his first class when all the students stood as one, balled their right hands into fists, and crossed one arm to press their fists against the left side of their chests. In unison, they spoke in the droning rhythm of something said so often by rote that it no longer carried meaning, but to Logan, hearing the words for the first time, it was chilling: "I pledge allegiance to the nation of Hallsburg and its righteous leadership. I swear my loyalty and service to protect my land and obey its laws unconditionally, in faith and courage, from this day forth."

Logan stood and did the motions with all the rest but found himself glancing around the room, looking for *anyone* who was as unsettled by the pledge as he was. No one blinked an eye, though; they all sat again, and the literature teacher continued without acknowledging anything that had just happened.

The second thing was the orientation. He scanned the transcript in bursts whenever the classes veered into familiar territory and he could afford to tune out. The very first line knocked the breath out of his chest: "Under the leadership of the Hallsburg Special Police Force, Childers Coast and the rest of the children's homes in Hallsburg—"

*ChilCo is run by the Black Lapels?*

Instinctively, Logan looked over his shoulder as if he'd see an officer standing at the back of the classroom. He hadn't seen any Black Lapels except those printed on the posters pasted at intervals along the walls since he'd arrived at the home, but that didn't mean they had no presence.

The remainder of the orientation described the perfect Chil-Co resident: studious, attentive, obedient, loyal to Hallsburg. The best of ChilCo's students, it said, would someday join the ranks of the Hallsburg Special Police Force themselves. Logan's lip curled at the thought. *Over my dead fucking body.*

The previous evening's raid, which had seemed like an exhilarating bit of fun, now seemed infinitely more dangerous. What if it had not been a janitor who caught them or a hold dean who questioned them, but a Black Lapel, pistol in hand?

When he finished the orientation transcript, he rolled it tightly, the sweat of his palms making marks on the paper.

Another bell rang, dismissing them to lunch, and Jace walked shoulder to shoulder with him through the halls. "So how's your first day? Learned anything yet?"

Logan opened his mouth to ask about the pledge or the Lapels, then chickened out and shrugged, changing his answer to, "Most of it I've done before. I got a little lost when the calculus teacher started talking about applying integrals, but I'll figure it out."

"You're smart," Jace said. He was messing with his lip again and didn't seem to realize he was doing it. It bugged Logan, though he wasn't sure why.

"I guess. Thanks."

Blue Hall was even more packed than it had been for dinner, the food—today a gray slab of meat, reconstituted and breaded, accompanied by syrupy pears instead of peaches—just as inedible, and the boys' eating equally voracious. Jace sat next to Logan and across from Randy, who ate quietly, eyes fixed on his tray like someone would take it if he looked up. *He has a nice jaw,* Logan thought.

"Oi, Randy! We've got our fullback," Jace said, clapping Logan's shoulder.

Logan considered what Ms. Lowell had said. What part was Jace playing now, as he chatted amiably with the other boys at the table, gesturing with a forkful of food? Good-natured, she'd said. But it was more than that. Logan could see the way Jace pulled in the people around them, creating a bubble that somehow included everyone who wanted to be a part of it and simultaneously built an "us versus them" mentality, making every boy at the table feel like part of an exclusive group. It wasn't just good nature; it was magnetism, hypnotism.

Jace looked at his watch, then shoveled food into his mouth, dropping the conversation he'd been carrying on. "We gotta go," he said around a mouthful of instant mashed potatoes. "I've gotta take you by the library before my chores."

He stood, eating off the tray as he carried it; Logan had no choice but to follow. "Uh, anybody want the rest of this?" His tray was snatched away, and he trotted after Jace.

They didn't make it out of the cafeteria before someone ran in, shouting, "Jace!"

A younger freckled boy Logan didn't know sprinted up to Jace, panting. The rest of the older boys at the Eagles' tables looked up. "Jace, some Panthers've got Ethan pinned up in the math wing bathroom. They said he stole something from their room, but he didn't do nothing!"

Like a mask had dropped down over it, Jace's face completely changed. Without looking back toward the tables, he raised two fingers, and Randy and a stocky guy Logan hadn't met yet jogged over.

Jace pointed to the messenger kid. "Sit with Squints. If Wolf sends anybody up to the math wing, head over to Green Hall and grab a couple of Bears. Shouldn't be a brawl, but Wolf's been itching for a fight since they rotated into Blue with us."

He set off with long, determined strides, face like storm clouds, and Logan and the others walked behind and beside him. What happened as they walked was strange: they were just four boys, slightly taller or heavier than most, but otherwise the same, yet when they set off together with purpose, Logan felt invincible. He wondered if that was Jace's doing.

It wasn't far from Blue Hall to the math wing. When they entered the bathroom, four older boys from Panther held a much smaller boy upside down between them. His head and shoulders were soaked, and Logan assumed the broken eyeglasses on the tile floor were his.

"Jace," one of the boys said with mock friendliness. He dropped the kid's left leg, and the small boy swung toward the floor with a yelp. "Figured you'd show up. You wanna teach your boys to keep their paws off other people's stuff?"

Jace ignored the Panther. "You all right, Ethan?"

"Yeah," the boy mumbled.

"Did you steal something from these assholes?"

"No!" The boy holding his right leg swung him into the stall divider with a clunk.

"Shut up, you. That's a lie."

Jace's voice was low. "Are you calling one of my boys a liar?"

"Nah," said the boy who'd spoken first. "We're calling him a liar *and* a thief."

Logan missed whatever cue made the other three boys explode into action. Jace was a striker, pummeling with fists, elbows, and feet. Randy was a grappler; he held the first boy who'd spoken in a chokehold the Panther couldn't wriggle free of. The third Eagle took the brute force approach, charging a Panther and tackling him hard to the tile.

Logan snatched the smaller boy out of the melee before pulling him to his feet and shoving him toward the door. With his back turned to the fight, Logan got a sharp sucker punch to the back of the head, staggering him.

No one had ever taught Logan to fight. He'd never built up so much anger that he felt the need to beat it out with his fists before, but the pure cowardice of punching a noncombatant in the back of the head filled him with fury that temporarily overruled his more logical thinking. His vision turning red, he seized his attacker's head and smashed it into first the cinderblock wall, then the mirror, then the sink. When he released him, the other boy slumped bonelessly to the floor.

He was ready to smash the whole world in, but the other Panthers were already under control. Periodically, Randy loosened his grip just enough to keep his Panther from going unconscious. Jace knelt on the chest of another, one knee planted against his throat.

He spoke quietly, almost companionably: "Repeat after me, little Panther. 'Eagles never lie.' Say it!"

The Panther choked out something resembling words, which was enough to satisfy Jace. He stood, straightened his jacket, and glanced around at the other Panthers. "God*damn*, Homeschool," he said when he saw the mess Logan had made of his attacker.

He glanced at his watch again. "Fuck, we're gonna be late. Come on, let's get you to library duty."

Without another glance at the Panthers, Jace swept out and Randy and the stocky boy dropped theirs to follow. Logan was the last out. Unlike the others, he couldn't resist looking back; he was surprised to see the boys cringe away from him. No one had ever been afraid of him before.

"Might want to tone it down next time," Jace said once they were striding through the halls again. They'd bid Randy and the other boy—Teapot, Jace had called him—goodbye as if nothing had happened. "We're trying to shake them up and keep them off our boys, not scar them for life. Moves like that'll get admin involved."

Logan's sweat went cold as if wind had blown over him, imagining the administration of this school—*Lapels? Would they be Lapels?*—paying any attention to him at all, but outwardly he only shrugged. "I didn't mean to. Just...got angry."

"Save it for the rugby pitch," he said, tempering the harshness of his tone with an easy laugh. "It was pretty badass, though. *Smash, smash, smash!*" He stopped outside the library and leaned back against the wall, propping one foot up on the paneling. "You're something else, Homeschool. Where you been all this time?" He chuckled and shook his head, his curls bouncing around his gorgeous, now-amiable face. "I'll meet you back here at four and take you to rugby practice."

"**I** am *not* wearing this." Logan stared down at himself, scowling. "You're putting me on. There's no way these are men's shorts."

"Come out, Homeschool. We're all wearing them." Jace sounded half amused and half impatient. "They're short. Whatever. You'll get used to them."

Logan stuck his head out of the shower stall he'd changed in. "Well, you're wearing sliders under yours, aren't you? It's different."

Jace laughed and jerked his thumb over his shoulder, gesturing for Logan to get out. "We don't have any spare sliders right now. You'll get yours when the rest of your custom clothes come in. In the meantime, you'll just have to—"

Logan stepped out, hands out at his sides, presenting the offending outfit for the entire team to see. The high-cut shorts were too loose and failing spectacularly to cover a particularly critical element of his anatomy.

"Is this really how you want me to play?" he demanded.

The entire team cracked up. Jace's head was bowed, his lower lip crushed between thumb and forefinger, his shoulders shaking with silent laughter.

After a moment he straightened, still laughing, and pointed to a boy standing next to Teapot who had a similarly stocky build. "Bud, give him your sliders. We know you've got nothing to hide."

"Oh, *ha*-ha, asshole," Bud said, but he stepped into another stall and peeled the tight undershorts off anyway, then tossed them to Logan before he tied his shorts back up. "Are we done ogling our fullback now? Can we all get moving?"

Chuckling, the team filed out while Logan changed.

Practice consisted of most of the team doing drills while Jace sat on the bench with Logan and a notebook, showing him the basics of the game.

"Worst case scenario, if you get totally lost, just listen. I'll probably be shouting some order or another at you."

"Great, so *everybody* will see how shit I am at this game."

"No, it's cool—I yell at everybody." Jace tossed the notebook to the other end of the bench and rubbed his forehead. There was a strange sort of tension in him, like he was working hard to stay focused on the moment. "You still want to raid the pantry tonight?"

Logan resisted the urge to rub his mostly empty stomach. "God, yes. I'm starving."

"Okay. Don't tell the others." Jace stood then jumped and stretched, warming up.

Logan should probably stretch too, but he didn't want Jace to order him out onto the field to learn by playing. "Why not?"

"They'll all want to go, and we can't do two big raids back to back." He snapped his neck to the left then the right with loud cracks. "Besides, the pantry's really a two-man job. Any more just get in the way." He swung his arms backward and forward in great arcs like a windmill. "And if you tell them, you'll have to split your share of the food."

Logan nodded. "Are you gonna make me play today?"

Jace laughed, enjoying the question—he clearly liked being in charge of people. "Nah, we're gonna play sevens because I feel like running circles around the forwards. Rules are basically the same as fifteen-a-side, so just watch."

That was fine by Logan; it was a pleasure to watch Jace play. He moved effortlessly, and *fast*, and seemed to watch everything at once. It was true what he'd said: he did yell at everyone, directing the backs at the top of his lungs. The game was over in fifteen minutes, but it was plenty of workout for the players. They tromped back to the bench drenched in sweat, some crowing victory, some good-naturedly bemoaning the failures of their teammates.

"Come on, Homeschool. We're done for the day," Jace called. "And you're gonna work out with us tomorrow."

As Logan trotted after them, he realized he hadn't thought about his parents once during practice. Between that and the knowledge that he'd be out on a raid with Jace that night, not alone with his thoughts, he could barely contain his gratitude to the curly-haired boy.

# 3

## ONE ON ONE

Logan and Jace waited into the wee hours for the rest of their roommates to fall asleep before they pulled on hoodies and socks and slipped out of the room. Jace yawned hugely as he slung a canvas bag across his body.

"We gotta make this quick. I'm getting too old for back-to-back raids," he said as they slunk down the stairs.

"Well, don't get us caught, old man," Logan whispered back.

He worried for a moment that the comment wouldn't be understood in the spirit in which he'd meant it, but Jace positively beamed at him, like Logan's light teasing was a generous gift. "Don't *you* get us caught, Homeschool. You any good at lock picking?"

"The incendiary kind?"

"The regular kind." Jace opened the common room door for Logan and shut it silently behind them.

Logan peered up and down the halls anxiously but saw nothing. "Can't say I know anything about locks. My parents never locked anything but the front door."

"Pity," Jace muttered. His crouched movements were eerily quiet with the socks on as he led Logan through the halls. "I could use another lock man now that Dodder aged out and got the boot. Neil—he's a twelve-year-old newbie bunked a couple doors down from us—has picking skills, but he's probably the least sneaky human being I've ever met. He'll take a while to train, maybe longer than I'll be here."

"Will someone be taking over this criminal enterprise when you're booted?" Logan tried to mimic the smooth, soundless stride Jace used to cross the open spaces.

"Probably Forrest. You haven't met him yet. He's next door to us. Does a lot of his own raids with his bunk. Most of 'em get blamed on us, but it's easy to tell the difference because they're sloppier." Jace started to turn a corner, then jerked back and threw an arm across Logan. Rapidly, they backpedaled and ducked into a water fountain alcove just as someone turned into their hallway, whistling tunelessly as he walked by. He didn't notice them pressed into the dark corner.

As soon as the guy turned into the next corridor, they darted out again and crept back up to the same corner. "Gets harder from here," Jace muttered. "A lot more people around."

Logan wasn't sure why that should be until he crept into the next hallway and noticed the nameplates on some of the doors. "Are these teachers' rooms?"

"Faculty and staff," Jace said. His words were almost all air, so Logan could barely hear him, even right next to him.

They continued, crouched and quick, until they reached a room with a nameplate that said, "P. Rollins." It stood at the end of the hall, somewhat by itself. Logan thought they'd be moving on, but Jace knelt and quickly pulled a rolled set of lockpicks out of his waistband. "The director's room?" Logan knelt next to him, watching him work on the lock.

"Yeah. Watch my six."

There were several long moments where Logan fully expected someone to step out of a room and discover them, but all was quiet. To his ears, the click when the door popped open sounded like a gunshot. Jace pulled him into the room by the shoulder, then quietly shut and locked the door behind them.

Inside, Logan froze. "We sneaking past a sleeping director?"

"He's got a house a couple miles east where he lives with his family. He almost never stays here," Jace said, pulling out his flashlight to guide them through the darkness of the room.

"*Almost* never?" Logan whispered, but he followed anyway. The director had not a single room but a suite. They'd entered a small salon with a door in each wall: bedroom, bathroom, cramped kitchen.

"Bingo," Jace murmured, opening the pantry to reveal shelves and shelves of food.

"Why stock it this well if you never stay here?" Logan asked as he pulled things off the shelves and shoved them into the bag on Jace's back.

"I've never seen it this well stocked actually," Jace said. He wore that thoughtful face again. Grabbing the light, he looked around the suite, taking in details they'd missed on their way in: the shoes lined up next to the door, the book propped open on the table by a half-full mug, the car keys tossed haphazardly on the counter. "Shit, we need to go. Now!"

He'd barely finished his sentence before someone was working the lock at the front door. They could hear voices just outside.

"You too, Jim. I want to meet Eileen at the next faculty dinner. We're going to Gianno's!"

The door started to open, and Jace shoved Logan hard in the chest, forcing him into the pantry. He didn't have time to say there was no room before Jace crammed himself in as well and pulled the door closed. It was an incredibly tight fit. They were too broad across the shoulders to fit side by side, so Jace's left side was crushed between the door and Logan's right.

With the door shut, there wasn't even a millimeter of give; wherever their bodies and limbs had been when the door closed, that's where they were staying.

They heard the director shuffle into his kitchen and prayed he wasn't peckish. "Ugh, cold," he mumbled to himself. They held their breaths as his footsteps moved past the pantry. They heard him set a kettle on the stove, the click of the burner lighting. Through it all, neither of them dared twitch so much as an eyelid.

Mr. Rollins hummed quietly to himself, bumbling about the kitchen, while Jace's hands twitched nervously. Logan wouldn't have noticed except that the fingers of Jace's left hand were pressed against Logan's thigh. When the director gripped the doorknob of the pantry, rattling it slightly, that left hand tightened into a crushing grip on Logan's leg.

"No, come on now, Paul," the director muttered. "Stick to your diet, you fat bastard."

It would've been funny if Logan hadn't been so heart-poundingly scared. His entire body thrummed with the cold burning energy of adrenaline. The kettle began to whistle, then the sound of liquid pouring into liquid, then shuffling toward the kitchen table.

"Oh!" Mr. Rollins's quiet exclamation almost made Logan jump out of his skin. He realized he had clawed into the back of

Jace's sweater, right where it ended at the small of his back, so hard his fingers ached. "Katherine, you forgetful old cow."

They heard the sound of him scooping up keys, then faster footsteps away from the kitchen. Both boys stayed tense, jumping at the noise of the front door being unlocked and opened again. It shut loudly, and then everything in the suite was silence.

Jace didn't pause to wonder if the director had actually left. He opened the door, looked both ways, and made a beeline for the front door. Logan shut the pantry behind himself and sprinted after, socked feet sliding on the hardwood.

"We have to go now, before he gets back," Jace said.

"Wait!" Logan grabbed Jace's wrist before he could open the door. "What if he's just outside? He said, 'Katherine.' Who's that?"

"That's Ms. Lee."

"Her room was right next door!" Logan pulled Jace away from the door as quickly as he could, making for the bathroom. He'd seen a window in the bathroom through the open door as Jace had shined the light past it.

He skidded in, followed a moment later by Jace, and ran his hands over the top edge of the lower half of the window, looking for the latch. Jace saw it first and flipped it, then flung up the glass and cupped his hand to give Logan a boost.

"Shit, Jace, we're on the second floor!"

"Go!"

Logan went. He flopped out of the window gracelessly, flubbed the landing, and rolled to a stop a few feet from the wall. Jace was right behind him.

Logan heard a call of, "Hey!" just as Jace dove out, landed uncomfortably, and immediately started running.

They bolted along the side of the building to the nearest corner, hoping to turn it before Rollins could get his head out the window and identify them. They turned but didn't stop running.

The two of them sprinted through the chilly night in their socks like hellhounds were chasing them. It was terrifying and electrifying, and Logan had never felt anything like it.

At one point he looked at Jace and saw the curly-haired boy grinning widely and wildly as he ran, showing off his missing tooth as he delighted in the pure act of getting away with something so closely. Logan wanted to kiss him just to taste some of that joy.

Finally, they stopped outside one of the rear wing doors. Logan thought it might lead to the hall where his literature classroom was. They both bent over panting, red-faced with exertion and the night's brisk winter wind.

"Can you pick this?" Logan pointed to the door that led back into the school.

Jace shook his head. "Not a chance. All the doors to the outside are alarmed."

"Then how do we get back in?" Now that they'd stopped running, the sheen of sweat that coated Logan's body was chilling in the breeze. Shivering, he wiped the sleeves of his sweater over his face, trying to warm it.

"We don't. They unlock the doors at first bell. Tomorrow morning we'll slip in at second bell with everyone else who's going to classes."

"In our pajamas?"

Again, Jace shook his head. His breathing was almost back to normal. "My guys know if I'm not in bed at first bell, I got stuck on a raid. We've got a clothes drop under the common room window.

They're smart—when they see you gone too, they'll drop some for both of us."

Well, they were stuck outside for the night then. Logan started to sit down next to the building, but Jace summoned him back up with a hand gesture. "We can't sit out here all night. It's too damn cold. There's a place."

They walked away from ChilCo into the stand of trees that marked the edge of the manicured lawn. The ground became rough, fallen branches and scattered stones stabbing through the thin protection of socks. As they went on, the ground sloped upward more and more steeply, and twice Logan lost his footing in the dead leaves and would have slid back down the hill if Jace hadn't caught his arm.

"How much farther?" he asked. He was in good shape, but a middle-of-the-night hike after a full day of school and a sprinting midnight raid had worn him out.

Jace stood still, appearing to count trees. "It's right...over here." He slipped into a thick copse of trees, shimmying between pale gray birch trunks, and disappeared. Logan slid in after him, bark scraping at his chest, to find the trees formed a half circle that hid the entrance to a little cave of sorts.

It wasn't deep; Logan could see the back just eight feet or so from the lip, but it was wide enough that they both could lie down end to end and not quite span the breadth of it.

"Nice spot," Logan said, sitting down in the dirt just under the stone overhang. And it was nice. Much warmer with the wind blocked, but you could see the star-strewn night sky through the bedraggled, half-shed branches of the trees. His stomach grumbled so loudly that Jace heard it and, laughing, dropped the bag of stolen food into Logan's lap.

"Thanks. I found it the first time I tried to hike to the lake." Jace stretched out along the edge of the shelter's opening, orienting himself so his head was at the end closer to Logan and folding his hands behind his head.

"Isn't the lake"—Logan said, pointing the way they'd come—"that way?" He unzipped the bag, pulled out the graham crackers that lay on top, and shoved three in his mouth. He was starving.

Jace laughed and waved away the cracker Logan offered. "Yeah, it is. I was, like, nine. My sense of direction wasn't so keen."

"But these days you're a regular forester."

As best as he could with his hands behind his head, Jace shrugged. "I just know where I'm going. You get good at certain things with practice."

"Seems like you're good at pretty much everything," Logan said, keeping his voice light, casual. He tried to make it sound like he was teasing Jace, not praising him.

"That's not true. Can't sing. Can't sew. Haven't got the faintest idea how to undo a bra."

"Everyone can sing," Logan rebutted, mouth full of a second fistful of crackers. "We can't all do it prettily. Same with dancing."

Jace laughed; Logan was growing very attached to the sound of it. "I can't dance either, prettily or otherwise."

"As for sewing, if you can get a button back on, you're golden. If your clothes need more than that, you should be throwing them out and buying new ones." Logan was on a roll now; Jace was laughing in earnest.

"What about the bra thing? Do you have an excuse for that too?" Jace's eyes were closed as he chuckled to himself.

"Who cares about undoing a bra?" Logan answered without thinking. Immediately, he regretted it. Jace opened one eye and tilted his head back to look at Logan. "I mean...with no girls around, what does it matter? You'll figure it out once you're booted." Logan's heart was pounding almost as hard as it had been in the pantry—he had to watch his stupid mouth.

Jace was chuckling again. "He says, 'Who cares about undoing a bra?' Ha! Boys in our room would flay you for that sentiment." After a moment of staring lazily up at the sky, he said, "Lie down, Homeschool. You're making me nervous sitting over me like that."

Logan finished the last of the cracker packet and obeyed, swinging his legs around and lying with his head next to Jace's, his hands folded under his neck in a mirror image of the other boy's position. "I'm tired but not sleepy. Does that make any sense?"

"Yeah, same. Still wired. I can't believe how close that was!"

Now that they were an hour or so and several hundred feet distant from the pantry, what Logan remembered most clearly wasn't the deafening fear, but Jace's hand on his leg.

If he turned his head just a little to the right, and if Jace turned *his* head to his right, they'd almost be close enough to kiss at this very moment. It gave Logan the same cold hands and heavy, thudding heartbeat he'd had in the director's suite.

He glanced at Jace. The boy was tugging on his lip again, worrying it until the pink flesh turned white under his pinching grip. Logan thought about pulling his hand away and freeing his lip, but he knew he shouldn't touch Jace now; he was way too close to him.

"What else are you bad at?" Logan asked, more to distract himself than because he cared about the response.

"No, I've answered. What are *you* bad at, Homeschool?"

"Me?" Logan thought about it. "I'm not a good singer. I have completely illegible handwriting. And I'm an awful liar."

"No, you're not. You were brilliant last night with Lowell."

Logan barked a bitter laugh. "I guess I'm just a different kind of liar than you are."

Jace looked over, offended. "I am *not* a liar. I'm an actor. Very different things."

"Okay, fine, I'm not a good *actor* then." He shifted, brushing a rock out from under his back. "I guess the difference is you've got full control of your face, so you can show emotions where there are none—I can't do that. I've gotta use what I'm already feeling about something. Might not be the thing I'm talking about at that moment, but I'm feeling that about *something*. I just have to dredge it up so it looks like it goes with my words."

Jace rolled onto his side, putting his face close to the side of Logan's. Logan froze. "That might be the best explanation I've ever heard of lying."

"*Thanke etu*," Logan responded. His voice was barely more than a whisper because it was hard to move air in and out of his lungs with Jace so close to him.

"*Etu sare...sare...* Shit, I forgot how to say 'you're welcome.' Lowell stopped teaching me ages ago. I think someone told her off about it."

"*Etu sare* is literally 'you are,' but the phrase for 'you're welcome' is *wicheer time*." Logan had closed his eyes so he wouldn't have to concentrate on not staring at Jace's mouth.

When Jace rolled away, back onto his back, Logan released a sigh of relief. "That's right, I remember now," Jace said. "*Wicheer time*." They were silent for a while, and then Jace spoke again, drumming his fingers against his stomach. "Tell me about life outside of ChilCo. Did you have friends out there, locked up in the basement with you?"

The panic that seized him at Jace's questioning eased as he redirected away from family. "Uh, friends? Not locked in the basement with me, no. Most of the time I didn't have anybody but Mom and Dad. But when I was younger, I did have this neighbor…"

Memories washed over him, and he blushed. Their next-door neighbors had fraternal twins, a boy and a girl. Both had snuck into Logan's yard after school every day, but it was Chris he'd spent time with up in the pecan tree, hugging branches and each other.

"You're blushing, Homeschool, so she must have been more than a friend." Jace had turned to look at Logan again, and his proximity combined with thinking about Chris was confusing to Logan.

"Yeah. Chris was…a really good kisser."

Jace quirked an eyebrow. "Chris?"

Flustered, Logan recovered. "Short for Christina. I called her Chris." He hoped it didn't sound like as much of a lie to Jace as it did to Logan's ears. But Jace seemed to accept the explanation; he only plucked at his lip thoughtfully.

Logan hadn't thought about Chris and Angela in a long time. Looking back, he supposed Angela might have been jealous. She was the one who'd told her parents about Logan and about what Chris and Logan had been up to. They moved away not long after that, and Logan's parents had a serious talk with him about keeping his head down. He'd missed Chris, and Angela too, terribly. No other kids his age ever moved in, and he wouldn't have been permitted to see them if they had, so he spent a lot of time alone after that.

"I take it that didn't end well?" Jace asked.

"What? Oh, no. Couldn't really, since I wasn't supposed to exist. Chris moved away. Her parents agreed not to tell the authorities about me, but they didn't want me near her when the Lapels did come down on us." It was too much, all the feelings in his chest at once. Logan closed his eyes and concentrated on his breathing.

"That sucks." Jace gave Logan the small privacy of turning away to stretch and yawn.

Logan tried to make light of it, to recapture the easy, companionable spirit they'd had. "It did suck. But I guess nobody really ends up with their first love, right?" Logan forced a chuckle, but beside him, Jace had gone tense.

"Don't say shit like that," he said harshly. It was the first time Logan had heard Jace use that tone.

"What?" Logan said, startled. "Shit like what?"

"Don't use that word. It's bullshit."

Logan ran his last couple sentences back through his mind, trying to determine what might have set the blue-eyed boy off. "Which word? Love?"

Jace shoved Logan in the shoulder, rolling him away. "Seriously, cut it out." He rolled over, putting his back to the baffled new boy, and said nothing more.

Logan watched Jace's back for a long time, waiting to see if he'd turn back and explain himself. But he never did.

"I can't believe he took you on a one on one," Squints said as Logan sat beside him at the lunch table. "He never takes newbies on one on ones. He hardly ever takes *anyone*."

"Well, it was probably just because I wasn't eating much of what they serve in here."

Squints's eyebrows shot up. "Did you go to the pantry? Ho. Lee. Shit. I thought he'd sworn off the pantry forever after last time." He rapped the table to get the attention of the Bens sitting a few seats down. "Bens, Jace and Logan raided the pantry!"

"What?" one Ben asked, just as another exclaimed, "No way!" The third looked confused more than outraged. "I thought he wasn't going back after he got caught last time?"

"Jace got caught?" This was news to Logan.

"Well, they didn't catch him in the act," Squints clarified. "A couple years ago, he slipped down the staff hall stairs trying to get away and broke his leg. He pretty much hopped and crawled all the way back to the dorms, then staged a fall down the stairs to our hallway." Squints took a bite of macaroni.

"Ms. Lowell knew it was him, though," he continued, his mouth full, "but she convinced Rollins to go easy on him, just switch out his rugby practice for a second chore rotation while his leg healed. I guess she figured a broken leg was punishment enough."

"I'm glad I didn't let him run back out the front door then," Logan muttered. "Though I guess we could have broken something jumping out the window."

"Out the window? What the hell happened on this raid?" Squints asked.

Jace arrived then, setting his tray down hard to stop the conversation. "Not in here, guys," he said, glancing around. He swung his leg over his seat, sat down, and leaned in close so only Squints and the Ben to his left would hear. "We were spotted but not identified, so let's refrain from shouting about adventures, shall we?"

"Sure thing, boss," Squints said, returning to his chipped beef with gusto.

Jace glanced across the table to Logan and grinned. "When you're done pretending to eat that, we can head to the dorm and see what real food we came away with."

"Do we get some?" one of the Bens asked. The roommates looked at Jace hopefully.

Jace sighed. "I told you not to tell them about it, Homeschool." To the rest, he said, "If there's anything left over, I'll leave it in my trunk. You're welcome to what's there."

Logan and Jace were the first two back to the dorm for the break between lunch and chores. Jace unslung his bag and dumped the contents onto his bed.

"When you've grabbed what you want, hide it well. The other boys'll be looking for it."

Logan glanced around helplessly. "I have no idea where the hiding places in this room are, much less which ones aren't already full of someone else's contraband. Any chance I could stow it in my trunk with a note that says, 'Don't eat this—it's mine'?"

"You can, but then it'll be a race between the boys eating it and Ms. Lowell confiscating it and reporting you for breaking into an admin room and stealing it. We didn't get away clean. She'll definitely be in here checking things out—if she hasn't already. I'm guessing she didn't come in to find we weren't in bed last night or we'd have heard about it already."

Logan sighed, staring around the room again. Although he'd watched the other boys hide their stash from the labs only two nights before, he could barely remember where half those holes had been—even then, the other boys obviously already knew about them.

Jace watched him with his crooked half smile. "You won't find any that way. Quit staring around like someone just dropped you on an alien planet. I trust you, so I'm going to tell you something the other boys don't know. But seriously—*seriously*—don't tell them. This is my spot for stuff they aren't allowed to find."

Logan nodded. "Okay, understood."

Jace knocked on his bed frame. "Sounds pretty solid, right?"

"Uh, yeah?"

"Everybody thinks it is. They think we can't move the beds because they're so heavy, but actually they're bolted to the floor. They're not solid at all."

He bent and ran his finger over the edge of the bed's leg, pressed hard on the back side of it, and the whole back of the leg came away with a click as a single panel. Inside, it was packed with jars, bags, and boxes that seemed to hold a little of everything.

"Whoa! Do all the legs do that?"

"No, just mine. I did it so I could get to everything easily. But they're all hollow." He pressed the panel closed again with a quiet snick and lifted the corner of his mattress. "You can slide out this metal piece here, and see? There's a hole that goes straight down through the leg. Drop your goods in there."

"That's brilliant! Thanks, Jace."

Logan stowed his food quickly before putting his bed back in order. He left out a pear and some saltine crackers, which he snacked on stretched out on his bed as the other boys came in.

They'd left a few things in Jace's trunk that they'd grabbed blindly but neither wanted, and the boys fished in to claim things as they filtered past.

"So what's the deal, Jace?" Squints said as he entered. He tossed his bag onto his bed and kicked off his shoes. "You swore you'd never go back to the pantry."

"And I probably should have stuck to that," Jace said with a laugh. "Look, we've got a new friend here, and I distinctly heard Ms. Lee tell me to give him a proper ChilCo welcome." The other boys chuckled, and any tension the moment might have held dissipated.

"Actually," Jace continued, "this guy saved my ass. I was about to run out the door straight into Rollins's arms, but he pushed me out a window instead." He smiled, his eyes crinkling and warm.

Most of the other boys nodded at Logan, and he felt like he'd passed some sort of strange initiation. He remembered what Ms. Lowell had said about Jace making life easier for newbies, and he got the sense Jace was going out of his way to show he liked and trusted Logan so the other boys would do the same.

And it seemed to be working.

# 4

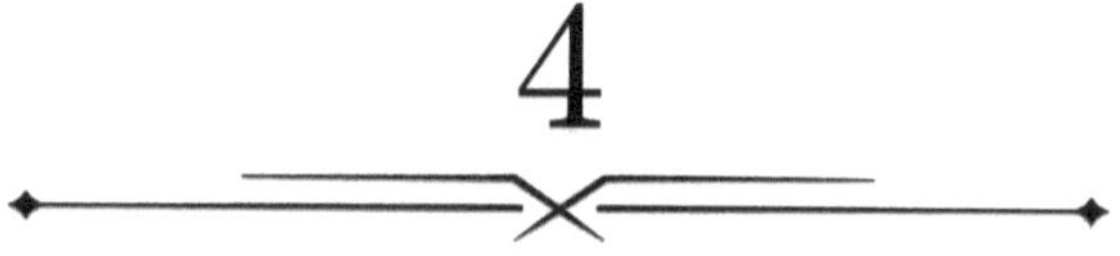

## APOSTATE

"Rise and shine, Homeschool," Jace half sung. Logan opened one eye, squinting into abnormally bright sunlight. It was later than he'd woken up during the first three days.

"Am I late?" he asked blearily, sitting up, but the other boys were all in the dorm room as well, and no one seemed to be moving with any sort of urgency.

"No, but you will be if you don't get up," Jace said. He lifted a folded stack of clothing then set it in Logan's trunk. "Lowell brought by your fitted stuff. It's all in here. Just in time, since you'll need your church clothes this morning."

"Church clothes?" Logan felt stupid repeating Jace's words, but he was at a loss. He'd never been to church in his life. Were special clothes required?

Jace's eyes widened slightly before he blinked and breathed out a muted laugh. "I guess your parents didn't smuggle in a priest once a week. It's chapel day. You need to wear…" He reached into the trunk and snagged a few articles of clothing, then lay them neatly at the foot of the bed. "…these. And comb your hair—you look like you were electrocuted."

As Logan self-consciously patted down his wild hair, he watched the other boys in the room. They laughed and chatted, some already dressed and others dressing. They did seem to have neatened up a bit from normal, and each of them wore a similar white button-down shirt, tucked into dark pants. Jace had rolled up the sleeves of his shirt, showing off tanned forearms, which Logan had to drag his eyes away from. "Is…church required?" he asked.

Jace's eyebrows quirked up incredulously. "I would assume so. I mean, I don't think anyone's ever said it's mandatory, but we all go."

Logan wasn't about to make himself the odd one out by refusing. His parents had told him that while Hallsburg didn't have an official state religion, almost everyone subscribed at least nominally to the beliefs of the Church of the Holy Sword. No one had ever been elevated to government leadership who wasn't a Swordsman.

His dad had always called it by the nickname B&B, short for "blood and blade," but neither of his parents had claimed any belief in it. Although they'd given him a brief overview of all the major religions on the continent, they hadn't been people of faith.

"Will I have to do anything? Or say anything? I don't…I've never been—"

"Don't panic, Homeschool, it's a dry couple hours of singing and sermons, and then we're back here with a free afternoon," Jace explained. He patted the clothing pile with one hand and glanced at the wall clock. "You need to get a move on, though."

Jace left him alone to get ready, and Logan tried to swallow his nerves. He wasn't entirely sure *why* he was so nervous—this wasn't any newer than a dozen other things at ChilCo—but by the time his shaking hands had tied the new, shiny shoes, everyone else was headed out the door.

Jace waited for him, waving the others out ahead of them.

"Are you okay?" he asked.

"Yeah. Just getting psyched up for the old B&B," he said with a hollow sort of laughter.

Jace's chin came up, eyes narrowing. He studied Logan for a moment as Logan got progressively sweatier under his scrutiny. Finally, he said, "Don't call it that where anyone else can hear. I don't want them to think you're an apostate. You're old enough to get in actual trouble for that sort of thing."

"Wait, what? What's an apostate?" Logan felt panic tightening his throat now.

Jace clapped his shoulder, steering him toward the door. "You don't have to worry about it as long as you don't say anything… uh…I guess as long as you don't repeat anything your parents ever told you about church. Just follow my lead, okay?"

"Okay."

They filed out, meeting up with other lines of boys from other rooms, until the entirety of Eagle Hold was congregated in the common room. Ms. Lowell gestured for them all to follow her into the halls, out the front door, and onto the sidewalk that ran alongside the road heading east. Other deans led other holds, and rows and rows of boys trotted away from the home, more orderly than anything else Logan had seen at Childers Coast so far.

The sidewalk was wide enough for two or three boys to walk abreast, though it narrowed and widened again at random intervals, squeezing walkers off into the grass at its most cramped points. Though Logan tried to walk next to Jace, he found himself gradually pushed back by the ebb and flow until he was alongside Squints instead. Some of the boys laughed and joked as they walked, but Jace was silent ahead of him, so Logan stayed quiet too.

It wasn't far—maybe half a mile—before the chapel appeared between the trees. A pretty place, larger than Logan had expected, with a towering steeple and white-paneled walls. It seemed to be built in a huge circle. Other people, not from ChilCo, milled around in a parking lot and greeted one another along the steps up into the church. Some of them—

Logan jerked to a halt, breath catching in his chest.

Some of them were Black Lapels.

A *lot* of them were Black Lapels.

What the fuck were the Black Lapels doing here? Were they here for someone? For *him?* Should he run? Hide? He couldn't catch his breath, and the blood in his ears was deafeningly loud.

Someone grabbed his wrist gently. Squints. "You're not in danger," the boy said quietly, pulling Logan forward so they didn't hold up the rest of the line of boys. "They're here for church. Here for the same reason we are. They're not gonna take anyone away."

Logan threw a spooked-horse glance at Squints. "You sure?"

"Yes," Squints said, blinking those huge brown eyes at him. He let Logan's wrist go but stayed next to him. "There's always some here. The Norford base is just a couple miles away, so this is the closest church."

"There's so many of them." Logan's chest tightened with the effort of trying to keep his tone normal, to not gasp like he'd just run three miles.

Squints looked over the crowd outside the church, now fil-tering their way in through the large double doors. "There are more than usual, but they're all dressed up. Probably came to get their blessing before they ship out. They do some kind of ceremony in their dress uniforms before they leave for wherever else."

With a fist, he knocked Logan gently on the upper arm; it looked like a playful shadow punch, but Logan felt the comfort intended in it. "You're okay. Keep your head down—do what we do. They won't mess with you."

"Jace told me to do what he does."

Squints laughed abruptly. "Don't copy Jace at chapel. Do what *I* do. It won't do as much to 'save your soul,' but it'll keep you from drawing any attention to yourself."

Logan nodded. "I don't want attention." He turned his eyes up to Jace, who was now two or three rows of boys away from Logan and Squints. "What does he do that draws attention?"

"Hm," Squints grunted, a noncommittal sound. "He does everything he does for his own reasons, and he draws attention wherever he goes, whether or not he wants to."

It wasn't an answer, but Logan could see from the blank set of Squints's face that he wasn't going to get any more by pressing. They were crunching through the pale gravel of the parking lot now, approaching the double doors. Lapels stood everywhere, chatting in knots or standing and watching the ChilCo boys file past. Logan was sweating through his button-down at the thought of any of those eyes turning to him.

Grinning, Squints nudged him with an elbow. "If there's one thing Black Lapels and church folk are good at, it's making you feel guilty even when you haven't done anything wrong. Don't worry about it—everyone gets nervous around them."

Logan exhaled shakily. "Thanks."

Then they were through the doors, entering a whitewashed hat box of a room packed with pews arranged in sections like segments of an orange, all turned inward toward a dais in the center of the room. On the dais stood a podium, and hanging above it, suspended point down from the ceiling, was a massive bronze sword.

"Homeschool! Squints!" Jace called them over to the far-left side of the room, where he gestured toward an open space in the pew next to him. Rather than scooting inward and letting them take the end of the pew, Jace stepped into the aisle, sent Squints and then Logan to wedge themselves in next to the boys already seated, and sat down at the end himself.

He stretched one leg into the aisle, but the other was crammed against Logan's; Logan was, in turn, packed in against Squints. All the boys sat practically on top of one another to fit into the high-backed benches, and more kept coming in from outside.

The pew directly in front of them was packed with Black Lapels, their usual gray-and-black uniforms replaced with white wool and sharp black trim, shiny silver buttons on their black epaulettes, and silver thread tracing the edges of their ever-present black lapels. As if he felt the weight of Logan's stare, one of them glanced over his shoulder at him, caught his eye, and tightened his lips in a slight smile of greeting before turning back toward the dais.

Logan wiped his sweaty palms against the stiff fabric of his dark pants. He didn't dare look at Jace right now, but from the corner of his eye, he saw the curly-haired boy crushing his lip between thumb and forefinger. He couldn't stop thinking about Jace's shoulder pressed against his, Jace's left hip against his right, the line of each of their thighs that made contact with each other.

Squints pulled a thin sheet of paper out of a wooden holder built into the back of the pew in front of them, plucked a half pencil from a slim hole in the holder, and balanced the paper on his knee to scribble a few words on the back.

When he was done, he handed it to Logan. "Those are the call-and-response things we all say," he whispered.

"Thanks, Squints." Logan felt a surge of gratitude to the bespectacled boy as he scanned the written phrases, hurriedly memorizing. If everyone else spoke and he didn't, would the Lapels in front of them notice? Would they do something about it?

As Jace shifted slightly, Logan's attention was drawn back to their points of contact. If he sweated any more, he'd drip visibly.

A fit, balding man in a somber oversize suit marched up through the aisle, and a hush fell over the room. At Logan's curious glance, Squints mouthed, "Father Robinson." When the preacher climbed two steps onto the dais and stretched his hands out to either side of him, the last whispers went silent.

"Good morning, Swordsmen, soldiers of God. We are blessed this morning with the presence of so many strong and courageous followers of the Holy Sword."

The man's voice carried to every corner of the room with an odd resonance. Slowly, he walked around the podium so he could speak to every segment of the radial array of pews. "I welcome you all to the whetstone, where together we will sharpen our blades and strengthen our arms. His might is great, amen?"

"Amen," everyone said in unison, Logan a half second behind.

"Stand with me and let us sing to the glory He grants us," the man said. Everyone rose.

Fortunately, the singing was closer to chanting, and Logan found he wasn't the only one making vaguely rhythmic noises instead of specific words. Standing, too, was a breath of relief, as they were able to spread out slightly. He relaxed infinitesimally as they chanted two or three more songs—hard to count exactly, since each sounded identical to the next.

When they all sat down again, though, Jace's closeness was more torturous than before. Jace had his outside arm flung over the high side of the pew and was leaning like he meant to climb over it, but they'd lost space in the shuffle. Logan's entire right leg was pressed against Jace's left, and he couldn't shift an inch without climbing into Squints's lap.

Logan missed the first call-and-response entirely, despite Squints's helpful guide, because he focused all his attention on not thinking about Jace. It felt desperately hot in the church. Jace shifted again as Father Robinson preached, his intonation a steady, almost musical cadence. Jace cast a sideways, uncomfortable look at Logan, but when he realized Logan was already looking at him, it shifted into a grin.

"Kind of snug in here," he whispered. "Hold on."

Jace shrugged his left arm up past Logan and swung it backwards so he could lay it along the top of the pew. It should have been a relief to have the extra room, but instead it just added to Logan's consciousness of Jace being next to him. Now he felt the warmth of Jace's arm along his shoulders and back.

The same Black Lapel who had turned around before glanced back again, and Logan froze like a rabbit in a hawk's shadow.

He'd had nightmares about emerging into the world unprepared, not knowing what to do or say in situations other people thought were common. He'd had nightmares about not being able to hide his attraction to other men, being caught and punished. He'd had nightmares about the Black Lapels coming back for him.

But his mind had never created a dream scenario as bad as this interminable morning in the chapel, experiencing all three fears at once.

"...His righteous vengeance down on those who question His authority," the priest said. "And let also His wrath fall upon the savage, the unnatural, the apostate, the weak, the cowardly. The Lord rains blessings down on those who raise up the sword to strike down His enemies. Think of the..."

Logan tuned him out again, concentrating on the top of his right shoulder where he felt Jace's pulse, pressed as it was against the inside of Jace's upper arm. Jace's heartbeat seemed to thrum faster than normal.

"We have with us today many of the Lord of the Sword's most treasured followers," the priest droned on. "Our Special Police wield His holy wrath and hold high esteem in the Lord's eyes. Stand, and let us send you with His blessing to the lands where you will bring his order."

The Lapels in front of Logan rose, standing at attention with their hands folded behind their backs. Logan drew back until his spine ground against the pew.

Without looking at Logan, Squints tapped the paper with a finger, indicating the third set of responses. Logan lifted the sheet and read along with the congregation.

"Blessed are the fierce of heart," the preacher said.

"For victory will be theirs," the room replied.

"Blessed are the strong of arm."

"For glory will be theirs."

"Blessed are those who enforce peace under His dominion."

"For all the earth shall be theirs."

"Blessed are those who bear pain without complaint and offer their life in service to the Lord of the Sword."

"For they will receive all they desire, in this life and beyond."

The preacher lifted his hands and spun in a slow circle, making eye contact with standing Lapels as he turned. After a long, long silence, he said, "Go, Swordsmen, and know that what you do in His name is blessed by Him."

Logan frowned. *Anything* you do? That sounded like complete freedom to be the biggest dicks on the continent and feel holy about it. The more he thought about the rest of the message, the more unsettled he became. No fucking wonder his parents hadn't thought much of the Church of the Holy Sword.

The priest said something else that Logan missed, and people shuffled out of the rearmost pews and toward the outside edge of the chapel. More men in suits and waistcoats awaited them, sword pendants hanging from fine bronze chains around their necks.

They knelt, and the priests dipped their thumbs in a glass bowl of something, then smudged it on the kneeling penitents' faces. As people rose and made their way back out the front doors, Logan saw that each person had a line of deep red drawn down the center of their lips and chin.

"Is that blood?" he whispered to no one in particular, but Jace answered him.

"No, it's oil. And do *not* let it get in your mouth."

"Also," Squints added, leaning toward both of them, "when they ask if you need to be purified before the oil, say no."

"Unless you need it," Jace whispered lightly.

Squints didn't take it as a joke. "He doesn't. None of us do."

Jace shrugged like he might or might not agree, then turned to watch as the people in the pew behind them rose and made their way to the back. Logan didn't want to turn all the way around and gawk, so he couldn't make out much of what was happening. "Our turn," Jace muttered, standing and waving for Logan to follow.

He approached a strange piece of furniture that ran the entire length of this section of wall: a long, carpeted bar low to the ground with periodic uprights holding up a similar velvet-coated bar a little lower than waist height. Jace knelt on the lower bar and placed his forearms on the upper, his hands dangling toward the suited man who stood behind the contraption. Logan mirrored him, kneeling next to him, and Squints took the spot on Logan's other side.

"Good morning, Jace," the priest said, smiling familiarly. "Do you need to be purified today before you receive the oil?"

Jace bowed his head for a moment before taking a deep breath, blinking up at the man, and saying, "Yes." He held his hands out flat, palms down, forearms braced against the bar.

The priest sighed so quietly Logan thought he might not have heard it. "Very well." He pulled a narrow rod out of his pocket, paused for a moment, then whipped it hard against Jace's knuckles.

Jace didn't flinch, but Logan did. Squints nudged him with an elbow, a warning, and Logan tried to school his face back into neutral as the man cracked down on Jace's fingers three more times.

When the first joint of his right index finger split, a bright line of blood appearing where the rod had struck, Jace folded his hands together and looked back up at the man wearing the sword necklace. "Thank you."

The priest nodded, pocketed his beating stick, and swiped his thumb through the ruby oil in his bowl. He drew a thick line down

Jace's lips and onto his chin, where it beaded up and threatened to drip. Logan watched it all with wide eyes.

Then the man turned to him. "A new parishioner, I presume?" he said, not unkindly, but still with a level of attention on Logan he'd prefer to avoid. He wasn't sure how to answer except to nod. "Welcome. Do you need to be purified before you receive the oil?"

"Um, no, thank you," Logan said.

With a faintly amused smile, the man reached into the bowl again and traced a line of oil on Logan's mouth. It burned. As the priest turned to Squints to repeat the process, Logan's tongue darted out by instinct to wipe away the slick stuff and instantly he regretted it. As much as it burned his chin and his lips, it lit the tip of his tongue on *fire*. It tasted of nothing but pain, and Logan made a small, involuntary sound of alarm as it threatened to melt his tongue away to nothing. He started to reach for it to wipe it away, but Jace reached over far enough to set his last two fingers against Logan's wrist and shake his head.

*Fuck*, what the hell was this stuff? Why were these people voluntarily painting it on their faces? He understood now why Jace had told him not to get it in his mouth, and he was afraid to part his lips enough to ask how to get rid of it, lest more drip in. He flattened them into a tight line and braced himself not to move or make any more noise. The priest was halfway down the line now. Surely he'd be done soon and they could escape this place.

After an eternity, the priest returned to the center of their section of the wall, raised his hand, and said, "Go and spread His message by any means necessary."

Jace unfolded and stood, and Logan followed right behind, pressing for them to hurry out the doors. He couldn't get out of this place fast enough.

His haste brought him right up to the back of some of the Black Lapels in their dress uniforms, and with difficulty, he fought his anxiety down. He had to get fresh air. He had to get this fucking fire oil off his face.

At last, they emerged, and Logan jogged away from the clusters of people standing on the gravel path and talking, some patting their faces with handkerchiefs while others simply left the oil where it had been placed. Logan stepped into the trees that ringed the lot and leaned hard against a trunk, searching his pockets for anything he could use to wipe the shit off.

"Here," Jace said, holding out a cloth as he leaned on the tree.

Squints was right behind him. "Sorry. We probably should have warned you about the oil. Heinous stuff."

Logan swiped it off his face, trying not to spread it further. He scrubbed at his tongue, but the cloth could do nothing for it.

"Get a lot of spit in your mouth and hold it there," Jace said. "It kind of dissolves after a while. Not much else for it once it's in your mouth."

He took the cloth back and wiped his own face before passing it to Squints.

Logan let saliva pool around his tongue, and it did seem to help after a minute or two. At the very least, he no longer felt he was openly bleeding from acid damage.

"You okay?" Squints asked.

"I guess," Logan said, though in truth he was furious about the entire debacle. More sharply than he meant to, he asked Jace, "How'd I do? Am I sufficiently proven not an apostate?"

"Apostate? Fucking hell, Jace, why'd you scare him with that?" Squints asked. "No one gives a shit if the ChilCo boys are true believers as long as we stay out of trouble. *Apostate*." He muttered the last in disgust, as if it were ludicrous.

"Homeschool wasn't scared. Were you?"

The look Jace gave Logan was fully unreadable, intense in some way Logan couldn't grasp. Logan stared back, and just like that, his ire faded into…something else. Confusion maybe. And an urge to prove himself the equal of whatever challenge Jace was setting for him.

"No, I wasn't scared," he said quietly.

Jace reached up to grab his lip and winced when he pinched skin already scalded by the oil. Though the wicked red stuff was gone, it had left a faint line where the priest had drawn it and Jace's lips looked swollen, like someone had punched him.

Or bitten him.

Squints cleared his throat, pink in the face for some reason. "We should get off the chapel grounds. People are leaving."

Logan and Jace turned away from each other to follow him toward the gathering exodus. There was less order on the return trip, though Logan noted the deans standing at the edge of the sidewalk, counting heads.

"Is that," Logan began as they tromped back toward ChilCo, "what it's always like?"

"What do you mean?" Jace asked.

"Like…'the strong and powerful can take whatever they want because it's God that made them that way and the victor's spoils are His blessings'?" Logan said, trying to keep his disgust from ringing through his words.

Squints laughed, but Jace spread his hands like Logan had proved his point. "See what I mean? Apostate." He said it lightly, though, not like he was pronouncing judgment. "Yeah, that's not *quite* how I'd have characterized it, but you've pretty much got it."

Logan frowned at the ground. "You don't seem to follow that philosophy, though. I mean, by that logic, *you* could stomp around and take anything from anybody, but Ms. Lowell said you look out for the smaller kids and the ones who are having a hard time."

Shrugging uncomfortably like he was being accused of something, Jace didn't answer, so Squints spoke up instead. "Jace isn't good with rules and authority, didn't you hear?" he teased. "And what's power good for if you can't use it to take care of your people?"

Logan considered that. He couldn't square the idea that Jace didn't believe what was preached with the boy holding his hands out, asking to be hit until he bled for "purification."

"Whatcha thinking, Homeschool?" Jace asked, interrupting his contemplation.

He couldn't say what he actually wanted, so instead he asked, "What's the deal with the oil? What's that supposed to represent?"

Jace shifted as he walked until he was bent like an old man, pretending to walk with a cane. Adjusting imaginary spectacles on his nose, he said, in a breathy voice dry as dust, "Larry Quintz, what is the source of all our sins, dear boy?"

He was clearly doing an impression of someone Squints recognized instantly. He laughed before answering, "Surely our minds, Father Thomas."

"No, *no*, dear boy," Jace said, the very image of a wizened clergyman. "Hearts, minds—*pshaw*. These are merely the malleable clay on which our sins write themselves. It is from our *mouths* that sin flows."

"Are you sure that's not food poisoning?" Squints quipped. To Logan, he said, "It's supposed to burn only if 'sin has crossed your lips.' A 'reminder of the burn that we shall feel in hell if we do not protect our precious souls.' I'm pretty sure it's made to burn like the Devil's asshole no matter what, though."

"Squints," Jace said, and Logan couldn't tell if the offense in his tone was real, "we're supposed to be teaching Homeschool here the way of righteousness. If you let them purify you of your sins before the oil, it doesn't burn."

Logan looked back at Jace's lips, still stained and swollen. They looked as burned as his own felt. "Is that true?"

Jace smirked at him, revealing no secrets. He tilted his head back and whistled—not a tune, but a signal, three high bursts and three low. Squints, on Logan's other side, echoed it, and so did a handful of other boys elsewhere up and down the sidewalk.

A minute later, the Bens, Randy, and Bails jogged up or fell back until they'd all converged in a clump too large for the sidewalk.

"Hiking this afternoon?" Jace asked when they'd all circled him. The upward intonation suggested it was a question, but nothing in his manner left room for disagreement.

Bails grumbled, though. "Every time we climb around in the woods, I end up falling down a mountain."

Jace waved a hand. "There isn't a mountain within thirty miles of here. You lose one chossy hold, fall five feet, and whine like you've endured a landslide. Anyway, we're just taking a mellow walk in the woods today. We've got new blood."

"Don't go easy on my account," Logan said, although the closest he had ever come to hiking was his and Jace's middle-of-the-night walk to the sheltered little cave.

Now that they had something ahead of them, the group picked up their pace. Logan stuck close to Jace. Out of curiosity, he looked at the other boys' hands whenever they were close enough; none of them seemed to have taken the "purification" option as Jace had. Why did he do that to himself?

"So where are we hiking? To the cave?" Logan asked, but Jace shook his head before Logan even finished the question, raising one finger like he would shush Logan, then stopping himself.

"No, that's mine. We'll head up and see the best view in Hallsburg. Maybe have a kite fight or something."

*That's mine,* he'd said, like he never shared it. But he'd shared it with Logan.

They marched into the dorm, changed, and pilfered food and water from the kitchen before most of ChilCo had even returned from the chapel, pouring back out again past Ms. Lowell as she herded stragglers through the front doors.

"We're headed to Trio Rock!" Jace called over his shoulder to her, and she waved them on with a fond half smile.

"They don't mind if we wander?" Logan asked, and Jace's eyebrows quirked like he didn't understand the question. "I mean, there's no security or anything keeping us from just running away?"

"Running away from what?" Jace seemed genuinely baffled, so Logan let it drop.

Jace set a blistering pace across the grounds and didn't slow until they reached the trees. He picked up a stick and hacked at the undergrowth as they walked. Since he, Logan, and Randy had the longest legs of the bunch, they ended up ahead of the others.

"Did you make that?" Logan asked Randy, nodding to the kite stuffed into the bag over his shoulder.

"No," Randy said ruefully. "I'm shit at crafts. I think Bails made this one."

"Don't remind him. If that one wins, we'll never hear the end of it," Jace said. He hopped onto a stump and steadied himself for a moment before flipping off of it, turning lithely in the air and tumbling into the grass and leaves ahead.

Randy muttered, "Always showing off." To Logan, he said, "You a showboater too?"

"Nah," Logan said with a mirthless chuckle. "I'm not much for attention." He hadn't really exchanged words to Randy. The redhead was soft-spoken, voice laced with a dry edge of sarcastic humor. He had nice eyes, warm brown like his freckles.

"So this week must have been a lot of fun for you," Randy said, eyes sparkling with almost-laughter. "Lots of stares. Lots of whispers."

"Lots of my entire life falling apart," Logan said, reflecting back the dry humor even though there was nothing funny about it at all. He wasn't sure how else to talk about it, though.

Randy looked away and dug around at the roots of a tree until he came up with a decent-size walking stick. "Yeah, that too," he said eventually. Clearly, he didn't know how to talk about it either. "Anything good so far?"

Logan stared hard at the ground, determined not to look at Jace. "This is pretty good. Walking around outside without, you know, being afraid the Black Lapels will scoop me up."

"Yeah, they don't mess with the school much outside of placement season. Unless you get in *real* trouble, but even Jace hasn't managed that, so..." Randy shrugged, stabbing at a patch of crab grass with his walking stick.

"What happens if you get in real trouble?"

Randy pressed his mouth into a flat line, making dimples in his freckled cheeks. "Nobody really knows exactly, do we? Lots of rumors. Lapels kidnap you and put you on the front line without a gun in whatever country they're fighting in at the moment. They tie you up in a tree and beat you with a stick. The make you drink holy oil. They put you to work on the walls at Shalecrest, shooting people who try to run."

Randy's dry tone suggested he thought these were all ridiculous, but Logan felt himself growing paler by the word. To him, any of those sounded plausible, minus some small amount of exaggeration as the tale was passed from boy to boy. Why *wouldn't* the Lapels take unruly boys and make them fight, either at Shalecrest or abroad? Why *wouldn't* they beat them or burn the sins out of them with fire oil?

"I'm teasing," Randy said, realizing how seriously Logan had taken him. "Those are just stories we tell to scare littles. The worst thing Lapels ever really do to you is bring you here. And it's not so bad, right? Your worst fears already came true. And you survived."

Logan swallowed, trying to work moisture into his dry throat. *It's not so bad?* It was the worst thing he could imagine, and he didn't *have* to imagine it. They'd taken everything from him. Because he had to say something, he said, "I did survive."

"Are we talking about yesterday's chicken surprise?" Jace said, finding his way back to Logan's left side as they caught up to him. "Survival was a near thing for me too. Can't imagine what it must have done to your tender innards, Homeschool."

Gratefully, Logan leaned into the lighthearted turn of conversation, fake retching as he said, "See, this is why I've avoided that damn cafeteria food."

"You can't dodge it forever," Randy said. "Soon you'll be slurping down brain-eating amoebas with the rest of us. One of us. One of us!" The others behind him heard him and picked up the chant, though they had no idea what he was talking about, and soon the whole group was picking their way through the woods chanting, "One of us! One of us!" After a few rounds, Logan started to say it with them, which he supposed fulfilled the prophecy.

Logan let the others draw him out of maudlin thoughts of Black Lapels and into the easy, untamed joy of being boys together.

They gamboled and climbed and swung and shouted and laughed their way through the woods, gradually stomping uphill until the way steepened and they needed their breath and sure feet. When they reached the top, they howled like a pack of wolves, listening to the echoes over the treetops.

They ate their snacks and scraps like feral creatures. They flew kites along the clear hilltop and tried to knock one another's sailing creations of wood and fabric down. When they failed, they'd simply knock one another down and wrestle for control of the string. They stayed out there all day, inventing games, talking about everything and nothing.

When at last they stood at the edge of the hill and watched their shadows grow long in front of them on the forest below, their pockets empty of food and their water all drunk, Logan *did* feel like one of them.

Jace shot him a mischievous look and pulled a rolled paper bag from his pocket. "Watch this, Homeschool." From the crackling bag, Jace pulled a small ball, trailing a bit of string.

"Bens, can I get a light?" Jace called, and one of the Bens tossed him a lighter. Tucking the bag under his arm, Jace held the flame to the end of the string until it began to spark and burn.

He held the ball for a moment longer, then reeled back and chunked it into the air as far from the hilltop as he could manage.

*Boom!* An explosion of colorful sparks lit up the sky.

The boys crowed appreciatively, watching the light dissipate, but Logan's eyes were all for Jace. The curly-haired boy was watching him, grinning, as he lit another, held it, threw it. Jace made fireworks. And though he knew better, knew Jace didn't have any reason to have considered Logan for one second when he made them, Logan felt like every one was lit for him.

Over the next several weeks, Logan's life settled into an easy, numbing rhythm. Wake up, shower, and dress; eat breakfast; mumble along with the pledge; sit through class; find the guys for lunch; relax in the dorm room or on the grounds with Jace, Squints, and Randy; refile books in the library; get his ass kicked at rugby practice; do his own pile of homework and several other boys' language and literature work as well; then read one of Jace's dozens of books until he fell asleep. Once a week, he'd hike to chapel with everyone else, chant the same words, try to tune out the most egregious messages, and watch Jace get his knuckles cracked open before enduring the horrid lip smear.

When it became clear that the Black Lapels weren't on campus, but instead sat above the home's administration in some nebulous hierarchy, Logan's anxiety abated slightly. As long as he stayed out of trouble, he'd be fine.

Although he ran out of the stolen food from the pantry, he didn't mention sneaking back in to Jace. He did ask if Jace would give him lockpicking lessons, which the curly-haired boy was happy to do, but Logan was slow to learn it. The cafeteria food was starting to taste okay anyway.

Every now and then, in the safety of the dark dorm room, the loss of his parents overwhelmed him. If the other boys heard him cry himself to sleep, they didn't say anything.

Sometimes it didn't come out in tears. Sometimes it was uncontrollable anger.

One afternoon, the third time he'd worked the same stupid calculus problem and gotten the same stupid—wrong—answer, an upsurge of such violent rage seized him that he picked up his textbook and hurled it with a wordless roar. It slammed into the wall corner first and put a sizable dent in the plaster immediately to the right of Jace's bed.

Everyone else had been silently working on their homework, so all eyes turned to him, which infuriated Logan even more. What the *fuck* were they staring at? Had no one ever lost their goddamn temper in this place? The more he thought about it, the angrier he got. He ground his teeth so hard he heard his jaw crack. If someone said *one* fucking word, he'd snap.

"Hey," Jace said, sliding off his bed, stepping over the textbook, and dropping an arm around Logan's shoulders. "Let's walk."

Logan shrugged him off. "I don't want—"

"Let's. Walk." Jace put his arm back around Logan and steered him out of the dorm, down the stairs, and beyond the common room. He took Logan all the way to the gymnasium at the opposite end of the school. Empty in the evenings, the gym was dark, with large squares of golden light from the setting sun painted across the hardwood floor by the high-set windows.

It wasn't until they stood in the center of the empty space that Jace let him go.

"Talk," he said.

"No."

Jace absorbed that with a nod. "Well, hit me then."

Unable to stand still, Logan paced. "I'm not gonna hit you."

"You looked like you were going to hit *someone*. Why not me?"

Logan shrugged. "Because I don't want to hit you."

"Who do you want to hit?"

He stopped abruptly, then turned and threw a dark look at Jace. It was an effort to summon any words at all. "Who the *fuck* do you think?"

"The Lapels?"

Logan growled. He hadn't known he could make that noise, but it vibrated through him naturally enough. He paced. Jace left him to it in silence, watching and waiting. Eventually the pressure built up until words boiled out of Logan. "What gave them the fucking right?"

"To take your family?"

"To take *everything*. And they stood there and pointed a gun at me and said it was all for *my own fucking good*. I...I..." He was overcome again, rage shaking into his limbs until he wasn't sure he could control them.

"Those smug fucking bastards are probably sitting at home, enjoying a nice cup of tea, thinking, 'Oh, I saved some kids today from the terror of parents that wanted them and cared about them, and I locked those fucking parents up in a death-prison and toted their kid off to the edge of nowhere to figure shit out on his own—'"

"Hey—"

Jace tried to break in, but Logan grabbed him by the shirt-front and hissed straight into his face, "*Do not try to comfort me.*"

Jace took hold of his wrists and carefully stepped Logan back. "I wasn't going to. I don't have anything to say to make that better." Slowly, he set a hand on Logan's chest, and then shoved him hard.

Logan shoved him back harder.

Then they were fighting. Logan swung for everything he had; Jace dodged most of it and absorbed the rest and didn't hit back hard enough even to bruise. He was just a little taller, a little stronger, and practiced from the thousand small brawls and wrestling matches he and his boys had had, so he didn't have to hurt Logan to keep him mostly at bay.

Logan had no idea how long he'd been in the red fog of pure barbarian rage when Jace finally wrapped him up in a choke he couldn't get out of. All the fight left him. He sagged, drained, and Jace let him fall on the floor. He sat down, pulling his knees to his chest and wrapping his arms around them, and Jace sat next to him.

"I'm sorry," he said at last, his voice catching. He knew he was crying; he hoped it was dark enough in the gym Jace couldn't tell.

"Don't be. I needed the exercise," Jace said lightly. Then, after a long pause, he added, "*I'm* sorry. About…all that. It isn't fair. And if beating the shit out of a Black Lapel would make you feel better, I could probably figure out a way to make it happen."

Logan laughed, a miserable bleating sound. "I'm sure that would turn out really well for both of us."

For a long time, the silence was broken only by Logan's occasional sniffles. Then Jace said, "Would it help to talk about them? You haven't said a word about your parents since you got here."

"I don't know."

"Do you want to try?"

Logan sighed out a sharp breath. "My mom…her name is—was—is Eleanor. She's a brilliant teacher. Took care of my dad after his accident and never complained for a second of it, even though I'm sure it was hard, with both of us.

"My dad: Frank. He used to be a really excellent carpenter. But there was an accident on a job site. A car drove through and pinned him to a wall, and it put him in a wheelchair before I was born. That's why they couldn't get the credits for a kid. They—" His face twisted, too many memories bearing him down into darkness. "It doesn't help. I can't…I can't—"

"Then don't," Jace said abruptly. "You don't have to tell me anything unless you want to. But you know, you're…you're not on your own. You don't have to figure it out on your own."

Logan looked at him, hoping to see what might be written on Jace's face, but the golden squares of light were gone now, and it was too dark to read. "Thanks."

After a while, they returned to the dorm room. They returned to their routine. And just as Squints had said it would, the repetition eventually deadened the grief. Gradually the tears came less often. The anger slowed. And ChilCo started to feel more like…not a home but at least a place where he belonged.

It helped that ChilCo was *Jace's* home.

Logan's initial crush on Jace didn't fade. In fact, the more he saw of Jace, the more he wanted to be around him. Half the nights he remembered his dreams, Jace was in them; Logan could only hope to God he wasn't talking in his sleep. He also was glad the curly-haired boy didn't seem to be sick of him yet.

In fact, Jace invited Logan everywhere, probably as part of his ongoing mission to ensure the other boys in his crew accepted the weirdly old newbie.

Time passed. Days melted into weeks, which slid into months. Other new arrivals at ChilCo made Logan look like a veteran. The boys of Eagle Hold started to treat him like he'd always been one of them, always been at Jace's right hand.

And Logan was getting altogether too comfortable.

# 5

## NOT A DISTRACTION

During the three months Logan had been at ChilCo, Jace proposed no more raids, though the other boys regularly brought up ideas for things to appropriate. Logan heard Bails and the Bens had gone out with Forrest's next-door crew. They were addicted to sneaking around and stealing things, pranking other holds, and generally being the vandals the administration thought they were.

Logan was surprised Jace hadn't said anything to them about it when they almost got caught—Forrest and three of his boys *did* get caught—but Jace seemed preoccupied and tired.

"What's wrong?" Logan asked abruptly one day while he and Jace messed around with a rugby ball in the courtyard after lunch.

"What do you mean?" Jace caught the ball, then put an arm out like he was defending himself against an invisible tackler and sent an ugly flick pass in Logan's direction.

Logan didn't make it to the ball in time, scooping it up off the grass instead. "I mean, you don't seem like yourself lately. Your guys are...drifting."

"I don't think anyone's ever complained I'm not controlling enough," Jace said lightly as he caught the ball and passed it back.

"I'm not making a judgment one way or the other about how controlling you are," Logan said, laughing. "I'm saying you used to be more controlling, and now you're less, and I want to know why."

"I'm thinking," he said simply.

Logan jumped for the high pass then punted the ball, dropping it very nearly on top of Jace. "Sure, and thinking is such a rare activity for you, it occupies all your time and energy."

Jace screwed up his face as he made the catch, then returned it with another punt. "It's something different. Usually I just think of something then knock out a plan for it. This is…different. Can't settle on what the idea is yet."

"Well, what are you thinking?"

Jace shook his head, denying his friend's unspoken offer to help. "It's *my* thing."

Logan spun the ball in his hands. "How do you know if you don't know yet what the idea is? I could help you narrow it down."

Extending his hands in a mute request for the ball, Jace frowned. "I don't think you'll like what I'm thinking."

Logan didn't throw, keeping the ball spinning between his hands. "Try me."

Making a frustrated sound in the back of his throat, Jace crossed the space between them in a few strides and slapped the ball up out of Logan's hands.

"Here's the thing," he said, spinning the ball as Logan had. "I…well, I used to think parents should never get kids. Everyone should be in places like ChilCo from the start." Logan felt a storm rising, and Jace clearly saw it on his face, as he hurriedly said, "But talking to you the last few months, I don't think it's right to take kids away from their families just because they don't have the credits for them. It's rehoming—and rehoming has to stop."

Lost in a maelstrom of thoughts, Logan missed the ball when Jace flicked it over and it *thunked* against his chest. The usual waves of pain when anyone mentioned parents crashed over him, now colored with horror at the idea of knowing nothing but the fluorescent, institutional-smelling halls of this place for his entire life.

Jace *wanted* that? But then, if this was all he'd ever known, maybe it was the best he could imagine. Maybe Jace was so happy here because he didn't know what he was missing.

Logan blinked, bent to pick up the ball, and said, "Okay."

Jace raised an eyebrow. "You're not gonna disagree with me?"

"Not yet." Logan threw the ball back. "I know nothing about rehoming except no one wanted me. Why do you want to end it?"

Immediately, Jace launched into what was clearly a much-considered rant. "Parents and families—they're a crapshoot. Even with all the licensing requirements, you get a lot of variation in how people are raised and treated. At ChilCo we've got structure, we've got boundaries. We've got everything a kid needs to grow up and be something worthwhile."

Logan laughed more cruelly than he meant. "Boundaries? You've never seen a boundary you weren't already planning to cross."

Impatient, Jace said, "Not boundaries for the residents. I'm talking about for the administration. They've got government oversight and random inspections; they have to submit curriculum, and they have to prove they're investing in us with their annual reports. They've got great facilities and lots of funding to keep them that way. The staff is all reviewed four times a year. They've got to undergo massive background checks and psych testing before they're hired. They do a damn good job here of making sure the right people are looking after us."

To Logan, this felt more like something regurgitated from a brochure than the experience he'd had at ChilCo thus far.

He balanced the ball vertically on his palm while he considered Jace's points. "Those things may be true, but there's no family here. With parents, you get personal attention, you get affection. You're not gonna get that from Ms. Lowell."

Jace sneered and spat. "Personal attention is the last thing we need." There was real venom in his voice. "We've got our bunkmates, our brothers. All parents are good for is fucking up the people they're in charge of."

Logan felt that like a slap. "I didn't end up too badly fucked up being raised by parents." He tried to keep his tone even. This was close to his heart, but his friend was clearly worked up over it too, and neither of them had any shared experience to argue from.

Jace didn't get angry, though. "It's not the same. Your parents were flesh and blood to you. They made you in defiance of the laws. They hid you. They wanted *you*. That's not what's happening at rehoming fairs." He sucked in a sharp breath, his face twisting in anger as his eyes went distant.

"They come in here and shop for a kid like we're fucking pets. 'Ooh, that one's so cute! Wouldn't that one's sad little story sound so good at parties!' They buy whatever kid they want, with no say at all on our part. And when something goes wrong—when the kid doesn't match their *aesthetic* or these 'parents' turn out to be fucking *monsters*—" He shook his head, clamping his lips together while he reined in his temper. "Did you know sixty percent of the kids who get matched at ChilCo's fairs are back here within a year?"

Logan whistled. "Whoa. No, I didn't."

"The system is broken, but they're still pretending like homes are somehow the preferred option and ChilCo's the fallback."

"Well, for the forty percent who find good homes—"

Jace squeezed the ball between his hands so hard his knuckles turned white. He exploded in fury. "What the hell makes you think they're good homes? Maybe they're just smart enough not to get CRS called on them! And do you honestly think it's fair to subject the rest of those kids to…to…whatever is bad enough to get them brought back here on the off chance that some kids *might* find parents who don't treat them like shit, *maybe?* You haven't *seen*—"

"Whoa, whoa," Logan said, raising his hands defensively. "I know I haven't seen it. I trust you. I'm not trying to argue. I guess you've probably known a lot of the kids who came back?"

Jace grunted, tossing the ball in Logan's direction. They backed away from each other and played catch in silence for a few minutes before Logan deemed it safe to speak again. "So if rehoming needs to end, what do you want to do about it?"

"It's got to start with the fairs. I want to put an end to the rehoming fairs before I get the boot," Jace said with finality, like pronouncing his goal was enough to achieve it.

It was an insane objective. Only a crazy person would think a teenage boy could do that. But if anyone could, Logan knew it would be Jace. He pursed his lips as he caught the ball and released it again. "How?"

Tucking the ball under one arm, Jace scrubbed his other hand through his hair. Suddenly he looked self-conscious, which was a strange fit for him. "Uh…I have some ideas, but…not anything I like yet."

"Ideas like what?"

After a pause, Jace pulled a small notebook out of his back pocket and crossed the grass to stand shoulder to shoulder with Logan so he could see the sketches. "I designed some…" He cleared his throat. "Some remote-detonated, uh, devices. If I put them here, here, and here, they'd bring the whole gym down. But it's got its own structure, so it wouldn't do much damage to the rest of the school. At most, take down the ceiling in that hallway."

The sketches were incredibly detailed, and at a glance, the margin math checked out. Jace had put a *lot* of thought into this.

"Bombs? This would kill so many people."

"I know." Jace snapped the notebook closed and shoved it into his pocket. "And not just the ghouls here to pick up a pet kid and their Lapel escorts either. There would be staff there and obviously kids themselves. Littles—that's all they ever trot out for the fairs. That's why I'm still thinking. Gotta figure out something better. Something longer lasting."

"Even if you *wanted* to kill people, how would you get your hands on the supplies?"

"Oh, I already have everything I need," Jace replied, seemingly surprised by the question. "I could take out the next fair if I wanted to. But unless I can figure out how to keep it from taking out Chil-Co staff and kids, I can't."

Logan stared too long before saying, "You're dangerous."

Jace smirked, raising an eyebrow in challenge. "You scared?"

"No, I'm not scared." *Hopelessly, desperately, dangerously attracted, yes—but not scared.* He handed the ball to Jace, enjoying the frisson of energy it sent up his arm when Jace's hand brushed over his.

"There's a lot of ways to bring about the end of something without blowing up half the school. We'll think of something."

"Oh?" Jace was an inch from smiling. "You're with me then?"

"Jace," Logan said, laughing, "of course I'm with you."

"Happy birthday, Homeschool!" Jace shouted, startling Logan out of sleep. Faces ringed his bed, and Jace knelt over him, holding a plate of snack cakes with a candle shoved in the top one.

"Holy shit. What time is it?"

"12:01," Jace said, grinning. "You've officially joined me and Squints in the land of the adults." The other boys let out a war whoop and dragged Logan into a seated position, then settled themselves around him.

"Hurry and light the candle so he can blow it out and we can eat some cake," Bails said.

Jace obliged, accepting a lighter from one of the Bens and bringing the candle to flickering life. "Make a wish."

Logan didn't look at Jace while he blew out the candle; he knew his wish was written all over his face, and Jace was smart enough about people to read it.

The boys were snatching cakes off the plate even before he opened his eyes. Jace laughingly scolded them. "Hey, you'd better leave at least two—the birthday boy gets a cake and so does the dumbass who took them from Rollins fair and square."

"You went back to the pantry?" Logan asked.

Jace's wide smile showed off that missing tooth. "Homeschool doesn't turn eighteen every day."

Only one cake was left when the boy-locusts finished swarming, but Logan didn't mind splitting it with Jace. He was warm from head to toe; Jace's grand, stupid gesture made those two bites of cake taste better than anything he'd eaten in a long, long time.

"**B**ack up, back up," Jace whispered urgently. Logan shuffled backward in his socks until his back was against the wall; Jace scrambled to stand next to him. Someone walked past their hiding place with a flashlight, but he wasn't shining it around like he was looking for night thieves. News of their break-in at the file room must not have spread this far.

"If I have to sleep outside again for nothing tonight, I'm gonna be pissed," Logan muttered once the wandering night guard was past.

"They're somewhere, damn it," Jace said. "I'm thinking it's gotta be the director's office itself. Maybe in his desk."

The two of them had done three raids in as many nights, each run riskier than the last: first breaking into Ms. Lowell's office, then Ms. Lee's, and finally into the file room. But the CRS files on the rehomed students who'd been returned to ChilCo continued to elude them.

They tiptoed under the sign-in window at the front door of the home, then slid past the cramped room the night watchmen used as a hangout because it had a table and coffeemaker. Once past, they broke into a shuffling sprint—they were lucky they hadn't had a footrace on any of the three nights, because men in shoes could move more quickly than they could in their socks.

But Jace had insisted on socks; apparently the older boy who'd trained Jace had been spotted by the whites of his feet in the dark on a raid and been booted. Getting caught was a more devastating outcome to Jace than slipping down stairs and breaking his leg.

"I must be losing my touch," he said as they got close to their dorm. "I've never been spotted this much before."

"You mean every fucking time you go on a raid?" Logan was irritated at their continued failure and the repeated close escapes. The night before, they'd gotten stuck outside again, and it had poured the whole night, leaving them drenched, cold, and miserable as they huddled, shivering, under the lip of the cave.

"Yes, obviously that's what I mean," Jace snapped, just as irritated. "Shit, it's Lowell!"

Their hold dean stood in the middle of the hallway, arms crossed, where she could see anyone who approached the dorm door.

"Oh, fuck," Jace said. "She'll wait us out. Let's go back out that first-floor bathroom window and come inside in the morning."

"No," Logan said. He wasn't going back outside. Even here, toward the interior of the building, the pounding spring rainstorm was clearly audible. "What good will that do anyway? She knows it's us. She probably already checked our beds and knows we're up."

He didn't understand what Jace was afraid of; from the many stories he'd heard, Logan's impression was that Ms. Lowell almost never actually reported the Eagle Hold boys for anything.

Jace grabbed Logan's arm. "I can sense that you're about to do something stupid. Do *not* do that stupid thing."

Logan shrugged apologetically, then stepped out into the open where Ms. Lowell could see him. "Good evening, Ms. Lowell. Man, it's really coming down out there, isn't it?"

"Mr. Cardot," the Eagle Hold dean said, no warmth in her voice; she wasn't surprised to see him. "I assume Mr. Evans is hiding around the corner, calling you three kinds of idiot?"

"You underestimate me, Ms. Lowell," Jace said, turning the corner with a sigh. "I speak several languages. I called him upward of a dozen kinds of idiot."

"What have you two been up to?"

"I read recently that night exercise is very beneficial for men concerned about their heart health," Logan said.

"Yes," Jace agreed smoothly. "And since we're getting on in years, what better time to take care of our health than now? Logan and I just had a very refreshing run. Would you care to join us, Ms. Lowell? The study was aimed at men, but I imagine women experience many of the same health benefits."

The corners of Ms. Lowell's mouth twitched like she was fighting a smile. "The two of you had better both be in bed by the time I get back from the ladies' room. *Someone* has been roving the halls at night, finding their ways into places they don't belong. I'd hate for a staff member to see you on your 'night run' and get the wrong idea."

As she turned on her heel and walked toward the women's bathroom at the end of the hall, Jace and Logan darted into their dorm before their luck could turn.

"See? That worked out," Logan said.

"You're still an idiot. Now she *knows* it's us. She's gonna know it's us when we break into the director's office tomorrow night."

"At least we're dry." Logan covered a yawn with his fist. "Do we have to do it tomorrow night? I could use a night of actual sleep."

Jace's eyes glittered feverishly. "Tomorrow night. We'll find the files in the director's desk, I'm sure of it." He slumped, and Logan realized how unused to failure Jace must be, especially in terms of his raids. He dropped an arm around the curly-haired boy's shoulders and squeezed.

"Buck up. The best-hidden things are probably the most worth finding, right?"

Jace shrugged out of Logan's hold and pulled at his lip. It was familiar enough that it didn't bother Logan so much anymore; he figured it was just Jace's tic when he was thinking.

"Thanks for coming with me," Jace said, voice muffled by his hand. He wasn't looking at Logan, instead concentrating on something entirely internal.

"I'm with you, Jace. Tomorrow night."

The next day, both boys were dragging ass after three late nights. Although Logan didn't look forward to another night deprived of sleep, it was clearly important to Jace, so he'd go.

He tried not to examine his devotion to Jace too closely, but he knew it wasn't only Jace's good looks that had him up raiding night after night. Everything about Jace—his passion, his charm, his brotherly protection of the other boys, his broken Old Dunisian, and that stupid, crooked smile—had him ready to follow the boy off the edge of the earth.

When at last the clock ticked the hour to roll out of bed, pull on the now-familiar socks and jacket, and slip out of their dorm, Logan's exhaustion had settled into his bones. Jace must have been tired too because they moved through the halls slower than usual.

Ms. Lowell remained in her office, or at least the light was on, and several other staff members wandered the halls in addition to the usual janitors and night guard. Their raids hadn't gone unnoticed and wouldn't go unpunished if they were caught. With each step through the corridors, Logan's nervousness ratcheted up.

The climb to the director's office took them up several of the largest, most wide-open staircases, well lit by windows that let in broad squares of moonlight.

"Of course it would pick tonight to be clear," Logan muttered.

Jace didn't respond; he was weirdly jittery, unfocused. Not an ideal condition for the lead man on a raid with this level of risk. Now that they'd both passed their eighteenth birthdays, ChilCo could boot them without helping them find a placement—basically condemning them to a hard life eking out a living and struggling to make rent on even the sketchiest, shit apartment. Logan had no idea if breaking into the director's office to steal his most secured files was grounds for such a dismissal, but he couldn't think of anything more deserving.

On their way up, they had no close calls, though they spotted the occasional person milling around from a distance. To get into the director's office, they had to get through Ms. Lee's office first, and since they'd broken into hers several nights before, she'd put a heavy padlock on the door in addition to the simple lock.

Jace had anticipated it. He bent to examine the lock. "They never learn," he whispered.

After pulling his satchel around to his front, he fished in for the jar of acid he'd brought. "Hold your breath," he advised, then unscrewed the lid and stuck the lock in it, hanging the jar with its thin metal handle around the doorknob to hold it in place. Immediately, it reacted with the copper in the lock. Jace waved for Logan to follow him to a supply closet, and they both ducked inside. "We'll wait here, give it time to work its magic. We don't want to be out there when it's smoking out anyway."

Logan shifted, brushing against Jace in the darkness, and noticed his friend was shaking. "You okay?"

"Yeah," Jace replied, too quickly. "Fine." His voice stretched tight, brittle.

Logan grabbed the fingers of Jace's hand. "You're shaking."

"I'm *fine*," Jace repeated, pulling his hand away. "Can we focus on what we're doing here, please?"

"I *am* focused on it. You're the one acting weird."

Jace didn't say anything, only peeked out of their hiding place, watching as much of the hallway as he could through the tiny crack he'd made between the door and frame. After another minute or two, he stepped out. "Let's go."

Logan pushed Jace aside when they got to the door, carefully pulling the acid away from the door and setting the discolored liquid on the floor. He didn't trust Jace's unsteady hands, and he didn't wish chemical burns on either of them.

The lock looked decidedly distorted. It was no challenge for Jace to use the pliers from his bag to twist the shackle until it broke. He didn't catch it as it fell to the floor, and it made a *clack* as it landed, very loud in the otherwise-silent hallway.

As quickly as he could, Jace picked the main door lock and slipped inside. Logan pulled a pair of gloves out of his own bag to pick up both the lock and the acid. He closed the jar, wrapped the lock in a plastic bag, and shoved both in his satchel before he followed Jace inside.

Jace crouched in front of the director's desk, head resting against the top edge as he fiddled with the bottom drawer's lock. Logan saw the dark circles under his friend's eyes and resolved that no matter what they found, there'd be no more late nights for at least a week.

"Got it," Jace said at last. Logan joined him as he dug through the papers hanging in folders in the drawer.

"Here, give me the picks. There's another drawer on the other side." Logan grabbed the bundle out of Jace's lap without waiting for him to respond, then worked on the other bottom drawer.

He'd just gotten the lock open when Jace grunted in frustration. "Shit. This isn't it either. Where the fuck do they keep them? They must keep files on the kids who get sent back. I know they do."

As soon as he opened his drawer, Logan knew it was what they were looking for. The first folder opened with a carbon-copied CRS form, stamped at the top with "Rehoming Failed."

"Jackpot. I've got 'em."

He scooped up a handful of the files from the drawer, but Jace tried to snatch the folders out of his hands. "Give them to me."

Logan stood, moving away from him. "What? We're both going to have to carry some—"

"Hand them over!" Jace said too loudly. He pulled; they both lost their grip on the papers, sending them flying all over the desk.

Footsteps in the hall outside—both boys froze. Then a voice, Ms. Lowell's. "No, I'll meet you there, I'm going to swing by and check it on my way to…"

"Oh, for the love of God," Logan muttered. "We'll never get out of here."

"Out the window?" Jace suggested, circling the desk to stand in front of it.

"We're on the fourth floor," said Logan. "Shit, shit, shit! We need a distraction!" They were going to get booted. If they could come up with *any* reason to be in the director's office other than stealing files, maybe they'd have a chance, but with the papers scattered everywhere, they needed a distraction, they needed the Bens, they needed *something*—anything—to keep Lowell from noticing what they were doing.

There was no time, no time. The footsteps were right outside Ms. Lee's door. She'd be inside the director's office in seconds.

Logan despaired. They were getting booted. There was nothing they could do. He would get sent away. He would be put in Shalecrest like his parents. He would lose everything *again*.

His mind filled with exactly one thought. He did the only thing he could think of doing, the only stupid, useless thing.

He grabbed Jace with a hand around the back of his neck and kissed him.

Jace jerked back in shock, then some recognition sparked in his eyes. "God, that's fucking brilliant," he said. "Take the files and run once the coast is clear."

Then he put a hand on either side of Logan's face and kissed him hard.

The world stopped turning. Logan forgot what breathing felt like. The earth must've turned upside down; all the blood was rushing to his head and his chest was bursting open and his stomach had disappeared. He didn't even realize he was pulling Jace against him, doing his best to crush him; he just wanted to be closer, closer, *closer*.

"Oh—oh!" A woman's shocked exclamation reminded Logan they weren't alone, but he would've happily kept going, caught or not, if Jace hadn't pulled away sharply.

The expression on Jace's face when he jerked back was like a punch in the gut for Logan. He looked surprised at the intrusion, but also mortified, disgusted, completely unsettled. Jace glanced between Logan and Ms. Lowell where she stood in the doorway with her hand over her mouth, and desperate horror grew on his face. He tried to step away from Logan, his hands raised as if to signal that he hadn't been touching the other boy, but Logan's hands were clenched on Jace's jacket.

Jace slapped his hands away, something between fear and fury flickering over his face. "I—we—it wasn't—" he choked out at Ms. Lowell. "It's not what it—God!"

Lurching as if on the edge of vomiting, Jace ran, pushing past Ms. Lowell and into the hall. Logan stood staring after him, every bit as stricken on the outside as he felt on the inside. Ms. Lowell shot him a baffled, unhappy look, then turned to follow Jace. "Mr. Evans?" she called. It wasn't an angry tone; she sounded concerned.

As soon as she was gone, Logan remembered his task: get the files, get out. He scrambled to gather those they'd scattered, scooping them into a loose pile and throwing them haphazardly into his bag. He seized another handful from the desk and tossed that in too, then kicked the drawer shut and ran for all he was worth.

When he burst into the common room, he could barely breathe, both from the exertion of the run and the flood of emotions trying to choke him. He pounded up to his bunk and shoved the papers into the slit he'd made in his mattress. Heart hammering, he pulled the sheet down over his temporary hiding place, tore off his jacket and socks, and stowed them.

Someone snored to his right, and he wanted to shake them and demand to know how they could sleep at a time like this—the world was still upside down.

There was no question of him sleeping. He headed out of the room and settled in a common room chair, waiting for Jace. As the large wall clock above the fireplace ticked away second after second, the incessant rhythm of it made Logan want to crawl out of his skin.

Several long, torturous minutes later, the common room door opened, and Logan shot to his feet. Jace and Ms. Lowell entered together, her hand on his shoulder in a half-mother, half-jailer gesture. Ms. Lowell gave Logan a smile altogether too warm for having just found them doing something against the rules, but Logan's eyes went straight to Jace.

Jace was a mess. His face flickered with expressions of fear and uncertainty, his eyes red from crying or near crying.

"I'll leave you two to talk," Ms. Lowell said gently. When she spoke again, her voice held a bit more steel. "Do *not* let me catch you anywhere you're not supposed to be again. I mean it. You *have* to be smarter than this."

As soon as she shut the door behind her, every element of Jace's demeanor changed. As he threw off his discontent like a costume, his shoulders straightened, his head rose, and his face split into a wicked, crooked grin. He lunged the distance between them and threw shadow punches at Logan's torso.

"You are a *genius*," he whisper-shouted. "That was some of the fastest thinking I've ever seen. Not many ways we could've thrown Lowell for a loop. God, I played her like a violin."

He adopted his miserable stance again but more exaggerated this time, a parody of himself. "'Oh, Ms. Lowell, I'm just so confused...we got so close and...well, there's something exciting about being somewhere you're not supposed to be with someone you're not supposed to be with—' She ate it up, Logan, I tell you what. 'Course, now she thinks we're gay, but I knew she'd let that slide, and I'd say that's better than being booted with no prospects." His laugh bubbled over with genuine delight.

Logan's stomach sank, but he mimicked Jace's laughter. It came out strangely hollow. "Yeah, now she thinks...we're gay. Funny."

"And don't tell me you can't act, Homeschool. That was *fucking brilliant*. Probably the best I've ever seen. Your face! You had Lowell convinced. Hell, you had *me* convinced."

All the pleasure drained out of the night like Jace had pulled a plug. Logan hated this. He hated how much joy Jace found in the idea that he'd been acting. It made his words more acidic than he intended. "Yeah, I had me convinced too."

Jace hadn't quite caught his mood, still grinning. "Huh?"

"Nothing. Forget it. Glad we made it out clean." He pushed past Jace to the stairs.

"Whoa, hey!" Jace grabbed his arm and held him back. "You're not nearly excited enough about this getaway. Take a moment and luxuriate in a good idea well executed!"

"It wasn't a good idea, Jace," Logan snapped. "It wasn't an idea at all. I just...did it." Seeing Jace didn't comprehend his meaning, he continued. "I racked my brain to come up with a distraction but came up with nothing. I knew we were goners. So I stopped trying to think of distractions and I kissed you. Those were separate events."

"I don't understand," Jace said, but Logan said nothing more to clarify. He only stared at the curly-haired boy.

Several ticks of the wall clock sliced up the long moment of silence between them. Some of Jace's overzealous glee drained from him, leaving an expression that vaguely resembled the one he'd worn on his way into the common room. At length, Jace said, "What are you trying to say? You kissed me because...you wanted to kiss me?"

"Yes." Logan couldn't hear his own words over his heart. He felt like he was hoisting a huge weight over the edge of a ledge and waiting for gravity to take it. "I did what I've been wanting to do since the day I met you because I thought everything was over. I thought we'd be booted."

Understanding dawned on Jace's face like he'd realized for the first time that night follows day. If Logan hadn't been breathing so shakily himself, he might have heard the way each of Jace's breaths came faster than the last.

"Logan," Jace said. That was all. That great, imaginary weight teetered on the edge of falling, and Logan knew it would take him down with it and destroy him.

Logan waited. He didn't feel like they'd made a getaway; it felt like he'd been caught and lost everything. When Jace said nothing more, Logan spoke past the lump in his throat. "I'm going to bed." All that weight pulled him over the cliff, down and down, an anvil around his neck.

"Wait." Jace grabbed Logan's arm again, twisting his wrist gently to turn him back.

"Just let me go. I've embarrassed myself enough tonight." He absolutely would *not* cry. Not in front of Jace. He wouldn't humiliate himself further.

"Logan..." Jace said again.

And Jace kissed him.

No oncoming administrators, no impending threats, no distractions—only the earth-shaking, feather-light pressure of Jace's lips on Logan's. Logan's bones liquified. If he hadn't grabbed on to Jace's shoulders, he might've melted into the floor.

It was perfect. Everything was perfect.

But an unthinkable thought intruded on the moment: Jace had just delivered the performance of a lifetime. For Lowell's benefit, he'd fabricated an entire relationship with Logan and all the emotions that went with it, then cast it off as easily as a jacket. If he thought he'd lose his friend and partner in crime otherwise, would he act like he wanted Logan?

The thought was nauseating. Logan broke away, shaking. "Don't—don't play with me. Don't you dare *act* with me."

Jace shook his head, reaching out, but Logan stepped back out of range. "I'm not."

"Two seconds ago, you were congratulating us both on how well we 'acted gay.'"

"Because I thought you were acting!" Jace looked desperately eager to explain himself, but Logan wasn't sure he could trust any expression on the chameleon's face. "I wasn't about to out myself to my *straight* best friend. I didn't know you were like me. How could I have known?"

"Oh, I don't know, maybe my *kissing you* could've been a clue?"

Jace shook his head. "I thought it was a distraction. You're the under-pressure thinker. I didn't want to assume it was real, and then you—what?—laugh in my face? Refuse to ever talk to me again? I didn't want another repeat of the Colby incident."

"The what?"

Sharp sigh. Jace rubbed his face. "Nothing. Never mind."

"What are you talking about?" Logan asked, irritated.

Jace's frown was tinged with skepticism. "Nobody's said anything about me and Colby to you?"

Surprised, Logan said, "You had a boyfriend?"

"No, no. *No.* Colby—I guess a lot of the guys weren't here yet when it happened, and most everyone else has forgotten or been booted by now. I had a crush on Colby Brown when I was little. He was my friend, and I kissed him one day in the courtyard. He was... not pleased."

Jace rubbed his hands over each other like he could scrub them free of the shame.

"He told our teacher, Ms. Adkins, what happened, and she told me how disgusting I was being and what a freak I was. The gravest of sins, she called it. She made me write five hundred times, 'Boys do not kiss boys.' She said if I ever got the urge to kiss a boy again, I should pinch my lip until it hurt," he said with a bitter laugh. "Like aversion therapy would make me straight."

"That's what you're doing? Aversion therapy?"

"Huh?"

"When you mess with your lip, that's what you're doing? It's not, like, a tic when you're thinking—you're actually doing what that teacher told you to do? Trying to fight 'sins' by hurting yourself?"

"Uh, I guess. I don't know—I don't really think about it. It's just something I do sometimes. I was upset for a long time about Colby not talking to me. He actually moved to another hold so he wouldn't have to see me anymore. So for a long time I'd do it whenever I thought about him. Now...I do it out of habit whenever I—" He let his expression finish the sentence for him, looking up at Logan with obvious want.

In his head, Logan ran back through their time together over the past months. Jace played with his lip *a lot*. Constantly. In fact, he was running his thumb over his lower lip now, pressing it against his teeth hard enough to leech the skin of color.

"Stop that." Logan slapped his hand away. "If you want to kiss me, kiss me. If you don't, then *please* don't. Just tell me if you don't, okay? Please be honest with me."

Jace reached for his mouth again then stopped and dropped his hand. "I am being honest with you."

The ticking of the clock marked another few seconds of silence while Logan thought. Could it be true? Could Jace honestly want him as badly as Logan wanted him?

"Okay." Logan took a half step closer to Jace. What else could he do? If there was any chance what Jace had said was true, he had to try. "Okay then."

Logan wanted to kiss him again, but they only stared at each other, a foot between them. Jace's eyes were so, so blue. He looked more uncertain of himself than Logan had ever seen him.

Something built between them, stretching the air so tight Logan was afraid a movement would tear the world apart. Jace opened his mouth as if to speak, then shut it again, looking embarrassed. He turned his head away, touching two fingers to his mouth.

"No," Logan said. Closing the distance between them, he pulled Jace's fingers away, holding that hand against his chest instead, and pulled Jace's face to his. This kiss was different—hesitant, honest. Jace brought his free hand up to Logan's jaw, and that stomach-less, upside-down feeling returned in the most pleasant way.

After a long, long time, Logan realized he couldn't get enough air in through his nose, and he pulled back a fraction of an inch to breathe and clear the dizziness from his head. Jace pressed forward and closed the gap again, pulling his hand away from Logan's chest so he could hold on to the other boy's waist.

Logan didn't notice they were moving until his back hit the wall. The air it forced out of him broke them apart. Jace leaned in, putting his hands flat against the wall on either side of Logan's body, and kissed him again, but it made Logan feel trapped.

He grabbed Jace by the shoulders and spun them both so Jace was against the wall with Logan leaning into him. Logan felt Jace's lips tighten against his as he smiled.

"You're not the boss of me," Jace said, the words puffing against Logan's mouth. He tried to turn them, but Logan had better leverage in his bare feet than Jace did in his socks.

Jace pushed harder, still kissing but laughing now too. Logan was forced back a half step, and then each of them grabbed the other and tried to push and pull simultaneously. They half rolled, half bounced against the wall, wrestling as much as they kissed. When Jace tripped over Logan's feet and slipped, they both went down, and they temporarily abandoned the make-out session, reveling in something more familiar.

But though they'd wrestled and grappled a hundred times, Logan had never been so fully aware of Jace's movements against him before. Now they felt intentional. He was too distracted to fight like he meant it. They rolled until Logan was wedged against a couch, Jace grinning victoriously atop him.

"King of the hill!" Jace crowed.

"I don't think so," Logan laughed, pushing Jace over. He snatched a kiss while they lay side by side for a moment, then pinned Jace's shoulders down and swung his leg over to sit on Jace's stomach. "Boom! Who's the king now?"

Jace laid his head back on the floor, breathing like he'd run miles. "I'm not sure this is how this is supposed to go."

"No?" Logan leaned over the curly-haired boy to kiss him again. "Seems right to me."

"No…" Jace grinned against Logan's mouth. "I'm supposed to be running this show."

Logan sat up, smiling but serious now because he realized Jace was serious, even if he'd said the words playfully. "You're not in charge of me, Jace. This isn't a raid. You're not my boss. I'm not one of your crew to order around. I'm your friend, and…" He waved a hand at their bodies, tangled up on the floor. "And whatever this is."

Jace propped himself up on his elbows, bringing his face back into Logan's range again. Logan took advantage of it. "Okay," he said between kisses. "That's going to be…" He paused and kissed Logan again. "…weird."

Logan laughed. "You haven't *always* bossed around everybody in the whole damn school—including the freaking dean! Think back to the last time you weren't in charge and try to remember how you handled that."

Like Logan had flipped a switch, Jace's good humor flicked off, queasiness washing over his face. He turned his head to the side and slid out from under Logan to sit up a few feet away.

"Whoa. You okay?" Logan was baffled.

"Yeah, I'm fine. Did you hide the files?"

Logan blinked, startled by the subject change. "Yeah. They're in my mattress. Are you sure you're okay? Did I say something…?"

"That's not very secure. We should swap them over to the panel behind my headboard."

Logan nodded. "Okay, I'll do it tomorrow while the boys are out. I can be late to history." He studied the blue-eyed boy's face, which was back under his control but no longer smiling.

"*Wor loqued ay?*" he asked, slipping into Old Dunisian the way they did whenever they didn't want the other boys to understand them: *What did I say?*

Jace shook his head. "*Notta.*" *Nothing.* As if to reassure Logan, he scooted back over to him and kissed him, but when he broke away and stood, his fingers had latched on to his lip again. "We should get to bed. Someone's gonna come down here and find us."

"Right…I guess this has to stay a secret." Logan wasn't sure how he felt about that. He certainly didn't want to draw any official attention to himself, but he wished he could reach out and hold Jace's hand or lean in for a kiss without panicking about secrecy. Then again, as weird as Jace was acting now, and as sudden as everything had been, did he really want to try to explain to anyone else what was going on? Even he didn't know what was going on.

"For now," Jace said. "Once we're out of Hallsburg…"

"But we're okay, right?" Logan didn't like how thoughtful Jace had become, how he'd turned internal and distant. Something felt wrong about it.

Jace gave him the full blast of that crooked, missing-tooth smile. "If you'd describe finding out your best friend likes you as much as you like him as 'okay,' then sure, we're okay. I'd call it something better than that, though."

It was sweet and perfect and exactly what he needed to hear, and Logan was absolutely certain it was a distraction from whatever was happening in Jace's head. Still, he was almost, almost reassured.

# 6

## A DISCOVERY

As Logan had known it would be, the dorm room was empty when he slipped in. He'd left bio early, since he'd finished his lab report already, and used the extra time to hike back to the bunk. If he hurried, he wouldn't even be late to history. Rushing, he peeled open the curtains, threw back the covers, and pulled the files out of the mattress, shoving the stuffing back in as he went. The folders were a mess, all bent corners and creases and mixed together.

Sitting on the floor next to his bed, he sorted them into stacks, grabbing papers with the same names and unfolding them neatly before tucking them back into their folders. He picked up one of the folders and his stomach dropped.

"Jace Evans: Rehoming Failed," the red stamp said.

Jace had been rehomed?

*Fuck*, of course he had. This wasn't just a campaign to protect the boys of ChilCo he thought of as brothers. This was personal.

Logan's fingers traced the edge of the manila folder, feeling how thick the stack of papers inside was compared to the other files.

He knew he shouldn't read it. He absolutely should *not* open that folder; he should put it in the stack with all the others. Of course, that's why Jace had fought him for them in the director's office; he hadn't wanted Logan to know about this. So Logan should definitely, definitely not read it.

He peeked over his bed at the door. Jace wouldn't come in in the next minute; he wouldn't have to know he'd read it. Curiosity drew him to the words like a magnet, and he was a helpless iron filing in its pull. He had to know.

As Logan opened the folder gingerly, the first page knocked the breath out of his chest. Two fuzzy pictures of miniature Jace, maybe eight years old, with the same curly hair and long eyelashes, were paper clipped to the top of the page. They were almost like mug shots: one from the front, one from the side. Except it was obvious Jace hadn't done anything illegal. Someone had done it to him.

His tiny, cherubic face was mottled with bruises down the left side, his left eye swollen shut and purple. Young Jace's bottom lip was swollen, blood at the corners of his mouth, and Logan wondered if this was what happened to Jace's missing tooth.

Fury filled him, heating his skin from head to toe. He started to read—he had to know what kind of fuckers would do something like this—and his blood ran cold all over again.

In clinical, matter-of-fact language, the CRS doctor who examined Jace wrote about the beating Jace had received, but worse— much worse—he detailed the devastating damage done to Jace's body and psyche over the course of eight months of sexual assault.

Logan read the transcript of the account by officers who had taken Jace from his rehome and choked back bile: "The kid was hiding in the back of a closet when we got there. We tried to pull him out, but he was so scared he threw up. Every time he'd heave, he'd sob about how sorry he was. Officer Fortson got Mr. Harris in cuffs and tried to get him out to the squad car before we brought the kid out of the master bedroom, but the bastard kept yelling at the kid, 'Remember I love you!' The kid threw up all the way to CRS."

Logan read on, though he could barely breathe around the lump of anger in his throat. He read about the school officials' recommendation of therapy for Jace and about Jace's violent refusal. He read about Jace's attempts to set fire to the gym where ChilCo held the rehoming fairs. He read several notes from Ms. Lowell to the director, expressing her concern about his ability to reintegrate with the other boys.

The door opened, and Logan slammed the folder shut before scooping up the rest of the stack and holding it to his chest.

"Jace!" Logan exclaimed as the curly-haired boy rounded the bed to stand over him. "You're not in class." He couldn't meet Jace's eyes. All he could see were the plum-dark bruises from the picture.

"I thought I'd help you move the files over," Jace said, so lightly it was obvious he'd hoped to beat Logan back so he could hide them himself. "Here."

He extended a hand to take the files from Logan, who passed the stack over uneasily. Jace's was on top.

Both of them stared at it for a moment. Jace swallowed hard, his breaths coming ragged, then shook himself and knelt next to his bed with its secret panels.

"Jace, I'm sorry. I—"

"Skipped bio?" Jace interrupted loudly, abruptly. "It's not me you need to apologize to, is it? You really shouldn't skip classes at this point in your education. Shame on you."

"No, I—"

"No excuses, Homeschool," Jace rolled over him. "They'll be looking at your schoolwork to make a good placement for you. You don't want to get stuck as a garbage man, do you?" He unlatched the back panel on his headboard and shoved the papers back there. His own file he held on to, gripped tightly in white-knuckled fingers.

"Jace, I read—"

"No!" Jace didn't turn to look at Logan, but his body drew tight as a guitar string. When he spoke again, his control was gone; his voice broke. "You just got here and pulled these files out. I was right behind you. You had no time to read any of them, but that's okay, because we'll read them later and figure out what we can do with them to bring down CRS."

He crumpled his own file into a manilla wad in his hands.

"But I—"

Jace spun on him, jabbing him in the chest with the crushed ball of paper. "You *didn't read anything, right?*" Logan stared, open-mouthed. Was Jace this desperate not to talk about it, not to acknowledge what happened? "*Right?*" Jace prompted again. A panicked sort of madness burned in his blue eyes.

"Uh, right," Logan said at last.

Jace's tenseness deflated, and he sagged, a kite in a lull between breezes. He kissed Logan lightly on the cheek, then pulled a lighter out of his back pocket, thumbed up a flame, and held it to the ball of paper in his hand. They watched it burn until Jace couldn't hold it in his hand any longer and dropped it to the floor. When it had shriveled into gray ash, Jace stomped it out and kicked the dusty remnants under his bed.

"Why are you looking at me like that?" he asked. "You never seen a fire before?"

Logan didn't have an answer Jace would want to hear, so he only kissed him. They both ignored Jace's shaking hands and Logan's too-tight hold on him. After a long while, Jace stepped back with a hollow laugh. "We gotta get to class. Lowell will kill us if she thinks we're skipping to make out."

"You know what we should do tomorrow?" Logan asked, picking up his bag and straightening his bed sheets.

"Hmm?"

Logan let Jace open the door for him and stepped through. "Skip class to make out."

Jace's laughter held a desperate edge. "I have been feeling a bit sick today. Maybe tomorrow I'll come down with the flu."

For several days, Logan and Jace were "sick," confined to their beds with a stomach bug that kept them from classes, meals, and chores. To avoid suspicion, sometimes one or the other attempted to attend morning classes, but they inevitably became too ill to stay and returned to the bunk, where the curtains were drawn around each of their beds to isolate them from the other boys, and they were blessedly alone for hours at a time.

Logan's fear of being caught was distant, vague; Jace was solid and present and warm and in possession of the finest pair of lips the world had ever seen.

The other boys in the bunk guessed Jace was up to something, though none of them could be sure what. Because Jace and Logan were in it together, the prevailing theory was that they'd somehow snuck a girl Logan had known on the outside into ChilCo. Jace neither confirmed nor denied anything when the other boys threw out ideas—he just smiled a tight-lipped, secretive smile while Logan tried not to laugh.

This morning, Logan grinned in the curtained tent of Jace's bed as he heard the door to the bunk quietly open and shut again. A moment later, Jace's head popped in, a gap-toothed smile splitting his face. "You should have seen Mr. Hutchins's face. '*Still*, Mr. Evans? I think this might be quite serious!' I even rubbed a couple handfuls of grass on my cheeks to give myself that nice green tinge."

Jace dove into the bed next to Logan, squirming and shoving until they stretched out comfortably side by side.

"We probably should go to class tomorrow," Logan said. "It's been almost a week—Lowell's definitely getting suspicious. Plus, the rumors are getting around about the 'girl' we've been sneaking in."

They both laughed, curled on their sides, foreheads almost touching in the narrow bed. "I think you probably threw Lowell off with that puke in the physics lab yesterday. Brilliant."

"Yeah, thanks again for the salt in my tea, by the way, dick!" But his complaint was good-natured. Logan had been annoyed at the time, but Jace had apologized very satisfactorily afterward.

"Well, if this is going to be our last afternoon alone for a while…" Jace seized Logan's face and pressed a kiss to his lips. After a moment's hesitation, he shifted to kiss Logan under the jaw, and a jolt of something new and unsettlingly good ran through Logan. Jace's mouth traveled down Logan's neck to the collar of his shirt, and they both laughed nervously when Jace tugged it down far enough to kiss Logan's collarbone.

"Should I…?" Logan started to unbutton his shirt, but Jace grunted and pushed his hands away impatiently, working the buttons loose himself.

"You worry about mine," Jace said. He really *was* impatient; he'd already opened Logan's shirt halfway by the time Logan could get Jace's top button undone.

A cold pit settled in Logan's stomach—it felt like fear but wasn't. Why were they rushing? He wasn't sure what he would do when his fingers finished fumbling open Jace's buttons, but he couldn't wait to get there.

Jace tried to push Logan's shirt off his shoulders, but he was lying half on it and still holding on to Jace's shirt, and he was well and truly tangled in it before it was all the way off. Jace didn't care; he returned to his interrupted path of kisses, pressing his lips to the space under Logan's collarbone, then to his breastbone.

Logan struggled to catch his breath, unsure where he'd lost it. Jace's mouth scorched his cold-pebbled skin. His abdominal muscles tightened further with every inch Jace traveled down his body—the soft, faintly ticklish brushes of lips against his stomach driving him insane. Jace drifted around Logan's side, nipping at his flank with a playful snap of his teeth.

When Jace's hands brushed over the waistband of Logan's pants, Logan shuddered. "What are you doing?" he asked, licking his lips and trying to fight down his nerves.

"Dunno," Jace said, twisting open the button at Logan's waist. When he glanced up at Logan, desire and uncertainty warred on his face. "Do you want me to stop?"

"No," Logan said immediately. A deep, overwhelming curiosity tugged at him; they were already well beyond anything he'd ever had with Chris in his backyard tree. And nothing Logan had ever imagined lived up to the sight of Jace kneeling over him, tugging his pants down centimeter by centimeter and bending to kiss each new expanse of skin.

"*Ay quara etu,*" Jace said, staring up the length of Logan's body: *I want you.*

Logan couldn't concentrate hard enough to come up with the Old Dunisian response. He couldn't concentrate on anything. He watched as Jace paused short of revealing Logan's very excited lower half, frowning with uncertainty. It was clear he wasn't certain what to do next or hadn't worked up the nerve.

"It doesn't bite," Logan teased hoarsely, jolting with anticipatory adrenaline. "And you'd better not either."

He'd meant it as a joke, but Jace's frown deepened, and he swallowed hard. The curly-haired boy hooked a single finger in the waistband of Logan's pants, tugging them out and down. Logan lifted himself up from the bed enough to let his trousers and underwear slip down to his thighs.

Hesitantly, Jace leaned down close to Logan's dick, his breath playing hot and ticklish against the sensitive skin. Logan wriggled.

Putting one hand on Logan's hip, Jace licked his lips nervously then brushed them over Logan's shaft, just under the head. Logan was dizzy, somehow drifting in a fog and laser focused on what was happening below his waist.

Was Jace, *his Jace*, really opening his mouth to drag a light, tentative lick over him? He panted and tried to keep still, although his whole body had broken out in a sweat, and his heart was breaking through his breastbone from below with a pounding hammer.

When Jace's mouth closed over him, he couldn't stop himself from bucking up, pushing deeper into the warmth of the other boy's mouth. Jace coughed and scrambled back, panic on his face.

"I don't think I can—" Jace's eyes were wide and troubled, his face twisted. He was, for a moment, the little boy from the file pictures, and Logan's concern for him threw a bucket of cold water on his lust.

He sat up, tugging his underwear back up to cover himself. "Hey, it's okay. You don't have to—" Embarrassed, he cut himself off.

"I'm sorry," Jace said, equally embarrassed. "I want to. It's not—I just—"

Rescuing him from trying to formulate a more complete answer, Logan pressed his lips to Jace's and ran the backs of his fingers up the other boy's bare chest. When Jace relaxed, Logan shoved him over on his side, then rolled him onto his back and knelt over him. Jace gave him a devastatingly sweet half smile, and when they kissed, the curly-haired boy held him so tightly it hurt.

He broke away and mimicked Jace's earlier movements, kissing his way down Jace's chest and stomach for an interminably long time. He had a strange desire to bite Jace's hard abs, especially when they flexed in response to Logan's featherlight fingertip touches. The tanned skin was dusted with fine blond hair that darkened the lower Logan traveled.

When, at last, he yanked Jace's trousers down, the blue-eyed boy arched a brow and smirked with obvious bravado. "Well?"

"You do want me," Logan muttered, and Jace laughed. Logan studied the length of flesh before him, an erection not so different from his own. In fact, when he took it in his hand, it felt almost as familiar as working himself, although at the wrong angle. Jace gasped, then half laughed, taking a shaky breath that turned into a groan when Logan moved his hand faster.

"I have no idea what I'm doing," Logan said, glancing back up to Jace for reassurance.

Jace had his eyes closed. "Could've fooled me," he said through gritted teeth. He wrapped his hand around Logan's and moved their hands together up and down his length. His grip grew tighter, his pace faster, until Logan ground their motion to a halt.

"Hold on," he said. "Don't get impatient. I still want to try…" Logan pushed Jace's hand away and bent his head, taking a deep breath before closing his mouth around the head of Jace's dick. Just as Logan had, Jace jerked his hips up, pushing himself an inch or two deeper. Logan frowned and tried to follow his motion, keeping his lips between teeth and flesh.

"Holy shit," Jace breathed. "Oh, God, that's…that's…"

Logan made a happy sound, almost a purr, in the back of his throat. Jace jolted again, gasping in pleasure. It was easy, making Jace feel good. He'd been afraid it would be difficult or weird, but it was the most fun he'd ever had, watching Jace writhe and pant and groan. For several long minutes, he tested the feel of everything in his mouth, or against his lips, or under his fingertips.

Logan ran his tongue all the way down to the base and back up, then sucked the head into his mouth again. He made a ring of his lips and ran it up and down the first four inches, as far as he could go before he felt like he might choke. Gradually increasing his pace, he kept up the same steady movement, up and down, lashing the head with his tongue on the upstroke again and again.

"Yes," Jace growled. "If you keep that up, I'll—" He didn't finish because he was already dropping over the edge, moaning low and gravelly in his throat as he came. Logan jolted at the first shot in his mouth, but he didn't pull off. He swallowed as quickly as he could—the taste was not altogether pleasant—and breathed through his nose until Jace lay still, spent, breathing unbelievably hard.

"I knew it!"

The exclamation from outside the curtained shelter of Jace's bed made them both jolt up in startled silence, Logan wiping at his mouth frantically. Frozen, the two boys stared at each other in wide-eyed terror.

Their dormmates had come back! And it was too late to pretend they weren't there or they were doing anything innocent in Jace's bed with the curtains drawn; Jace's finish had been loudly, obviously sexual.

It was Bails shouting, and at least two more shushed him. He ignored them, continuing, "I knew you were smuggling girls in. Why have you been holding out on us?"

Logan and Jace frantically tried to reassemble their clothes. "Uh, no," Jace said, clearing his throat as he wrestled his pants back up. "Definitely no girls. I was, uh—"

"Bullshit!" Bails said.

"Can you guys leave me alone for a minute?" Jace growled out while he tried to get his belt back through the loops.

"We *could* do that," Squints said. "But…if you do have a girl in there, you'll need our help to get her out before Lowell gets up here. She decided you and Logan were sick enough to need a nurse."

Logan mouthed to Jace to get *out* of the bed and pretend Logan wasn't there, but Jace shook his head and mouthed something unintelligible back. He pushed Jace in the chest, trying to point him out the curtains on the far side from the guys, but Jace gestured back with increasing ferocity.

"Uh, Jace? Lowell's gonna be here any minute," Squints reminded them.

They were both still wrestling back into their clothes, but the space was too small for two guys their size. Leaning to the side to give Jace room to shrug his jacket back on, Logan tried to pull his shirt back up onto his shoulders, but he was sitting on one of the arms, and when he shifted his weight to pull it out from beneath himself, he started to slip backward. Jace couldn't catch him in time.

"Shit!" he shouted as he fell off the side of the bed, crashing ungracefully through the curtain and landing on his back with an impact that drove the air out of his lungs.

Several pairs of eyes looked down at him as he sprawled on the floor, one leg still caught in the sheet, his shirt half open. Confusion was written on the faces of Bails and Randy, but by his level stare, Squints wasn't lost at all.

"Hey, guys," Logan gasped out.

From inside the curtained shelter, Jace's voice could be heard, tightly strung. "Nice going, Homeschool."

"You were *both* with the girl?" Bails asked incredulously.

Squints rolled his eyes and stuck his hand out to help Logan to his feet. "God, you're slow, Bails."

Blushing from his hairline down, Logan turned back to the bed and saw Jace paralyzed, hiding behind the curtains, terror in his eyes and his thumb pressed to his lips. When he met Logan's eyes, Logan extended a hand toward him, a mute offer—pleading, really—for Jace to come out and face this with him. He watched Jace pull the mask down until his face was smooth, unruffled, and cool, like this was something he got caught doing every day.

He slid out of the bed much more gracefully than Logan had, his mussed clothes looking intentional and rakish. He threw open one side of the curtains to reveal the empty, rumpled bed. "I'm not importing women. Obviously." He straightened Logan's shirt on his shoulders so he wouldn't have to make eye contact with anyone.

As Jace fastened the top buttons on his shirt and ran his fingers through his unruly curls, Randy reached out to brush lint off Jace's shoulder. "You were *together* together? You're gay?"

Jace's eyes flicked to Logan, and he inhaled like he was drawing strength. "Yup," he said in the cheeriest voice he could muster. Then he cleared his throat and changed the subject. "You said Lowell's on her way up? Logan, get in bed and look sick. The rest of you, I'd better hear about how much Logan and I have been throwing up all night when the nurse gets here."

With a wave of his hand, he dismissed them all, and after a stunned moment, they obediently dispersed. Logan appreciated the way Jace had handled it; as long as he acted like it wasn't a big deal, maybe his crew would do the same.

"*I'm* gonna throw up," Bails muttered, not quietly enough.

Ignoring the boys' stares, Logan slid into his own bed, pouring a sprinkle of water into his hands to rub over his face and neck to make himself clammy, then dropped his head and limbs heavily onto the mattress like he was weak with sickness. He doubted it was as good as what Jace was doing on the other side of the room, but it should be enough.

The guys sat on Bails's and one of the Bens' beds, silently staring at each other. Logan rolled his eyes. There was nothing natural about Bails not talking.

A moment after they were settled, the door opened, and Ms. Lowell and Ms. Timmons, the ChilCo head nurse, stepped in. While the nurse went to Jace, Ms. Lowell drifted to Logan's bedside. Belatedly, he realized he should've pretended to sleep to avoid interrogation, but it was too late by the time she stood beside him.

"Four days sick?" she said, an eyebrow raised. "That may be some sort of record."

Logan gave her a hangdog smile. "The unfortunate side effect of too many late nights in a row, I suspect," he said very quietly, for her ears only. He was surprised by how hoarse his voice came out. He did sound raw, like he'd been vomiting for days.

She pressed the back of her hand to his forehead, frowning at the dampness there. "Overheated and sweating," she muttered, and he was fleetingly grateful for the full-body blush that had heated his skin. "Ms. Timmons, what do you think?"

"A stomach flu, as you suspected," the nurse said, tucking the blankets up around Jace, who appeared unconscious and faintly green. How did he do that? "I hope you two are drinking enough water," she said to Logan. "You're in terrible danger of dehydration."

Logan picked up the water glass from his bedside table and waved it weakly at her.

"Good. Make sure he gets some as well." She pointed to Jace. "Wake him up to drink, if you need to. I'll have the kitchen send you up some bland food, potatoes and such, that you can try to eat."

She glanced up at the other three boys, who watched the whole scene with uncharacteristic silence. "You boys will want to stay clear of these two until this passes, unless you want to be in the same situation."

Bails giggled uncontrollably until Squints elbowed him hard in the ribs. "They've kept the curtains closed, and we've stayed away from them, Ms. Timmons," Squints said. "Though they still wake us up every hour or two all night, getting up for the bathroom."

"Hmm. I'll need to call up to the chemist to get some stronger anti-nausea drugs than I've got here. Ms. Lowell, let's leave these boys to rest."

Lowell glanced back once at Logan, who gave her a smile he hoped conveyed honesty, gratitude, and a fair bit of illness. It mostly felt lopsided and unnatural, though.

As soon as the two women were gone, Randy, Bails, and Squints pounced on Logan, full of questions.

"You're both gay? Like *gay?*"

"When did this happen?"

"Is this what you've been up to all this time you've been 'sick'?"

Logan raised his hands, warding their words off like physical attacks. With a cautious grin, he joked, "Slow down. I can't take all these questions. I'm very ill. You heard Ms. Timmons."

Jace grabbed Bails and Squints by the back of the neck, then shuffled them to the side so he could slip past them and sit on the edge of Logan's bed. To Logan, the muscles of Jace's shoulders appeared tense, and he realized Jace was parking himself between the guys and Logan as though protecting him. "This really isn't any of your business, boys."

"Like hell it isn't!" Bails said. He was wildly animated, shaking his head and hands without any attempt to convey meaning. "We've all been—and you've…you've been…gaying it up this whole time?"

Jace's shoulders drew up, tenser than Logan would've thought possible. "Bails," he said seriously, "shut the fuck up."

Randy patted Bails patronizingly on the head as Squints took a seat on Logan's bed next to Jace. Jace drew in on himself, seeming to hold his breath.

Squints stared at them for a second before saying, "So I guess Colby wasn't a fluke, huh?"

"Nah," Jace said.

"How long has this been going on?" Randy asked. He waved at first Logan, then Jace.

Jace glanced a side-eye at Logan, who raised an eyebrow back. He wasn't going to answer any questions until he heard what Jace had to say about it. After a pause, Jace went with honesty. "About a week. We only recently found out we were...so alike."

Squints shrugged. "Glad you figured it out." He got up and wandered to his own bed, where he'd dropped his bag.

Bails watched him go with wide eyes and a wide-open mouth. "You're *okay* with this?" he cried.

Squints frowned at him. "What does it change? They've been inseparable since Logan got here. The raids were already slowing down. We've been wondering why the hell they keep disappearing without us for weeks. Now we know. Hell, we'll probably see *more* of both of them now that we know and they don't have to hide. From us, at least." He turned to Jace with questioning eyes. "Right, Jace?"

Logan felt a pang for Jace's crew, who clearly had missed him while he gallivanted off with his new toy. Not enough of a pang to want to share Jace's time, but a twinge nonetheless.

"Sure," Jace said. He smiled at Squints, then turned to Bails, arching an eyebrow and daring the loudmouth to say something else.

Bails seemed legitimately at a loss for words. Deeply troubled, he held more concern on his face than Logan had ever seen.

Randy dropped an arm around Bails's shoulders, shaking the younger boy slightly. "You're not going to say anything about this, Bails," Randy said. "You're not going to go spreading rumors outside our crew. You're not getting our boys killed for this."

*Killed?* Logan shot a glance at Jace, who didn't react.

"Well, no," Bails said vaguely, a hard line drawn between his eyebrows. "I'm not going to…spread…" His voice trailed away to nothing. He eyed Logan with a curled lip, barely masking his disgust. With a blink, he seemed to snap back to himself. "I mean, *shit*, do you think I want anyone to know this? They'll think our whole crew's gay."

"It's not contagious," Logan muttered, trying to lighten the mood, despite how much Bails's horror stung.

Bails sneered at him, a harsher expression than he'd ever turned on Logan. "Well, Jace caught it! You're gonna drag him right to hell with you."

Violent energy buzzed from Jace, but it was Squints, stretched out on his bed with a book in hand, who sighed noisily and spoke. "Oh, for fuck's sake, Bails, Jace has been gay for as long as you've known him. It's never bothered you before. Why should it now?"

Bails deflated slightly, looking lost. "But I thought…" Logan saw it written on the boy's face: his childhood hero was no longer shiny and holy and superhuman. He was legitimately crushed that Jace was "less" than he'd been before.

"You thought what?" Jace said, sitting forward. His voice vibrated with an edge of danger, and Logan wondered if he would need to intervene to protect Bails.

The door to the room opened, and the Bens filed in, roughhousing and laughing. They slowed when they saw the weird, tense tableau Bails, Randy, Logan, and Jace had created around Logan's bed. "What's going on?" one of them demanded.

"Logan and Jace are gay!" Bails whisper-shouted. "Not, like, 'they pussed out on a bet' gay either. Like 'they *fucked*' gay."

Jace's fists tightened at his sides, a vein jumping in his temple as he ground his teeth. Logan set a hand on his arm to hold him back from whatever he was itching to do. It wasn't exactly the way he would have hoped to break the news to the rest of Jace's crew. If they'd *ever* broken the news. *Killed?*

But the Bens just blinked over at first Jace, then Logan, in almost synchronized consideration.

"Duh," one of them said, as another said, "Obviously."

"Wait, what?" Logan spluttered. "You knew?"

The Bens laughed. The one in the middle said, "You've been staring at Jace like Bails stares at cake since the day you got here, Homeschool." A muted "Hey" came from Bails.

The Ben on the right said, "And Jace went to the pantry *twice* for you."

"He's a good friend but not *that* good," the last Ben said.

Logan blinked at Jace in astonishment, and Jace smirked back, his rage dissipating. "We're not as subtle as we thought, I guess," he said. "Should've asked the Bens and saved ourselves months of pretending not to like each other too much."

"Eugh!" Bails said, grimacing horribly. "How's everyone pretending this is okay?"

Randy clapped Bails hard on the back. Although he looked troubled himself, he spoke with confidence when he said, "Because it *is* okay, Mouthy."

"Bullshit," Bails spat, his face dark. He shrugged out from under Randy's arm, scowling for all he was worth. "Do you even hear how ridiculous this is? *Jace Evans* is gay? The king of this whole goddamn school is a goddamn fa—"

Jace shoved Bails hard, cutting off the younger boy's words as he staggered backward. When Jace stood, towering over Bails, the loudmouth cringed, his deeply unhappy face crinkling further as he retreated another step. Jace's arm whipped out like a snake strike, seizing the front of Bails's shirt and dragging the smaller boy forward until he could get right in his face.

"Listen to me," Jace said, "I have stood up for you every god-damn day since you got to ChilCo. Who had you transferred into Eagle Hold to get you out from under Martin Sneed's thumb? Who beat the *shit* out of that ginger kid from Bear when he shaved off your eyebrow? Who's done your fucking history homework for the last six years so your dumb ass wouldn't fail out? Huh?" He shook Bails and the kid's head rattled on his neck.

"I *made* you, Bails. If it weren't for me, you'd be a sniveling, snot-nosed idiot shoved in some bigger kid's trunk because you could never learn to shut your *goddamn* trap. If you ever want to enjoy the privileges of being friends with Jace Evans, 'king of this whole goddamn school' again, you will play nice. And you will *keep this a fucking secret.* Not one word about Logan. Not one word about me. Do you hear me?"

Bails snuffled, scowled, then wrestled out of Jace's grip and darted for the door. Sighing, Jace shook his head as the younger boy fled, red-faced and furious. One of the Bens tried to stop him, but Jace waved him off.

"No, let him go," Jace said as Bails slammed the door. "He'll come back or he won't."

Jace sat down hard on the end of Logan's bed. After a mo-ment, he picked up Logan's hand, threading his unsteady fingers between Logan's. Logan knew it was for effect, a symbolic gesture, but it filled him with warmth anyway.

"Anyone else have an issue they want to air?" Jace asked, his voice sharper than Logan had ever heard him speak to the boys.

They all shook their heads.

"Good," Jace said. "Good."

# 7

## THE LAKE

Later that night, Bails returned and dropped straight into bed, drawing his curtains closed. Everyone ignored him and the earlier revelations, acting for all the world as if nothing had changed. For the Bens, at least, nothing had: they'd already guessed about Jace and Logan in theory, and they hadn't walked in on any evidence of the relationship in practice.

Logan made Jace follow him downstairs to the common room, where they sat in an empty corner with their textbooks, pretending to do math homework.

"What's wrong?" Jace asked, drumming his pencil against the table with nervous energy.

Logan stared at the pencil until Jace noticed the sound and stopped. Then he said, "What did Randy mean by 'killed'?"

Jace frowned, and then his eyes grew wide. His cheeks inflated until he blew the air out in a long, uneasy sigh. "You…don't know?"

*Obviously*, Logan thought.

He stared until Jace checked there was no one in earshot and spoke again. "Did your parents know about you?"

Logan shrugged. "Kinda."

"And they didn't tell you it's illegal? 'Unnatural' relationships—having them, wanting them. It's all illegal. The Lapels will arrest you, and they're not too careful about making sure you get safely to a work camp either."

Logan pictured the men's camp at Shalecrest as he'd heard of it in stories, imagined his fingers raw, his back bent and broken by labor. He was big and young; they'd work him hard. But if Jace was right, he might never even make it that far. A Black Lapel would crack his skull open on the pavement and say he'd fought them when they tried to put him in the car.

He looked at the common room floor, where he and Jace had rolled about with absolutely no concern for who might walk down the stairs. Now the room was half full of boys laughing and studying and playing games. None of them were paying any attention to him and to Jace, but what if they'd already spotted them?

"Your entire crew knows," Logan said quietly, anxiety gripping his throat like a vise.

"They won't talk," Jace countered.

"Bails?"

Jace paused, working his jaw side to side as he thought. "Even Bails knows better. We take care of our own."

*But am I one of "your own"?*

Logan didn't want to say it, but he couldn't shake the thought. They seemed to like him well enough, but he wasn't one of their brothers. They accepted him because Jace accepted him. And if their relationship made Jace an outsider, they'd *probably* protect Jace, for the sake of their friendship, but Logan would be chopped liver.

"You scared, Homeschool?" Jace asked. He tried for a playful tone, the same challenge he'd been issuing since Logan arrived.

Only this time, Logan *was* scared. And he could see that under the bravado, Jace was too.

He took a deep breath then forced a grin. "I'm not scared."

Jace chuckled, dropping his head to his chest and shaking it. "Then you're a braver man than I am." When he looked up again, his eyes were honest, showing his uncertainty. His fingers crushed his lower lip to paleness. "Do we have to stop?"

"Absolutely the fuck not," Logan said. When Jace's eyebrows shot up, he leaned forward across the table, dropping the volume but not the intensity of his voice. "You think I'm going to let a Black Lapel tell me whether I get to be happy? Not a fucking chance."

Jace let go of his lip to give Logan a crooked, fatalistic smile. Logan saw his lip, reddened from his constant abuse of it; he saw the scars on his fingers; he saw the split along one knuckle that hadn't yet healed, and he realized it wasn't the Black Lapels who were stopping Jace.

"They say 'unnatural' a lot at chapel, don't they? Harp on it every fucking week. Is that why you let them beat the shit out of you?" Logan asked.

In an instant, Jace's smile was gone, and he jerked his head away, looking out over the room. His hand returned to his lip, but he noticed it immediately and made a frustrated sound, dropped it to his lap with a thump. Logan pushed on. "Do you think there's something wrong with you, Jace? Something they can 'purify' out of you if they hit you enough?"

Jace turned back, stormy, but still said nothing. His jaw muscles flexed. More gently, Logan said, "I know I wasn't raised in it, but I've heard what those priests say about their god. He's the god of 'anything you can take is yours.' He's the god of conquerors and bullies and rapists. That's not you. If *that* god told me there was something wrong with the way I cared about people, I'd honestly take that as a compliment."

Still, Jace said nothing, but his eyebrows rose plaintively, his eyes fixed on Logan's. His hands stayed in his lap, far away from his mouth. Logan leaned closer. "There's nothing wrong with you, Jace."

The curly-haired boy shuddered, a small, involuntary noise catching in the back of his throat. He licked his lips and half laughed as he said, "I think you're probably the only person in the world who thinks that."

"Bullshit." Logan shook his head vehemently. "Maybe they're not saying it in those exact words, but your crew worships the ground you walk on."

Jace's shrug was uncomfortable. "They don't know me."

"Even Squints?"

Exhaling sharply like Logan had scored a hit on him, Jace said, "Maybe Squints, but—"

Logan rolled over his protest. "Did Squints seem disgusted or angry or upset earlier?"

"No, but that's just Squints. He's always been like that. He accepts people as they are. Doesn't try to fix them. That doesn't mean they don't need to be fixed."

"You don't, though," Logan insisted. When Jace scoffed and then laughed uncomfortably, Logan asked, "Do you *want* there to be something wrong with you?"

"Of course not," Jace snapped, then sighed and softened again. "Sorry—I know you're trying to be nice, but you don't understand. You didn't even know this shit was illegal, and you don't know the first thing about Swordsmen."

Logan sat back and drummed his fingers on the table. "True," he said. "But I feel like I've gotten to know *you*. And I say nothing's wrong. If you'd rather take the opinions of soldiers who hate you or priests who want to hurt you, that's your prerogative. But *my* opinion is you're…exactly right."

He stared at Jace until Jace finally made eye contact with him, blinking and squinting like he was looking into the sun.

Jace shook his head, but a faint, baffled smile spread across his lips. "Well," he said. He folded his hands and tapped them against his mouth. "Well, then…I guess…I guess—"

He laughed, then seemed surprised by the sound of it. "I don't know what to say to that. No one's ever thought that before."

Logan shrugged. "Don't have to say anything. Just believe me."

Jace stared at him, scanning over every part of Logan's face like he was looking for the lie. At length, he said, "All right, Homeschool. I will."

Going back to classes the next day was difficult, but Jace and Logan agreed it wasn't worth the increased scrutiny from Lowell to continue their faux-sick seclusion.

Instead, they snuck out that night in their usual PJs and hoodies—though this time they wore shoes, since they wouldn't be sneaking around inside.

Squints stirred as Logan slipped out of bed, turning over to watch them dress for an adventure. When Jace stuffed his blanket into his bag, Squints said quietly, "Camping out?"

"Yeah," Jace replied, barely any voice coloring the exhale of the word. "The lake."

Squints sat up. "Stuff your beds and pull your curtains a little. I'll cover for you if Lowell comes through." He raised his fist toward Jace, who knocked his own against it gratefully before suiting action to Squints's advice.

"Thanks," Logan whispered, as the pair slipped out of the room and made their way to the open first-floor window at the end of their residential hall to clamber out into the night.

They hiked in the direction of the lake. It was a clear night, glittering with millions of stars, and the air still held the warmth of the spring day despite the cool evening breeze.

When they reached the lakeshore, Logan stopped, looking out over the dark, diamond-studded water, but Jace grabbed his hand and kept walking around the edge.

"Not here," he said. "There's a better place."

Logan found it challenging to concentrate on anything else with Jace's hand warm in his, so he did a lot of tripping over lake-smoothed tree branches and small stands of pampas grass.

The farther they got from the ChilCo buildings, the more they were forced to pick their way through heavier brush and scrubby trees whose roots made tangles in the water like a nest of snakes.

Jace beaned himself on a low-hanging branch and reeled back, cursing and laughing. Logan pulled Jace's forehead down and kissed it. This led to more kissing, standing thigh-deep in lakeside greenery.

Logan marveled at the difference between Jace's soft lips and his rough grip.

"Come on," Jace said, laughing breathlessly as he broke away. "Where we're going is much cooler than here. And I think I've got spiders on me."

Jace was right: his spot was cooler. Much like the narrow cave on the other side of the campus grounds, it was almost entirely hidden by trees, and it took serious wriggling to get through the underbrush and dodge reaching branches. But once inside, they were enveloped in foliage, with an arm-span opening onto Lake Childers's sparkling water.

With a snap of his wrists, Jace spread his blanket out over the ground, which was soft with years of accumulated leaf litter. He sat, tossing his bag aside then pulling Logan down next to him.

"How do you find these places?" Logan said, reveling in the serenity of the hideaway.

Jace shrugged. "I've spent most of my free time exploring." He glanced at Logan with suppressed laughter sparkling in his eyes. "And before you came around, I had nothing but free time."

"Do you miss it?" Logan asked, lying down, his hands tucked behind his head.

"What? The free time?" Jace laughed. "Not even a little." He copied Logan's posture, spreading his long legs out toward the water and lying back comfortably on his folded hands. "Do you remember lying like this out at the cave, that first time I took you there?"

Logan exhaled in an almost laugh. "I remember battling a very strong urge to kiss you."

"Same," Jace said. "I wish I'd known. We've wasted so much time pretending."

"You like pretending, though," Logan said, idly tearing up a couple of pale purple water irises and plucking petals off, one by one.

Jace turned his head toward Logan but didn't answer.

When Logan looked up, Jace seemed bewildered. "Why would you say that?"

Logan raised an eyebrow at him. "Don't you?"

"Whether I like it or not," Jace said, "a certain amount of pretending is necessary."

Logan grunted, a noncommittal sound. He disagreed; Jace's acting seemed to be mostly a habitual pastime, not any sort of necessity. He was well-liked, smart, gorgeous, athletic. He didn't need to pretend to be anything to get what he wanted.

"Don't grunt like it's not true," Jace said, scowling and raking up a handful of water flowers for himself, shredding them as Logan was doing. "You're as much a pretender as I am. And it's not because you're deceitful or anything like that—you just know that putting everything out there in the open is never a good plan."

"I wouldn't say *never*," Logan said.

"No?"

Logan reached over and pinched Jace's lower lip, a playful imitation of the other boy's habit. "I think we're both glad I finally fessed up to wanting to kiss you."

Jace grabbed Logan's wrist, tugging his grip on his lip away and kissing Logan's fingers. "But that's not laying *everything* on the table. Single truths, sporadically given out."

Logan frowned. "I want everything out. Ask me a question, anything. I'm not interested in pretending. I've spent most of my life pretending not to exist, and most of my time here pretending not to be obsessed with you. I'm thoroughly sick of it."

"Obsessed with me, eh?" Jace said, a wry grin showing off his missing tooth. He rolled onto his side and propped himself up on his elbow so he leaned over Logan. He seemed to be thinking of what questions he might pose to Logan, studying him with hooded, thoughtful eyes.

At length, he said, "I don't think it's fair to ask you questions."

"Why not?" With Jace so close, his blue eyes so bright with moonlight off the water, Logan's body was heating up. He knew he should be concentrating on Jace's answer, but he was distracted by the chameleon's mouth.

"Because I…don't want to answer yours," Jace said, his words hot air on Logan's lips as he leaned down to kiss him lightly.

Confused, Logan smiled into the kiss. "What do you mean?"

Jace pulled back, arching an eyebrow. "Just what I said. You're not interested in pretending? Well, I'm not interested in dredging up things that are better left buried."

Logan slid back and sat up, drawing his knees up to his chest and hugging them. Jace was so matter-of-fact in the way he shut Logan down, the deep cut of knowing Jace wanted to share nothing with him, and wanted to know nothing more about Logan, either, was made so quickly and with such a sharp blade that it took the space of several breaths before it hurt.

"Oh," was all Logan could find to say.

Jace was quick to soothe and bandage. "It's not that I don't want to talk to you or anything like that. Talking to you is the best part of my day. I just…" He sighed, tousling his curls as he scratched at his scalp.

"I know the sort of things you'll be curious about. And I don't want to talk about them." He exhaled and quietly added, "I like that you know little enough about me to think there's nothing wrong with me."

Logan nodded, his mouth still set in a grim line.

"Hey, don't look so serious." He strong-armed Logan, pushing his legs flat so he could crawl up Logan's body and press a kiss against his jaw. "Doesn't this make you happy?"

"Yes," Logan said, his voice faint because Jace's warm proximity had stolen his breath.

Jace's smile was triumphant. "Good." Shoving Logan down hard on his back, he knocked out what remained of the air in Logan's lungs. Holding his shoulders down, Jace kissed him hungrily, aggressively. When Logan tried to shift them onto their sides, Jace kept him pinned with a low growl.

"Jace," Logan gasped, trying to shove the other boy back far enough to get space to breathe. "You've got me trapped."

"Mm-hmm," Jace hummed. He lifted up from one of Logan's shoulders to wiggle his hand under Logan's hoodie, then flicked the buttons open on his pajamas. He pressed Logan's head hard against the ground with the force of his kisses.

"Jace," Logan said again, more emphatically this time. He grabbed the arm that had unbuttoned him almost to his waist. "Stop. You do this to me a lot. I get it—you're stronger than me. But that doesn't mean I like being pinned down."

Jace stared at him, blinking owlishly as he processed what Logan had said, so Logan continued slowly, enunciating each syllable. "I don't think I'm the kind of person who likes to be dominated."

Finally reacting, Jace frowned slightly, turning to stare into the trees while he thought. He forced a ghosted grin, trying to summon a sarcastic comment, but when jokes eluded him, he lapsed into quiet confusion. When he turned back, his face was dark, inscrutable.

"What if…I need you to be?"

Jace's low-spoken words hung in the air between them as they eyed each other, minds churning and foreheads creasing. When a minute ticked by without Logan responding, and then two, Jace let him up, sitting back on his heels and resting his arms across his knees. The curly-haired boy wouldn't meet Logan's eyes. After a moment, he reached up in that constant, subconscious movement and pinched his lip again.

For a long time, the pair sat in silence, Jace staring into the crush of trees surrounding them, Logan staring at the canopy of branches as his mind whirled. Could he handle that? He'd never considered the role he would play in a relationship, never wondered before how far he would bend to adapt to someone else's needs. Of course, he'd never imagined being involved with someone as dedicated to being in control as Jace was.

But Jace was…Jace. Logan was crazy about him, and if Jace needed someone he could overpower, so what? It didn't prick Logan's pride to let Jace manhandle him—it just wasn't what he preferred. But it was infinitely preferable to not having Jace at all.

Logan made a decision. Sitting up, he pulled Jace's hand away from his mouth and brushed a kiss across Jace's palm.

"I guess," he said, "I could try."

Jace's grateful smile nearly broke Logan's heart. For a moment, he lost some of his hunger and dominance as he kissed Logan sweetly on the forehead, nose, and finally his lips.

"Come on. Strip down. Let's go for a swim," Jace said. He didn't really leave Logan with a choice, as he practically tore the other boy's clothes off him. Jace took his own pajamas off with no less haste, and it was pure joy to watch him undress, seeing each smooth stretch of tight-cable muscle appear from under the baggy black clothes.

Once he'd dropped his discarded clothes and kicked his shoes onto a corner of the blanket, Jace leapt backward with a happy cry, plunging into the lake. Logan followed, toeing the water with a cautious foot before letting Jace seize his arm and pull him under. They wrestled in the shallows good-naturedly, each dunking the other a half-dozen times, splashing and laughing.

Soaked and spluttering, Logan was caught by surprise when Jace kissed him again, this time pulling the full length of Logan's body up against him with his hands on Logan's hips. Jace's erection pressed insistently against Logan's thigh and vice versa.

The contrast between cool water and the heat of Jace's skin everywhere it touched made Logan feel lightheaded, short of breath.

"All right, I'm following orders," he said, nudging Jace's head to the side so he could nip at his neck. "So what do you want?"

"Everything." Jace's fingers dug in so hard it hurt; his kisses were insistent.

Logan fought the urge to reassert himself, consciously relaxing under Jace's grip. He moved slowly, breathed deeply, tried not to be overwhelmed by Jace's almost desperation. Something in the way Jace was crushing him, consuming him, broke Logan's heart. The curly-haired boy didn't just want him—he *needed* him.

Jace broke away, panting, breathless. "Could you...do what you did yesterday?"

A faint sensory memory of Jace coming across his tongue made Logan lick his lips. "Yes," he breathed, bending to kiss Jace's shoulder. Grinning widely, Jace released Logan and kicked himself up so he floated horizontally in the dark water, tiny waves lapping against his tanned, goose-bumped skin.

With his arms stretched out to either side, he looked like the picture of relaxation, but his too-quick breaths and bright eyes made his anxiousness apparent.

When he knelt in the water next to Jace, Logan couldn't quite reach him, so he towed the floating boy a few feet closer to the shallow shore. There, he sank to his knees, took a deep breath, and sucked in earnest—less testing and playfulness than there had been the day before, and more pleasurable urgency.

At first, Logan focused only on the head, but as he got used to the feeling of Jace in his mouth, he bent to take more of Jace in. Jace yelped and jerked when Logan pressed him deeper, dunking himself and spluttering, shaking water sprays in every direction. He laughed when his flailing made his waist sink in the water, drawing his dick out of Logan's reach.

"Well, this is working," he said lightly. He dropped his feet to the lake floor again and latched onto Logan, kissing him while he pushed them both toward the water's edge.

They stumbled and scrambled out of the water before flopping onto the blanket. Jace threw himself onto his back, grinning in anticipation of Logan beginning his task again. Logan didn't disappoint; it was extremely pleasurable to watch Jace lose control of himself when Logan touched him. He stretched his mouth uncomfortably wide around Jace's erection, fighting the urge to gag when the tip pressed past the back of his tongue. Jace's eyes were closed, and he seemed to be concentrating hard on not thrusting wildly.

Everything was unfamiliar, wonderful, strange.

Although Jace wasn't touching him as he bobbed his head, working to bring the curly-haired boy off, Logan hardened beyond anything he'd ever felt—he was almost painfully aroused.

After a while, Logan's jaw ached, but when he pulled back, Jace's hands rose from his sides and interlocked in Logan's hair. "Please…" Jace said, eyes still squeezed shut. He wasn't quite pinning Logan's head down but nevertheless made his preference that Logan continue his work quite clear.

Logan murmured acquiescence, a low rumble in his throat that made Jace groan. He held his head still and nudged Jace's hips up and down for a couple of beats; Jace needed no more hint than that. He thrust up into Logan's mouth—first slowly, then harder and more quickly, his teeth gritted and his moaning almost pained.

"That's—it's—right—" Jace gasped, his fingers curled and tangled in Logan's hair. Finally he came with a wild, primal sound that made Logan lightheaded all over again. Logan swallowed, ran his tongue over Jace's head, swallowed again, sucking the other boy dry.

When at last Jace released him and he could lift his head, he took a deep, grateful breath, laughing as he stretched his jaw experimentally, rubbing at the joint under his ear.

"That was…" Jace said, breathless. "That was…that was the best thing, ever. Ever." He laughed, shaking his head. His chest rose and fell with his panting. "Sorry. It's hard to…words."

"Always happy to render you speechless," Logan said, crawling up Jace's body to kiss him. While Jace recovered, Logan ran fingertips over his abs, his chest, his shoulders, enjoying the taut smoothness of every inch of Jace's body.

"You do have a habit of draining the blood out of my head," Jace said. He rolled them over, pressing Logan's shoulders into the ground and straddling him. "Now I return the favor."

Logan's eyebrows shot up. Hadn't Jace just the day before established that he wasn't up for sucking dick? Ah, but he wasn't going to. Jace scooted down Logan's body, sitting on Logan's thighs and jerking Logan with one hand.

Being touched that way by Jace—by someone Logan had fantasized about for months and never imagined he'd be near like this—was overwhelming. As soon as Jace's hand moved up and down his length, Logan's body bowed, his back arching and his head pressing itself back into the hard ground. It was only a hand; it should've been roughly the same as working himself, but it wasn't. Not at all.

It was a hundred, thousand, million times better.

"Jace," Logan croaked. His throat felt raw, his lungs barely able to take in air. He wanted to close his eyes and give in to the feeling, but he couldn't bear to look away from Jace's smirking concentration and the bright, intent light in those blue eyes. It felt like he should be memorizing this moment, the outline of Jace's face and body in the moonlight.

After all the playing they'd done the past week, and the drawn-out teasing of sucking Jace off, it was over more quickly than Logan wanted it to be. He tried to grab Jace's arm and slow him down, postpone the inevitable, but Jace pinned his hands out of the way, then moved the fist that gripped Logan mercilessly faster. With a thunderous rush in his ears, Logan came.

The last few spurts trickled over Jace's hand, and Logan held his breath as the curly-haired boy lifted his fingers to his mouth, taking a tentative taste. If he liked it, maybe he wouldn't be so hesitant to reciprocate. Maybe—

But Jace shuddered, frowning at the taste and clenching his sticky hand into a fist at his side. Logan's euphoria dimmed. Even in his post-orgasmic delirium, Logan saw Jace's face visibly oscillate between strongly positive and equally strong negative emotions.

Jace stood abruptly and extended his clean left hand to Logan to help him up. "Another swim?"

"Sure," Logan said with a sigh, avoiding Jace's eyes. He wasn't even sure why he was embarrassed, but he was. He tried very hard not to feel disappointed.

"Hey," Jace said, stopping Logan from brushing past him with a hand pressed to Logan's chest. "I'm sorry. I didn't mean to—"

"It's fine," Logan said, cutting him off. "That felt good. Let's leave it at that."

He dove past before Jace could speak again, letting the water of the lake close over him, blessedly cool against his overheated cheeks. He tried to diagnose his sudden self-consciousness. Was it because he'd been so puppy-dog enthusiastic to suck Jace's dick, or because Jace so obviously wasn't willing or pleased to do the same for him? He felt a little stupid for even thinking the question; how was it possible that he was dissatisfied with his *fucking hot* best friend giving him an orgasm, who cared how?

Logan's head broke the surface again, returning him to the night sounds of the lake: bullfrogs and chirping cicadas, water quietly lapping, the wind rustling the reeds. Jace sat in the shallows, rubbing his hands over each other in the water, his expression distant as he stared blankly across at the opposite bank.

Floating on his back, Logan let the gentle wind push him slowly to the middle of the lake, far from Jace. He wished he weren't naked, but he wasn't willing to paddle back to the blanket and dress.

A quiet splash resounded as Jace lay back in the water, floating like Logan was. The curly-haired boy pushed off from the water's edge before easily cutting through the lake's surface until his body butted up against Logan's and sent ripples out away from them in every direction. Jace took Logan's hand, interlocking their fingers so they didn't drift apart in the water.

His grip was strong, warm. Logan couldn't get his feelings straight. On the one hand, having Jace next to him was perfection. On the other, he couldn't shake the feeling that Jace was acting again, playing along as much as necessary to get what he wanted.

Logan needed something real, something genuine and open from the chameleon. "Answer a question," he said. "Tell me something about you." He said it quietly to the sky drifting past overhead.

"I can't," Jace said.

Logan let out a long, steady sigh, sinking lower in the water as the air left his lungs. "What if I need you to?" he said, echoing Jace's words from before.

The blue-eyed boy wriggled, antsy, uncomfortable.

Taking a deep breath, he folded, letting go of Logan's hand to drop beneath the water's surface. He balled up and spun so he swam downward, touching the bottom with both hands then bobbing back up again. When he surfaced, he shook glittering droplets off his heavy, wet ringlets and spread his mouth in a wide, toothy grin.

"Okay. I'll try."

And Logan felt his heart start up again.

Treading water next to Logan, Jace reached out to run his hand over Logan's chest, just enough pressure to be felt without pushing him under the water. He followed his fingers with his tongue, tracing the shape of Logan's muscles, drawing lines of fire across his skin. Logan shook under the assault, gasping. Jace kept him breathless with a long, bone-melting kiss.

When Logan pulled away to tread water as well, he bubbled over with laughter. "I know what you're trying to do, trickster. You can't make me forget all my questions forever."

"You'd like the attempt, though," Jace said, smirking. He slipped his hand underwater and palmed Logan's hardness, his fingers sliding up and down its length.

Logan let Jace draw him closer, but he grabbed the back of Jace's neck so he could kiss him on his own terms. When Jace tried to wrap him up and pin them chest to chest, Logan danced back in a swirl of water. "Nuh-uh," he said. "Brace yourself for a question: who was your first friend at ChilCo?"

Jace's hands skimmed the lake's surface, drawing patterns that caught moonlight. "Easy one. Squints. He's known me longer than anyone. I don't remember ever not being friends with him."

Logan paddled in a circle, enjoying the feel of water against his skin. "Your turn then. What do you want to know about me?"

"I already know everything about you, Homeschool," Jace said, grinning a challenge.

"Oh? I doubt it. I'm sure there's something in that tiny brain of yours worth asking."

"Tiny brain, huh?" Jace laughed and dove after Logan, dunking both of them. He nearly drowned Logan when he grabbed the other boy's legs and held them above him out of the water so Logan hung almost upside down in the lake. Logan hooked his knees over Jace's shoulders and paddled furiously, flexing his abs hard to hold his head out of the water while he spat out what seemed like gallons of the lake.

The position put Logan's dick close to Jace's face, and Jace surprised them both by leaning down to swipe a fierce lick along the bottom edge of it. Logan was so shocked by the sudden pleasure that his back arched, plunging him back into the water. Jace laughed and let Logan's lower half go so the other boy could recover. "That's what you get," Jace said as Logan shook the water out of his ears.

Logan didn't try to verbally spar with him; he jumped on Jace, wrapping his legs around Jace's waist and grabbing the curly-haired boy's face in both hands so he could kiss him ferociously. Jace staggered back a step before reciprocating, opening his mouth to Logan's tongue and clutching Logan's body closer to his.

"I've got a question," Jace gasped between kisses.

"Hmm?" Logan hummed against Jace's lips.

Jace dragged Logan toward the water's edge again. He threw him down in the shallows, laughing when Logan pulled him down alongside him. Rolling over Logan, pinning him down again, Jace bent close to Logan's ear and whispered, "Can I fuck you?"

"I—" Logan's mouth went dry, a jolt of adrenaline making his chest flare with sudden heat. "I don't know. I mean, yes, but—"

"But?"

Logan's face flushed hot. "I don't know what I'm doing."

"Me neither," Jace said, chuckling.

"But you've at least—" Logan bit his tongue hard to shut himself up. *Stop talking, you moron.* He "hadn't read" that CRS report, after all, and there was absolutely no good reason whatsoever to bring up what he "hadn't" read in there at this moment.

Jace watched Logan, wide-eyed, waiting for the sentence to end. Logan croaked, "You at least have some idea of what's supposed to happen, right? Because my entire knowledge of sex is from a couple magazines I found in the basement, and there was definitely supposed to be a girl involved."

When Jace visibly relaxed, Logan's own muscles loosened. He'd very nearly ended this whole evening's adventure with a few thoughtless words. He hadn't anticipated it being so hard not to address Jace's past; the words on that page were burned into Logan's mind, nicotine stains yellowing every interaction between them.

Jace didn't seem bothered, though. He grinned mischievously. "I've got the basics, at least. We can figure out the rest." His bravado faltered for a moment. "That is…if you want to?"

"I want to." Logan sounded a lot surer than he felt. "Just tell me what to do," he said, as if that weren't exactly what Jace would have done anyway.

Jace grinned, punched Logan lightly in the chest, then climbed over him and out of the water. Dripping wet and gloriously hard, Jace looked like a mythical creature as he picked up his back-pack and dug through it.

"The Bens were right about a lot," Jace said, "but they were wrong on one point. I didn't go to the pantry for you twice—"

Victoriously, he pulled out what looked like a half-empty bottle of vegetable oil. "I went three times," he said with a grin.

Logan raised an eyebrow and waited for the explanation.

Jace's lip pressed out in a pout when Logan didn't seem to appreciate his offering. "It's oil," he said, as if that explained why he looked so pleased with himself.

When Logan shook his head, shrugging, Jace continued, "Like, lube?"

Logan nodded slowly, trying to look as though the explanation had made an impression on him. "Oh. Okay. Uh, cool."

"Goddamn, Homeschool," Jace said. He dropped his bag on the ground with a *whump* and sat on the blanket, holding the vegetable oil like a trophy. "You really *don't* know what you're doing, do you?"

"That *is* what I said," Logan said stiffly, crossing his arms.

"I'm not making fun of you. I'm just surprised. Come here." He patted the blanket next to him, and after a moment's hesitation, Logan slopped out of the water and lay down on the comforter, stretched out on his side facing Jace.

Jace kissed him, then turned him until he lay flat on his back. "So first I kiss you all over," he said, and he did exactly that, pressing his lips against Logan's collarbone and nipples and abs and the *V* of muscle between his hip bones. He nipped lightly at Logan's thigh and ran his nose along the length of Logan's shaft. "Not so bad, right?" Jace muttered, and Logan wasn't sure if he was talking to himself or Logan.

The breeze off the lake chilled the water droplets studding his skin, and Logan shivered. Jace brushed his lips against Logan's, then bent to murmur, "I'll warm you up—don't worry."

Kneeling up, Jace said, "Now you have to bend your knees a bit." One eyebrow cocked, Logan did as he was told, sliding his feet toward himself along the ground to raise his knees.

"Uh, farther," Jace said, pushing Logan's legs back until his heels met his body, then, with a frown, lifting Logan's knees back toward his chest.

Logan laughed uncomfortably and tried to drop his legs again, but Jace held him where he was. "Hold your knees," he commanded. Then he smiled and said, "Please?" And just like that, Logan had no other choice.

"I feel...kind of dumb," Logan said, looking up into the trees. He tried not to think about how exposed he was, tried to remember he trusted Jace, but his enthusiasm flagged. The cold wind brought goosebumps up over his whole body.

Jace considered him for a moment, then pulled his legs back down. "Let's try something else. Here, lie on your side."

Logan rolled over and shivered happily as the curly-haired boy settled in behind him, one arm around Logan's waist and the other slipping under Logan's head. Jace pressed a kiss to the back of Logan's head and pulled him tightly to his chest. The hard line of Jace's erection lay along the cleft of Logan's ass, a preface that made Logan both nervous and painfully excited.

When Logan relaxed, Jace's hand drew slow circles from Logan's waist to his hip, and then he was holding Logan's length in his hand again, working it with slow, insistent pressure that made it hard for Logan to breathe.

Jace kept up his steady rhythm until Logan was writhing; it was a pace designed to frustrate, too arousing to let Logan lie still and enjoy it, but too slow and easy to bring him to climax. Through his teeth, Logan groaned, "Jace," and tried to grab Jace's hand and force him to speed up or to tighten slightly.

But at Logan's touch, Jace released him. Instead, he dragged his fingers up and over Logan's hip, fingernails tracing teasing lines. Then his touch vanished altogether, the night wind rushing in between them as Jace half rolled away. Jace rustled around, cursing quietly to himself as he fumbled with something, and then he was back, his smooth skin radiating heat against Logan's back.

"You'll have to really relax," Jace said.

Logan laughed, more air than sound. "I'll do my best."

Despite his intentions, when Jace slid a slippery finger inside him, every muscle in Logan's body clenched against it. "Oh—I—"

He couldn't catch his breath. Jace moved it so slowly, but each minute shift and twist was more sensation than Logan had ever felt.

Jace stilled. "Is it bad?"

"No."

"So...it's good?"

Logan wasn't sure how to answer that. He wouldn't call it good, but he thought...he wanted more. When he told Jace so, the blue-eyed boy smiled against Logan's skin, bit him gently on the shoulder, then leaned back to watch a second finger slip inside Logan. Logan squeezed his eyes shut, biting down on his lip to hold in the moan trying to escape him.

Jace's fingers pressed in as far as he could reach, scissored apart, twisted out and back in again. Logan rocked back against Jace's hand, shivering with the waves of hot and cold that had overtaken him, focusing every bit of his attention on how it felt to have any part of Jace *inside his body*.

It was unreal.

Logan had never been so hard in his life. He wanted to reach down and jerk himself, but he was afraid he'd come at the first touch of his hand, and he wasn't sure he could bear to have Jace inside him if he climaxed now—and he wanted Jace inside him.

"Jace," he said, "please—"

He didn't need to tell Jace what he wanted. Jace slipped his fingers free and rolled away again, long enough to shock the oil-slicked skin of Logan's body, and then he was back, and something else pressed against Logan's hole.

He gritted his teeth until his jaw popped. The pressure was intense and painful, and there didn't seem to be any way Jace would fit himself in, and oh, God, it was becoming more than he could bear, and any second now he'd have to call Jace off, and it hurt and it wasn't going to—

The head of Jace's dick slipped inside him, and Logan let out all the air he'd been holding in a wordless exclamation. Jace pressed his free hand—still wet with oil—to Logan's chest and asked, "Are you okay? Does it hurt?"

Logan nodded, not trusting himself to speak. No matter; it was a yes to both. Consciously, he tried to relax, focusing on letting down his defenses, but he couldn't seem to release the tension in his body. Jace reached down again, taking Logan's hardness in his hand, and Logan groaned at the combination of pain and pleasure.

As Jace stroked Logan, he also pulled himself back slightly, until he barely remained inside him. Then he pressed in again, pushing deeper until Logan gasped and recoiled, then retreating again. He shook with effort, as though he had to physically fight the urge to shove himself in to the hilt.

"Feels…so good—" Jace managed through clenched teeth. Logan moaned in response.

Then, suddenly, Jace was pressed against him, as deep as he could reach, and Logan felt…perfect. Like a switch had flipped, the unbearable penetration became everything, everything he wanted. Jace fit inside him so snugly, and how had he ever, ever felt complete without him?

"Oh, God," Logan whispered. Jace clutched him ferociously, pressing his forehead to the back of Logan's neck, panting. Jace kissed him, bit him, echoed his astonished words.

It wasn't fireworks; it was just wholeness. Logan felt *right* so intensely that he wanted to cry for how empty and gray the world had been before. And Jace's arms around him, crushing him, bruising him with how close Jace wanted to be to him—it felt like they were moments away from Logan folding right into Jace, making one person out of two.

"More," Logan said.

Jace exhaled a laugh. "That's all there is." Still, he ground his hips harder against Logan.

Logan growled and rocked away from Jace, then shoved back again hard. Jace groaned like he'd been punched. "Oh," he breathed.

Gasping like he was contemplating a plunge off a precipice, Jace drew his hips back, then pushed himself back in with steady, unyielding pressure. They both groaned, and Jace clamped his teeth on Logan's shoulder as he did it again and again and again.

It was too much.

It was not enough.

It was almost—almost—almost—

"Jace!" Logan half sighed, half wailed. His entire body locked up, a trembling starting in his thighs and rippling up through his abdomen. Everything was pure, perfect sensation. The wave of pleasure tightened his toes, swept all the way to his scalp. Behind him, Jace choked out something that could have been Logan's name, his arms so crushingly tight, his hands clawing into Logan's skin. Then Jace shook, too, jerking against Logan.

As the roaring in Logan's ears died down, their panting in the otherwise-silent night seemed incredibly loud. Jace hadn't loosened his grip at all, and he hummed almost like he was purring as he nuzzled against the back of Logan's head and neck.

"I love you," Logan said into the night.

Jace flinched, then drew his head back stiffly. The sudden cool breeze in the space he created made Logan shiver. Logan couldn't bear not to see the curly-haired boy's face. He turned, gasping anew as Jace slipped out of him, and lay on his side facing Jace. The other boy's blue eyes were wide, troubled. He lifted a hand to his mouth, pressing his lower lip against his teeth with his thumb.

"No," Logan said, pulling Jace's hand away, replacing it with his lips. "Don't do that. I'm sorry. I shouldn't have—I'm sorry." His stupid, stupid mouth. Everything had been so perfect, and he'd had to go and—

Silently, Jace pressed closer, wrapping his arms around Logan and nudging Logan's nose with the tip of his own. "I like you," he whispered. "I adore you. I'm...charmed by you."

Logan smiled, dropping his eyes. Jace's slow, lazy kiss made him shudder, made him want to jump right back into what they'd just finished doing. When they broke apart for air, Logan whispered back, "I'm infatuated with you. I'm captivated by you."

"Don't forget 'obsessed.'" Jace said, laughter in his voice.

Logan chuckled as the potential tension that had crackled between them vanished. "How could I forget? I'm obsessed."

Jace paused, thinking. "I'm enchanted. I'm enamored!"

"Fascinated," Logan shot back.

"Bewitched."

"Beguiled."

They threw synonyms at each other until their vocabularies ran out and they'd exhausted every similar word in Old Dunisian, Tychan, or Freelan. Eventually they were too shaken with laughter to come up with more.

Jace ran his hand over Logan's cheek—such a soft, guileless motion that Logan's heart could snap in half from sheer happiness.

Jace's gentle contentment sharpened into something wicked. "I've got the sudden very strong urge to fill you up again," he said.

Logan yawned and stretched, feigning tiredness. "I don't know," he teased. "I mean, are you even up for such vigorous activity this soon? Maybe you should take it easy an—"

With a snarl, Jace slammed Logan onto the ground and knelt between Logan's legs. His kisses were sharp, hard, hungry. He pressed himself closer and closer until his thighs were under Logan's, forcing his legs back in almost the same position they'd first attempted. It didn't feel dumb now—it felt like Jace wasn't close enough to him yet.

"Yes or no, Homeschool," Jace growled.

"Yes, Jace," Logan said. "Always yes."

Logan woke up sore. He groaned, trying to favor his aching shoulder and hip, his tight back muscles, and his bruised-feeling ass all at once as he sat up. Jace opened his eyes and grinned, then pulled a face as he sat up and stretched his shoulders.

"I'm not built for sleeping on the ground," Jace rasped, then yawned loudly, like a lion. He levered himself up until he was seated, then pressed his forehead to Logan's. His eyes were so close all Logan could see was blue. "How do you feel this morning?"

Logan tilted his head up far enough to kiss him. "Like I fucked my best friend."

"So…awesome?"

Grinning, Logan said, "Yeah, pretty awesome."

"Good," Jace said, clunking his head against Logan's. "Me too. Ready to head back?"

Logan cast a longing look at the blanket. "I guess. Wish we could stay."

Jace stood and brushed a few dry leaves off his pajama pants. The sun peeked over the horizon, and the light gave Jace's hair a pink glow. He offered Logan a hand to help him up. "I know. It'll be nice once we're placed and we can be together all the time. Maybe we'll have a break where we can travel for a while or something."

Jace's words—and the future together that they implied—warmed Logan like a plunge into a hot bath. "You think we'll be placed together?"

Jace shrugged and grinned as he slung his backpack onto one shoulder and bent to pick up a corner of the blanket. "Doesn't really matter, does it?" he said as he shook the comforter out. "I'll go where you go or vice versa. I'm not about to leave this place without you."

# 8

## WHATEVER JACE WANTS

As if Jace speaking about placements had been a summoning ritual, Logan started hearing the word everywhere. Boys their age talked excitedly in the halls and classrooms about one another's rumored universities and jobs, comparing test scores, and speculating wildly about where their respective deans would be able to get them into.

When Logan received a summons to Ms. Lowell's office, Jace nodded sagely and only said, "It's that season."

Slightly baffled and with trepidation, Logan knocked on Lowell's door, waiting for her cheery "Come in!" before he pushed his way past precarious stacks of papers to a seat.

The dean of Eagle Hold had more stacks of folders and paper covering her desk, and though they seemed neatly labeled and even color coded, it was so overwhelming that Logan wondered how she could possibly find anything.

"Ah, Mr. Cardot," she said brightly, gesturing toward the chair he was already lowering himself into. "Thank you for stopping by.

We need to talk about your placement. I'll admit we're behind on yours. Usually I've had a half dozen conversations about it by this point, but you arrived very close to the end of your ChilCo career."

"Uh…sorry?" Logan settled heavily on the seat and dropped his bag between his feet.

"No, no-no-no, I don't mean to imply it's your fault," Ms. Lowell said, hurried and harried. "I know this is all very, um, involuntary for you. Which is why I *do* want to make sure you get my full support in finding an appropriate placement. I have your academic record here…"

She raised a finger as if to pause his response while she plucked a file from a stack with her other hand and flipped it open. "And to be perfectly honest, Mr. Cardot, I could place you nearly anywhere. You're an exemplary student. So tell me: where do you want to go next?"

*With Jace*, he thought, though he didn't dare say it. He cleared his throat, searching for an answer. What *did* he want next?

He knew his parents had had a plan for getting him out of the country when he turned eighteen, a smuggler who had agreed to falsify documents and help him get at least a full country away.

It was part of why he'd been so diligent in studying languages—so he could escape. All he'd ever really dreamed about was getting far away, seeing the world outside the oppressive, gray nightmare of his home country.

Nothing here was worth staying under the thumb of the Black Lapels.

"Anywhere out of Hallsburg would be a good start," he said dryly, thinking of what his parents had told him of Tycha and Thoglain. Both countries were reportedly less militaristic and more open to his kind of person—gay, intellectual, with a bent toward literature and languages. None of those things were particularly highly valued in Hallsburg.

He expected her to think it a flippant answer, but she nodded.

"Yes, I agree. Any future here would be exceedingly…guarded." She pulled a sheet of paper out of yet another stack and slid it across the table toward him. With a yellow highlighter, she circled three names on the crisp white page.

"These are some of the highest-rated schools on the continent. Each has different programs they're well known for. If you give me an idea of which direction you'd like to go—which classwork you enjoy most or which profession you want to point toward—I can help you narrow this down."

Logan looked at the list, feeling overwhelmed. Was he supposed to pick his whole life, his whole future, right now? "I…like languages. I like reading and writing. Is there a job that does those things? Not a teacher. I don't think I want to be a teacher."

"Of course," Ms. Lowell said. "Writers, editors, translators, librarians—those are the more obvious choices. But you could excel in other careers because of those interests as well. Legal representatives do quite a bit of reading and writing, if you've got a bent toward justice and law. Research analysts, if you prefer the sciences. Administrators—" She chuckled, gesturing at the papers around her. "Do more documentation than you could possibly imagine."

Logan nodded in acknowledgement of the sheer volume of paperwork packed into the room, though that wasn't quite what he'd been talking about when he said "writing."

There were too many options. He glanced at the list again, floundering. "I don't…I'm not sure I—" He slid the paper back onto her desk. "Do I have to tell you today?"

"No," Ms. Lowell said. "Take a little time. Think about it. Maybe talk to your friends about what they're going to do. But I will caution you against making any large future decisions to align with what someone else is doing."

She eyed him beadily, and he knew she was talking about Jace. He was glad he hadn't told her what he *really* wanted at the beginning of this conversation. But actually he didn't much care what he was doing, as long as he and Jace were together. Any of the things she'd named would be fine; it was just work.

"I'll think about it," he said, gathering his things before stepping out of the office. "Thanks, Ms. Lowell."

He escaped the overwhelming stacks into the overwhelming press of people in the hallway and headed straight for the courtyard, where he knew Jace would be waiting for him. The first breath of fresh air through the heavy metal doors felt like surfacing from underwater. Jace whistled and waved from the far corner of the courtyard, where he and Randy were bent over a notebook, but Logan paused in the doorway for a minute, enjoying the quiet. Squints trotted across the courtyard toward him.

"Hey," Logan said as the boy got close.

Squints held out a fist and Logan knocked his against it. "Hey. You okay?"

"Yeah?"

Squints shrugged. "You looked a little spooked. We need you over there. Jace designed something and now none of us can convince him he's crazy."

With a laugh, Logan followed him toward the other two. "He probably won't listen to me either, but I'll do my best."

As soon as Logan was within range, Jace grabbed him by the arm and yanked him down next to him on the bench. "Homeschool, you'll see the vision," he said, snatching his notebook out of Randy's hands and shoving it into Logan's. Logan blinked down at what seemed to be detailed blueprints, albeit sketched hastily with a combination of blue pen and silvery pencil lines. He lifted it, turned it slightly, frowned at it.

"Is that a treehouse?"

Jace laughed victoriously. "It's *the* treehouse. The ultimate hideout and headquarters."

"The amount of material we'd have to steal from the woodshop alone—" Randy interjected, but Jace was already snatching the notebook back, flipping to what looked like a materials list so he could stab at a few lines and vehemently explain what they could source from what stockpiles. Logan glanced up at Squints, who smirked and shrugged helplessly.

"—right, Homeschool?" Jace said, swinging back toward Logan. His eyes were wide and hopeful, and he looked so earnest and so sweet that Logan fought the urge to kiss him there in front of everyone.

His hesitation made Jace frown. "What is it? You don't like the house?"

"There's nothing wrong with it. It looks cool. I'll even help you build it. Or steal the stuff for it or whatever." He hadn't really been paying attention to Randy's and Jace's argument, so he wasn't sure what exactly Jace was looking for support for.

Jace's frown deepened as he sat back, looking over Logan for a minute. He wasn't used to people not paying attention to him, and he was clearly searching for a reason why. "You got a note from Lowell last bell," he said at last. "What did she want?"

"Uh," Logan said, scratching behind his ear, "she wanted to talk about my placement. Wanted me to tell her what I wanted."

Jace's chin rose. "What'd you tell her?"

"That I didn't know," Logan said with a laugh. "I've never really thought about it. There were so many options, I—" He shrugged. "I don't know."

"What options did she give you?" Squints asked.

"Everything," Logan said with another breathy laugh. "Do you all have your placements picked out? She said she's already talked to everybody else."

"Yeah," Squints said, "she's been talking to us about it for years. I think she's got mine narrowed down to three anthropology programs, depending on which she can get me into: Leonyl, Durhoss, or Hurst." Seeing that the names meant nothing to Logan, Squints continued, "Those are the three best research programs since I want to stay in academia. Leonyl is in Thoglain, Durhoss is in Tycha, and Hurst isn't too far away from here. It's on the east coast."

Logan remembered seeing the first two on the list Lowell gave him, but Hurst hadn't been one that she circled, probably because it was in Hallsburg.

Randy snorted and said, "I'm not sitting through classes in another fucking language. It'll be Hurst for me, definitely, then Kepler for medical school."

"Aren't you worried about getting in?" Logan asked. Lowell and Squints had made it seem like they needed a backup plan.

Randy smiled smugly. "I'm already in."

Jace knocked him in the chest with the back of his hand. "You didn't tell us! When the fuck did that happen?"

"I don't feel the need to tell you everything about my life," Randy said primly.

He laughed and dodged Jace's attempt to grapple him. Jace's notebook hit the ground with a slap as they play-fought, gamboling around the end of the courtyard while Jace shouted, "That's what you get when you keep secrets!"

As they wrestled, Squints dropped onto the bench next to Logan. "Ms. Lowell will sort you out. She's good at her job. And I can't imagine you'll be hard to place. You're all brains."

"Thanks," Logan muttered. "I'm not really worried about getting in. I just don't know where I want to get *into*. A few months ago, my plan was 'disappear so completely the Black Lapels will never come looking for you.' I didn't, like, even think about colleges."

"Well, forget about colleges then," Squints said. "What do you want to *do?* I don't mean as a job. I wouldn't have picked anthropology off a list. Lowell asked me, 'What change do you want to make in the world?' I said I wanted people to understand each other better. She gave me a bunch of options—counselor, diplomat, that kind of thing. But I wanted to study people, not deal with them one on one. So…anthropology it was."

*What change do I want to make in the world?* Logan wanted to bring his family back. He wanted to introduce Jace to his parents, to live happily in a house by the sea somewhere with him, to fill their home with books and animals. He wanted to live his life without Black Lapel interference.

But that wasn't something he could tell an administrator at a school run by Black Lapels, even one who seemed as genuinely interested in her charges' well-being as Ms. Lowell.

"I don't want to change the world," he said. "I just want to live and be left alone."

Squints's eyes dropped and he frowned. "You know," he said after a minute, "if you stay with Jace, you'll end up changing the world along with him. He's never been able to leave things alone—and you'll be right beside him all the way."

Logan exhaled an almost-laugh through his nose. "True. I guess that's it: I want to make sure nothing gets in Jace's way while he changes the world. Is there a program for that?"

"You talking about me?" Jace said, plopping down on the bench next to Squints. He scooped his notebook off the ground.

"You didn't tell me your placement options," Logan said.

Jace lit up, and Logan felt he was looking at the *real* Jace: pure enthusiasm and honesty he wasn't sure he'd ever seen before. "Durhoss—the college Squints talked about in Tycha—has this crazy engineering school. Like, nine out of ten of their grads lead major programs straight out of school. They only take twelve students a year. No chance I'd ever get in, but, man, can you imagine?"

Of course Logan could imagine. "Don't be stupid. You'll obviously get in. It sounds perfect for you."

Jace grinned. "It's a good school for other stuff too. I'm sure they'd have a good program for you."

"Lots of language and literature options," Squints said.

Logan smiled, but the pressure of the longing in his chest made it hard to speak. In Tycha, could they live the way they wanted? Could he and Jace have a place together? He pictured the two of them studying side by side: Jace sitting cross-legged on the couch, doing math in the margins of his textbook; Logan stretched out with a novel propped against his chest, his head on Jace's leg.

He muscled past it and said, "I can tell Lowell that's where I want to go, but I might not get in. I'm not sure if schools will like the fact that most of my education came from being homeschooled in my basement."

"If you didn't get in, I wouldn't go," Jace said.

Logan rolled his eyes, trying to keep it light. "If you got into your *dream* school, you'd—"

"I wouldn't go." Jace's face was serious but still open, still honest. "I told you already: where you go, I go. I'm not leaving this place without you. Not for school, not for money, not for anything."

Squints swiveled to stare at Jace seriously, deep concern etched on his face. Logan leaned past him so he could speak more intensely but drop his voice, as other people were crossing the courtyard. "Jace, if you were one of *twelve* people picked from the entire continent to study in the best program in the world, you would go. You'd *have* to."

Jace smirked. "Then I guess you'd better tell Lowell to get you into Durhoss."

"Oof!" Logan grunted as Jace tackled him hard, then snatched up the ball, cackling, and ran on. He was slow to get up—it wasn't the first hit he'd taken this practice, or the hardest, and they added up—and his teammates shouted at him to get a move on.

Although he wasn't playing his best, he could hardly be expected to maintain his focus when Jace was playing on the "skins" team, showing off the entirety of that bronzed, lithely muscled torso.

Someone smacked Logan in the back of the head as he ran past, and he scowled up to see Randy casting an eyebrow-raised look of mixed irritation and amusement over his shoulder. *He* knew why Logan's reactions were slower, why his mind was wandering.

The practices had been this way for days; to Logan, every aspect of this stupid game took him back to the lake. It wasn't as though he cared about the outcome of the scrimmage; he wasn't terribly competitive.

So how could he possibly maintain an interest in chasing the ball down when he could be chasing Jace down instead, tackling him to the grass, dragging his tongue across the smooth expanse of skin between neck and navel?

Jace was unaffected, of course. If anything, he seemed to thrive off the tension, becoming more intense, more competitive. With what seemed like no effort at all, he scored another try, and he caught Logan's eye while he did his goofy, celebratory dance.

"I think that's enough humiliation for one day," Jace called so his voice carried over the entire field. He spun the ball on his middle finger, caught it when it wobbled off, then spun it again until Teapot snatched it up to shake over his head like a victorious ape. "Hit the showers. And practice is canceled tomorrow. We all need a day of rest before Saturday's game."

That pronouncement was enough to put even the losers in a good mood as they headed to the locker room. Logan hung back behind the rest, lifting his shirt hem to wipe the sweat off his brow. Jace fell in step beside him, carrying the whiteboard under one arm and a pair of balls under the other.

"You need more practice, Homeschool." He dropped his voice. "Anyone would think you liked being tackled by half-naked men."

Logan smirked. "Just the one man. And only half naked is only half the fun."

A rough humming rumbled in Jace's throat, though his face wore a placid expression, suitable if anyone turned to see them together. "What do you say we skip dinner?"

"Why? Aren't you hungry?" Logan asked in mock-surprise.

"Very," Jace growled.

They showered and redressed quickly, though the other Eagle Hold ruggers were already mostly gone by the time they gathered things to leave. Logan would have loved to strip Jace back down and shove him into the showers, feel what it was like to press their bodies together under the running water, but the Mustang team had booked an evening practice, and they'd be filing in soon.

They emerged into the late afternoon light, giddy with excitement at the prospect of being alone together again. Logan wondered if that would ever wear off.

Going back to their dorm was out of the question, as was wandering to one of their far-flung hideouts on the grounds.

After a moment's contemplation, Jace hoisted his book bag higher up on his shoulder and said, "There's a pretty big supply closet at the end of the math wing. No one should need to go in there right now."

Logan needed no more convincing than that. He set off at a fast pace that Jace soon matched, then outstripped. They half ran the length of the sports fields before lurching through the double doors into the building. Grinning, they tried to keep haste out of their steps once they were inside, but they kept erupting into a rush, darting forward a few jogging steps at a time.

When they reached the dark, cramped closet with its astringent air, Logan barely had the door shut before Jace was unbuckling

Logan's belt and untucking Logan's uniform shirt. His hands were too urgent, too frantic, and he tore one of the buttons off the shirt.

"Slow down," Logan breathed.

"No," Jace said. He bent to kiss the spot where Logan's neck met his shoulder, then bit it—hard.

"Ow, Jace."

"I need to try something. Now. Before I lose my nerve."

Logan felt Jace's nervous energy in the other boy's restless hands roaming over his body, never settling, feeling him all over as if to reassure himself that Logan was there or to find some sort of handhold. "Okay," Logan said. "Do whatever you want."

Jace nodded, taking a deep breath, blinking too rapidly. He was scared; Logan felt it. What the hell was he scared of?

Suddenly Jace dropped to his knees all at once in a too-abrupt motion, clutching Logan's hips to steady himself. Was he really going to…? Logan lifted his hands to the back of his own neck to keep them out of the way as Jace yanked his pants down, then planted his hands on Logan's thighs; Logan didn't dare move or even breathe.

The curly-haired boy bent to plant a kiss on Logan's dick; it bobbed appreciatively, making Jace flinch. Logan was about to stop him—tell him it was all right, he didn't have to do this—when Jace shoved his mouth down over half of Logan's length, plunging him into damp heat that rendered him incapable of thought.

Logan shoved a fist in his mouth, trying to smother the incoherent sounds that strained to leave his mouth. In his head, a steady refrain of *ohmygodohmygodohmygodohmygod* drowned out everything else as Jace drew back, flicking his tongue along the underside, then sucked Logan back in again.

If the world had ended at that moment, if lightning had struck him or a sinkhole had opened up beneath his feet, he would have died euphoric. Gingerly, he lowered one hand to Jace's head, feeling the curls slide under his fingers as Jace bobbed up and down the length of him. His fingers clenched involuntarily, catching at Jace's hair, tearing at the back of his own neck as he struggled not to seize Jace with both hands and thrust for all he was worth.

"Yes, yes, yes, Jace, *yes*," he whispered, a litany of gratitude, of purest pleasure.

He was going to come. He was so close, so close to the edge. His fingers jerked, skimming across Jace's hair, his face. Jace's face was...wet. Logan's climb to orgasm stuttered, faltered. He ran the backs of his fingers over Jace's cheek more intentionally, but Jace slapped his hand away. Not playful. Defensive.

With a grunt of effort and muffled disappointment, Logan pulled himself free of Jace's mouth and tried to turn the other boy's face up to look at him. "Jace?" he said hesitantly, quietly, mindful of the thin door that stood between them and everyone else.

Jace jerked out of Logan's grasp. "I can do this. I can do it. Just let me do it."

Logan paused, then knelt in front of Jace, squeezing himself down in the confines of the closet. Jace had tears in his eyes and a mulish set to his mouth. He wouldn't let Logan catch his eyes. "Hey, look at me."

"I *can* do it," Jace said. Still, he wouldn't meet Logan's gaze.

"Of course you can," Logan said, refastening his pants. "But...I don't want you to. You clearly don't want to."

Jace rolled his eyes, frustrated. "It's not fair. You do everything I want while I pick and choose because—"

With a kiss, Logan silenced him. "Shut the fuck up. Seriously. I do everything I do because I enjoy doing it, and you enjoy me doing it. Nothing feels good to me that doesn't feel good to you. If someday you decide sucking me off makes you happy, I'll be very, *very* eager to give it a try. But right now, I don't want it."

Jace rested his forehead against Logan's, eyes shut. Logan realized Jace's thoughts were still turning and knew with absolute certainty this beautiful, stupid fool would try this again and *act* better next time. He sighed. "Look at me, Jace. I want you to promise me you will *never* touch me if you don't want to. I mean it. Promise."

With a wry grin, Jace sat back, scratching at the blond stubble on his cheek. "Relationships require sacrifice, right? I recall reading that somewhere."

"No," Logan said flatly. "I swear to God, I will never lay another finger on you if I can't trust that you actually want me."

What flickered over Jace's face was hard for Logan to read in the light from the crack under the door, cool white along the bottom edge of Jace's jaw. Hurt? Confusion? It vanished as quickly as it appeared, though, and Jace got to his feet, dusting off his pants. "I promise," he said, his voice small.

"Good. Now…" Logan threw open the button on Jace's fly, then pulled his warm length out with a flourish. "If you'll excuse me, I am *very* happy sucking dick."

He worked up as much saliva as he could, slathering it over Jace's length as he inched his mouth down. He pushed himself down more forcefully, swallowing harder, opening farther than he ever had. Gulping against the urge to gag, he had three-quarters of Jace in his mouth before he felt the twinge of panic that he couldn't breathe.

Logan ran his hands up under the edge of Jace's shirt, loving the smooth, hard planes of his abs under his fingertips. Jace groaned and staggered, grabbing a shelf with one hand to steady himself and running the other along the back of Logan's head. "Oh, fuck," he breathed. The muscles under Logan's hands rolled as Jace rocked his hips, sliding his dick in and out of Logan's mouth.

Logan kept up, breathing in time with Jace's out strokes, feeling every pant and moan from Jace like an electric buzz along his spine. Making Jace whimper felt so goddamn *good*.

Then, abruptly, his mouth was empty, and he grunted in confusion as Jace yanked him to his feet. They teetered, unbalanced in the tight quarters, and then Jace spun Logan around, shoving him hard against the wall and yanking his pants down again. Logan leaned on a forearm to keep Jace from crushing him face-first into the cinder-block wall and made himself relax as Jace slid the slick tip of his cock against Logan's tight hole.

"I need…I need…" Jace whispered, almost to himself.

Logan understood. He felt Jace's need in the desperate way his arm came up under Logan's, clutching at Logan's shirt to hold him tighter. He relieved his own need by pushing back against Jace, rotating his hips slightly as he put more and more pressure on that place where the two of them met, and then—

He hissed, half pain and half, "*Yes*, Jace."

Then Jace was fucking him. Hard…harder.

Where Logan's arm against the wall trembled under the weight of Jace's thrusts, Jace rested his own atop it, threading his fingers through Logan's. Jace's other arm wrapped tightly around Logan's chest, pulling him mercilessly back against each thrust. It was brutal. It was transcendent.

Logan was in a fog. He couldn't feel any one part of his body anymore; he was just a shell, trembling, melting, burning, taking a cock made for him. When Jace cursed and jerked and flooded him, Logan felt it more profoundly than any orgasm of his own.

His arm gave out, and Jace flattened him against the wall, still buried inside him. When Jace shifted, pressing his face to Logan's shoulder, Logan could pick out the words in the low stream of sound Jace made: "Logan, Logan, my Logan, mine."

"Yes," Logan said. "I'm yours."

They stayed that way until Jace softened and slid free of him. The cool air of the room reminded Logan of what Jace had left behind inside him. He laughed quietly as he pulled up his pants and redressed. "I'm going to be full of you for a while," he said.

Jace's eyes sparkled, then darkened hungrily. "You like that?"

"Very much," Logan said.

A low, happy rumble vibrated in Jace's chest, and he nipped Logan's ear. "Let me know next time you start to feel empty. I'll happily fill you up again."

# 9

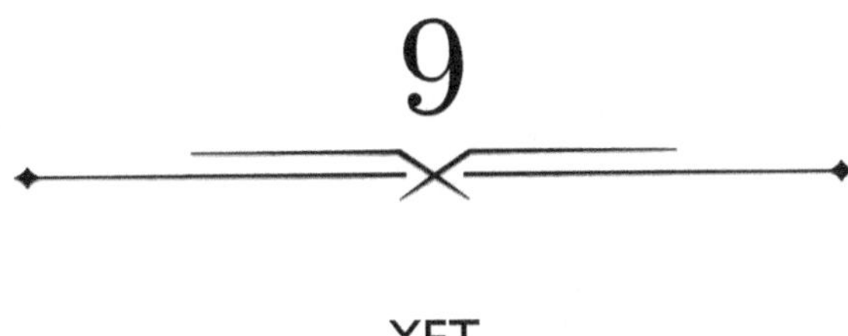

## YET

"Durhoss," Logan told Ms. Lowell, standing in her office. "Tychan lit at Durhoss."

Blearily, the dean looked up from the paperwork she was filling out by the light of her small desk lamp and blinked a couple of times before she processed what he'd said. Then she frowned, one eyebrow rising skeptically. "I take it you spoke with Mr. Evans about his plans?"

"And Squints and Randy," he said, his voice rising defensively. "It's Durhoss. That's the one I want. I'm good at Tychan already."

"You're practically fluent," she said, her words agreeing with him but her tone clearly disagreeing. "But even for Tychan lit, most of the classes will be in Freelan. Mr. Cardot, this is not a decision to be made…with too much external influence. Things change. People change. Your future shouldn't be based on anyone else."

"I hear you and I want Durhoss." Logan's face and voice were resolute, and Ms. Lowell sighed. Even as she shook her head, though, a faint, fond smile crossed her lips.

"I typically apply students to three or four programs, since there's no guarantee of being accepted. Shall I select some other options for you that have similar programs to Durhoss's?"

Logan hesitated, but she already knew he was doing this to stay with Jace. "Just…put me down for the same schools you applied to for Jace. I'm going where he goes."

"Mr. Cardot—"

"I'm going where he goes," he said, meeting her eyes as seriously as he could. "Thanks for being worried about me, really. But I don't have any big dreams about what I want to do someday. Jace does. So I'm going where he does. The only thing I *do* care about is—" He paused, sudden fear icing over his vocal cords.

She knew about the two of them, and she'd made no move to report them or punish them, but she was still technically the enemy. One word from her, and he and Jace would both be in Black Lapel custody. He had to trust in how much she cared about Jace. "—is staying with him. I know you're gonna say we're too young or inexperienced or whatever, but if you asked me what change I want to make in the world, the only thing I can think of is, I want to change it so I can be with him for the rest of my life. I don't have anything else, anyone else. Just Jace."

Ms. Lowell's face softened, and she pressed her hand to her mouth, taking a long, slow inhale and exhale through her nose. Still short, her nails were painted bright green now.

"I understand, Mr. Cardot," she said at last, then smiled. "Mr. Evans was in here not an hour ago, telling me something very similar. Against perhaps my better judgment, I'm already doing my best to find you something together. You're both so bright, I shouldn't have too difficult a time. And as for Durhoss, I have high hopes for both of you getting in. It *is* a good program to fit your interests, even if you might have selected it for other reasons."

Logan grinned. "Thanks." He started to duck back out, then paused and shut the door again. "Can I ask you a question?"

"Of course, Mr. Cardot." She folded her hands on her desk.

He studied her for a moment, understanding why Jace trusted her so much. Jace would never have acknowledged it or possibly even recognized it, but it was obvious in the way he teased her, the way he sent the other boys to her, the things he asked her for. "Why didn't you report us? Why are we getting help finding a placement instead of getting booted or arrested?"

She took a long, deep breath. She held it. When she finally released it, staring down at her hands on her desk, he thought she wasn't going to answer him.

But she said quietly, "I have no control over the laws of this country. I have no control over the policies of this school; they are set above even Headmaster Rollins's authority. But I am charged with the care of hundreds of boys who have no one else in the world advocating for them. I watch them grow up. I see their hearts get broken by things I can't change about the world.

"I have so little time with each of them to make them feel that someone cares about them. And then they're grown and they go out into the world, and many of them—most of them, I'm afraid— are crushed under its heel.

"I refuse to be another force crushing children, Mr. Cardot. It may be that I'm ultimately acting against your best interests. Perhaps you'd be better served by being disciplined for your actions. But I don't think so. And so…I've chosen not to bring you to the attention of those who would see you punished.

"Besides—" she said, then cut herself off with a rueful grin before shrugging and powering through. "Besides, I…might understand better than you know."

Logan absorbed that. "You have a good—" He wanted to say *woman* but chickened out, glancing at the door as if someone might overhear through the wood. "—person at home that you love?"

"The best in the world." Her small smile was fond and sad and Logan could feel the longing in it.

"Then why don't you run away and be with…her?" He dropped his voice on the last word until it was only air. "You could go anywhere."

"Because my place is here. Protecting my boys."

Logan loved her then. "Would it be all right if I hugged you?"

Ms. Lowell smiled, warmth radiating off her. "Of course." She stood, and though she was much smaller than him, she hugged him so tightly and so comfortingly that he felt, for a moment, safe.

But that spell was broken when she pulled away, frowning. "Please be careful in the next few weeks, Mr. Cardot. It's placement season. The school will change. Black Lapel recruiters will be on campus. Please don't draw attention to yourself for any reason."

He swallowed, nodded. The last thing he wanted was attention. He slipped back out of the office with a murmured, "Thank you," and went to find Jace and his crew.

"Where did it all come from, though?" Logan asked, looking at the heaps and piles of wood and corrugated metal on the ground around the massive oak tree. They were deep in the wildest parts of the ChilCo grounds, the Sunday afternoon light making glitter out of the fresh green leaves overhead.

Jace held his notebook up to the tree, squinting, making small notes with his pencil. "Don't worry about it. Anybody who wasn't involved in getting it should hold on to their plausible deniability." Sparkling with energy, he grinned at Logan. "Help me get those concrete blocks where they need to be. They're heavy as shit."

As they laid out the foundation for the treehouse, Squints and Randy trotted up among the trees. Randy threw a look at the pair of them, sweating copiously and palms bleeding from the work they'd already done without gloves.

Logan thought the boy would comment on their stupidity in getting started before everyone else arrived to help, but as he slipped his bag off over his head and dropped it, Randy said, "Is it required that we're all shirtless for this? Because I didn't sign on for that."

Logan tensed. Randy said it jokingly, and it shouldn't matter at all, but Logan had seen the crew running around ChilCo wearing much less than he and Jace were now, and no one had thought a thing of it. They'd gone swimming at the lake; they'd changed in front of each other hundreds of times—the only thing that had changed was him. Well, him and Jace, and their…togetherness.

Squints scoffed in the back of his throat, then grabbed the back of his collar and yanked his shirt off over his head, tossing it on top of his school bag. "If you want a farmer's tan, just say it," he said scathingly as the Bens emerged from the trees. "Those of us who'd like a tan for college have to take advantage of any day where the sun's out to get some color."

After an awkward pause, Randy said, "Well, *sorry*, some of us are bitter we don't tan, I guess." He laughed, shaking his red hair back from his face, and pointed up at the posts Jace and Logan had erected. "All right, what's next?"

With seven boys—Bails didn't join them—working with seemingly boundless energy and zero concern for building codes, the treehouse stood, solid, by the time the sun had sunk down to its last sliver of visible light.

They'd built a single, sprawling room around the central pillar of the trunk nearly ten feet off the ground, with one huge window and several smaller peepholes in the other walls. Jace scrambled up first, climbing along the short handholds they'd nailed into the tree trunk, and stood on the platform under the peaked roof. He leaned out to look down at them and let out a war cry, half wolf howl and half pure boy-joy.

The others echoed him and climbed as well, testing the creaking boards with the weight of all seven of them. It held, and they rejoiced by pretending to shoot invisible enemies in the trees, shouting at the descending sun, and collapsing, exhausted, to the planks of the floor.

Logan sprawled across Jace on one side and Randy on the other, and as he absorbed the warm sense of belonging that came from puppy piling with six chatting friends, he got the shivers from Jace's hand on his leg and, surprisingly, Randy's on his shoulder.

As night descended, the other boys left—first the Bens, then Randy, then Squints—until only Jace and Logan remained in the home they'd built ten feet off the ground in the boughs of a massive oak. Logan stayed mostly where he'd dropped when Randy had slid out from under him, his arms tucked behind his head and his legs sprawled over Jace's lap as Jace sat propped against the back wall of the treehouse.

"You built this," Logan said, smiling.

Jace turned away from where he'd been watching the sky purple through the large window hole in the front wall. He returned Logan's smile. "Well, we *all* built it. But it's nice to see my design come to life. I like building things. Harder than blowing things up, but more fun."

"Is this what you'll be doing if you make it into Durhoss?"

Jace chuckled. "Not building treehouses. But yeah, something like this. Building things that make people happy."

"You know what you should build?"

"Hmm?"

"A library," Logan said, picturing rows and rows of books, vaulted ceilings and sliding ladders, cozy nooks and stained-glass windows. Jace could build a beautiful library.

Jace shifted, running his fingers over Logan's shin. "That's more architecture than civil engineering. Why a library?"

Logan shrugged, staring up at the roof of their treehouse. "I don't know. I've always wanted to see a real one. Don't get me wrong, I love the library here, but it's—"

"ChilCo's library is the only one you've ever seen?" Jace asked, aghast. "We have, like, twelve books and a stack of old newspapers. Lowell's office is better stocked than that."

He clicked his tongue in disapproval of the home's priorities.

"Well…" Logan pulled his right leg up and propped his foot on Jace's thigh so the other boy could touch more of him. "…haven't had a lot of opportunity for exploring the libraries and bookstores and coffee shops and whatever else in the world."

Jace's fingers drew delicious pressure along Logan's calf muscle. "Make a list. We'll go see everything. Starting with a library."

"How have you seen them? Does ChilCo do, like, field trips?"

"Yeah. Every couple years they take a batch of us to Fairview for a 'Life Skills Tour.' They teach how to grocery shop, how to navigate street signs, that sort of thing. We get to explore the city for a while. They don't want us to be completely useless when we get out of here. Did your parents ever…?"

"Kinda. They were really worried about me being able to blend in when I grew up. Obviously they couldn't walk me around town, so they…" He was suddenly inexplicably embarrassed. He tried to pull his legs away so he could sit up, but Jace held him tight, thumbs making soothing circles along his skin.

Face heating, Logan continued. "My dad pretended to take up photography as a hobby, and my mom pushed him around town, taking pictures of everything. They had these big prints developed, and they'd quiz me with them. 'What is this called? How would you use it? Who would you expect to be here? What kind of conversations could you have with them?' It drove me nuts, but…I get what they were trying to do."

When Jace remained quiet, hands roaming gently up Logan's thigh, Logan found himself speaking again. "They couldn't teach it all from pictures, so they did other crazy stuff. My mom would take me out in the middle of the night in her old car and let me drive around. She'd pretend there were other cars on the road with us. 'Oh, they're stopping fast! What do you do?'"

She'd clutch at the door like he was going too fast, gasping and squealing and pretending to stomp on a brake pedal from the passenger seat. He missed her. *God*, he missed her.

Staring at the ceiling from his back, he pretended he wasn't crying, that Jace couldn't see it. Jace pretended with him.

"Did she teach you to swim?"

"My dad did, actually," Logan said thickly. "He loved to swim. There was a pond down the block from our house. It was tiny and half goose shit, but no one was ever around after dark, so we'd go out there at night and swim. Once I was old enough to help my dad in and out of his chair, it was always just me and him."

"Sounds like they tried to make your life…normal."

Defensiveness rose up in Logan. "They made it great. I don't know as much about the world as everybody else, but it was great."

Seeming to realize he'd touched a nerve, Jace went silent again and tapped Logan's knee so he'd switch legs. He worked the muscle of Logan's left leg with his fingers for a while before saying, "You probably know more about girls than I do. Because of…" He paused, a frown creasing his forehead. "Oh, shit. I'm an idiot. It *just* occurred to me that Chris was a boy."

Logan laughed, rubbing a hand over his face to rid himself of evidence of tears. "Yeah, Chris was a boy. He did have a sister, though, and I spent time with both of them. So I probably *do* know more about girls. Actually, have you ever even *met* a girl your age?"

"Yeah. When we were littles, they'd take us to visit our sister school, Ambrosia Hall, once a year for this, like, open house party thing? We'd play games and the girls would cook this big dinner we all had to get dressed up for, and then there was a dance. They stop taking ChilCo boys when we hit thirteen. I, uh…" Jace's grin twisted, face turning pink. "I actually got disinvited a year early, though."

"Oh?"

"Yeah. They thought I would cause trouble, I guess."

Logan smirked. "Did you try to light the dance hall on fire?"

"No." Jace's face grew redder. "Apparently, there were quite a few girls, uh, writing 'Evans' on their notebook like it was their last name. I don't know if they thought the girls were gonna fight over me or I was gonna sneak off with one of them or what, but…" He shrugged and tugged on his ear. "I didn't go to AmHall anymore."

Logan laughed hard enough that Jace looked genuinely offended. "I'm sorry," he gasped out between chuckles. "It's just, the idea of so many girls getting a crush on you that they felt you were a danger to the school—" He cackled again.

"Yes, well, they didn't know I was more of a danger at my own school," Jace said with a scowl, his blush spreading down his throat to his chest. "And I was pretty torn up about it at the time. The AmHall Open House was fun. I don't like having things taken away, especially when I didn't actually *do* anything."

"Sorry," Logan repeated, trying to get his giggles under control. "That is pretty unfair."

Still scowling, Jace resumed his hands' gentle stroking over Logan's leg. "Aren't you supposed to get jealous about stories like that? Not *amused?*"

"Why? *Would* you have snuck away with one of the girls?"

Jace paused, frowning. "I don't know. Maybe. If they were fun. I'll try anything once."

Logan's brows rose. He couldn't tell if Jace really meant it or was trying to get a reaction from Logan, so he elected to treat it as the latter. "Well, consider me jealous, then."

"Don't patronize me, Homeschool."

"No, no. I would never." Logan pulled his legs free of Jace's hands and sat up. "I'm *extremely* jealous. Point me in the direction of AmHall and I'll track down every girl who ever imagined you proposing and…I don't know. Compliment them on their good taste?"

"You are such a pain in the ass," Jace said, grinning as he leaned in to kiss Logan. It was so tender and familiar it made Logan ache for a past they didn't share.

Resting his forehead against Jace's, Logan said, "I wish we'd met back then. I wish you'd moved in next door to me so we could have spent our days together."

"We'd be proper trouble by now. I'd've snuck you out." Jace ran the tip of his nose along the bridge of Logan's. His voice dropped into that divine honeyed bass he only got when he was burning up with lust. Into Logan's ear he whispered, "Shown you the entire fiction section at the local library."

Logan laughed, knocking Jace back playfully. "You joke, but you breaking the rules to show me something cool has been, like, the main turn-on of our relationship to date."

"Oh, I know. I'm not joking. I've never fucked anyone in a library, but I'll try anything once." He smirked, and Logan collapsed onto the floor, enjoying the dizzy, cozy feeling of flirting shamelessly.

They lapsed into comfortable silence as darkness descended, turning the shelter they'd built into an inky cocoon. Eventually, Jace said, "We should head back. We're cutting it close."

"I want to stay here," Logan said drowsily.

"We didn't bring a blanket or anything. It gets cold at night."

Logan reached blindly into the dark until he found Jace's arm, then tugged the other boy down to lie beside him. He snuggled up against him, forehead to forehead, wrapping his arms around Jace's middle. "Then we'll have to keep each other warm."

Logan got his first formal write-up the next morning, as he trotted into class still straightening his shirt on his shoulders. The boys had dropped them some clothes beneath the window, but one pair of socks and one shirt were missing, so they'd scrambled back to the dorm room before they could make it to class.

"Tardiness is unacceptable, Mr. Cardot. Mr. Evans, you ought to know better by now," Ms. Gillian, the literature teacher said as they crept around the back of the room to their seats. "You've missed the pledge. You will both stand at the front and recite it now."

Logan shot her an incredulous look—he'd never seen anyone have to do that, and this certainly wasn't the first time someone had been late to class—but Jace trotted obediently to the front of the class, and Logan had no choice but to follow.

They said the words in rough unison, and then Logan found his seat, but he almost misstepped again halfway through class when he simply spoke the answer to one of Ms. Gillian's questions aloud instead of raising his hand. It was exactly the way he'd answered a dozen times since he'd arrived at ChilCo, but Ms. Gillian gave him a sharp, unhappy look. She held them after class to sign the write-up, and as he and Jace jogged to their calculus class to avoid yet another tardy, Logan finally got the chance to ask what was going on.

"It's placement season," Jace said, as if that explained everything. "Everything gets all formal during placement season. Just follow my lead."

It was easy enough in classes, but at lunch, instead of lining up for food as usual, Logan found himself standing in several long rows of boys inside the cafeteria doors.

"What are we—" he tried to ask, but Jace shushed him urgently just in time. One of the lunch ladies, wielding a ladle like a riding crop, walked up and down the lines of boys, inspecting their uniforms and stances. Logan imitated Jace's straightened shoulders and straight-ahead stare as the ladle-laden woman passed by him, narrowed eyes seeming to look straight through him.

When they were, at last, released to line up for food, Logan tried to question Jace, but the lunch room was held to silence by the periodic bellows of the same patrolling lunch lady. It wasn't until they tossed their trash and escaped to the dorm room that Logan was able to say, "What the *fuck* is going on today?"

Jace shrugged. "Sorry. Like I said, it's placement season and—"

"Everything gets formal?" Logan cut him off. "Any other surprises for what 'formal' means before I get my ass written up again?"

Jace set a hand on his arm. "Hey, it's not that big of—"

"It *is* that big of a deal," Logan snapped. "Ms. Lowell told me not to attract *any* attention, so I'd like to stop stumbling around like I have no idea what's going on. Help me!"

"Hey, okay," Jace said soothingly. He tightened his grip on Logan's arm, giving him a little shake. "I promise it's not that crazy. No one's looking at you twice. But here's the deal: no one skips the pledge, and every meal we line up for inspection before we get to eat. In a couple of weeks, the Lapels will be on campus, and they'll be observing us during meals and practices.

"And there's also the games. They host these competitions—winners get cool prizes. I think last year's grand prize was, like, a year's supply of chocolate, but it's usually better than that. It's always some huge thing. Worth competing for."

"Competitions?" Logan repeated numbly. The idea of the Lapels wandering around this campus where he'd come to feel at least partially safe was abhorrent. "Are they mandatory?"

"Nah, but nobody skips unless they can't compete."

"I don't want to compete," Logan said. It came out too loud, too rushed. Panicky.

"You don't have to," Jace said. His thumb rubbed reassuringly against the inside of Logan's arm. "Like I said, it's not mandatory. It's really okay, I promise. It's not…they're not here to make an example of anybody or anything. They're just recruiting."

*Just recruiting*—like that wasn't Logan's worst nightmare. He nodded, waving Jace off because he couldn't summon the words to explain the dark imaginings that plagued him, images of Black Lapel guns pointed at him—or at *Jace*—memories of his parents' helplessness, of his own trapped terror.

Just because they were on campus to recruit didn't mean they wouldn't arrest or shoot or beat or… And what if they did try to recruit him? What if they wanted him to be one of them? Logan wanted to run for the lake, the treehouse, the cave—anywhere he could hide. He wanted nothing to do with the Black Lapels for the rest of his life.

For several days, things got "more formal," as Jace had described it. Logan didn't even think Jace realized how much the school changed as it prepared to host the Black Lapel recruiters. Everything tightened up; everyone walked on eggshells. Even the language the faculty and staff used changed—now more legalistic and in line with what poured down from the pulpit during chapel each week. Logan constantly felt nauseous, crawling with anxiety. It felt like danger lurked behind every corner.

And, in part, that was because it *did*.

It was hard to notice at first, but there were whispers, side-eyes, extra scrutiny on whatever Jace and Logan did together.

Then it became snide remarks in classes, particularly from Wolf and Tiger Holds, which seemed to hold the most enmity for

Eagle and Jace in particular. Violent, late hits in rugby games; feet stuck out in the hallways to trip them; small acts of vandalism, like rotten food shoved into their backpacks or foul-smelling mystery fluids slathered on their common room doorknob—these things built up until Logan spent the day in a state of constant alert and vague, directionless fury.

"Is this normal?" Logan asked Jace one evening as he shoveled mashed potatoes out of the side pocket of his bag after rugby practice. "Is this 'placement season' behavior?"

Jace, eyes dark, watched him with a grim expression. "No."

Freshly showered, Randy pulled his day clothes back on and sat on the bench beside Logan. "Need any help with that?"

"No," Logan said bitterly. "I need assholes to keep their shitty cafeteria food to themselves." Rage boiled under his skin, but what the fuck could he do? He didn't even know who had done it, and he couldn't do anything about it even if he had.

Randy took the bag from him anyway, lifting the books out so he could carry it to the sink and rinse it out.

"You both need to watch your backs," he warned, not looking at Jace or at Logan. "I've been hearing some things. Martin Sneed's been talking about finding a way to tell the Lapels about you. I don't know what he knows or how he knows, but—" He shrugged, handing the rinsed bag back to Logan. He made eye contact with Jace. "Watch out."

Everything in Logan's body seized up, so cold he expected to see his breath when he fought an exhale out of his chest. Someone was trying to report them to the Black Lapels? His worst nightmare, and it was coming true.

Logan didn't know much about inter-hold politics, but he knew Jace and Martin had been at odds for almost as long as Jace had been at ChilCo. The informal Tiger leader held sway over his hold with fear and violence rather than force of charisma, and he was clearly envious of Jace.

"What would make him think there's anything to tell?" he choked out. He wanted to grab Jace, stuff him into a box somewhere and climb in after, hammer the lid shut and hide until the world forgot about them.

Randy shrugged. "You two…aren't that subtle. Just watch your backs. I'll watch 'em too, if he tries anything while I'm around. The rest of the crew will too. Well—" He cut off and his lip curled, and Bails's name echoed, unsaid, through the room. "Most of us will."

They didn't have to wait long for the threat to materialize. They had rotated lunch assignments again, and they now shared green hall with Tiger: Martin Sneed's hold.

Almost as soon as they'd been inspected and waited their turn through the line, someone reached over Logan's shoulder and shoved his tray off the table, scattering his meatloaf and corn across six feet of floor tile in an unappetizing smear.

When Logan spun to confront the perpetrator, he saw three Tigers, only one that came near to his height, but all broad shouldered and probably old enough to be booted. The trio smirked at him like each of them held a particularly nasty secret.

In a second, Jace was around the table and at Logan's side, and the two Eagles who were seated nearby—Squints and Bud—stood up, ready to jump in if necessary.

"You need to get the fuckin' boot already," one of the Tigers said, eyes narrowing at Logan. "What are you still doing here?"

"What the fuck is your problem?" Logan demanded. "I don't even know you." Next to him, Jace was drawn tight as a bowstring but held his silence.

Logan gave the room a quick scan and saw a couple of the teachers and Director Rollins sitting at one end of a table near the door. Although they hadn't noticed the trouble yet, they would when voices got raised. The middle Tiger, the one who'd shoved Logan's lunch, inclined his head so he was staring down his nose at Logan. "The fucking problem is *you*, queer."

Logan had read the word, but he'd never heard it said. He had no idea it would drip with disgust like that, no idea a single syllable could contain so much contempt. It *hurt*.

Jace growled—actually *growled*—next to Logan. "You're going to want to shut your fucking mouth, Martin."

Ah, so *this* was Martin Sneed. Broad shouldered and long armed but stick thin, ears too large and nose too long, he looked altogether too goofy for the serious expression he was painting on. Pure hate radiated off him, and the fact that he was picking a fight now, with the director in the room, told Logan what he was up to.

Martin continued to speak to Logan as if he hadn't heard Jace, but Logan watched his eyes flick over to Jace and his evil little smirk grow. Martin kept his tone conversational as he said, "What are you still doing at ChilCo? Shouldn't you be in the shithouse with your parents? I heard it was close, getting you in here instead of Shalecrest. I bet the Lapels would be very curious to hear their little illegal is *also* a boy fucker. They're not too big a fan of your kind."

Logan had been prepared for Martin's insults, so he merely gritted his teeth against the rage that welled up, but Jace lunged at Martin. Logan grabbed him in a bear hug, holding him back with all his strength.

"He's baiting *you*, Jace," he said quietly. "Rollins is here. Start a fight and you'll get booted. Maybe both of us."

Jace shook with rage, head to toe. "I'll fucking kill you, Martin," he hissed, low enough that no one outside their little circle would hear, but full of venom. "I'll *fucking* kill you."

Squints rounded the table and helped Logan wrestle Jace back as Martin's shit-eating grin spread. Jace took a few breaths to recover himself, then cast a glance over his shoulder at Rollins and seemed to understand he was being played. Though his muscles remained strained under his skin, he pulled a mask of calm over his face.

Martin, seeing his opportunity to get his rival punished or booted slipping away, stepped forward to deliver his last jab. "The Lapels would love *you*, though, Jace. You're a magnet for kid fuckers and queers, aren't you? Set you out on the corner and they'd just have to arrest whoever shows up to drill you. They'd clean up."

Jace's face went very, very pale.

Logan didn't remember deciding to let go of Jace and tackle Martin to the ground, but he must have, because when he came to, he was getting hauled off Martin's body, arms swinging, trying to get in another hit across the other kid's bloody mess of a face.

His hands throbbed; he'd definitely broken a bone in there somewhere, and his knuckles were split and bleeding.

The cafeteria was in riot mode. Jace held on to Logan—he was probably the only person physically capable of pulling Logan away from Martin in his fury—and bellowed at his crew, trying to get them to back out of the fight. Squints was snarling and beating one of the Tigers with a ferocity Logan wouldn't have expected, and Logan snatched him away.

The three of them lurched toward the door as Director Rollins wrangled his way to the center of the brawl, shouting for everyone to stop and physically separating boys where he could. When he spotted Martin on the ground, unmoving and mulched, he frantically called for one of the teachers to retrieve the nurse.

"We need to get out of here," Jace whispered urgently, hauling at Logan as if he meant to carry him out. "Get you cleaned up."

"They're gonna know it was me with or without the blood," Logan said numbly. He turned back toward Martin, who hadn't moved. "Did I kill him?"

"No," Squints said, "he's still breathing. I could see him blowing bubbles. He's right, though, Jace. Everyone saw Logan jump on him. Even if the Eagles don't say a word, all the Tigers will point to him." Squints looked legitimately freaked out.

"I shouldn't have taken the bait. Stupid," Logan said with a dry, humorless laugh. "Looks like I'm getting the boot."

Jace didn't answer, but Squints muttered, "At least." Jace held Logan's upper arms, and he kept a constant door-ward pressure on them, trying to pull Logan out of the cafeteria.

Fingers pointed in their direction. Although the fighting had stopped, voices were raised in argument and accusation. Director Rollins stood in the middle of the boys, his hands out in a calming gesture as he tried to sort through everything being shouted at him.

"We should probably tell him our side of the story," Squints said, but none of them moved closer to the director.

Instead, they waited as Ms. Timmons appeared, helping Martin to his feet and out of the room. Then Rollins and the two teachers that flanked him crossed to Jace, Logan, and Squints.

"Mr. Cardot, we need to have a conversation," Rollins said. "Let him go, Mr. Evans."

Reluctantly, Jace did. "Director Rollins, you should know Logan didn't—" he began, but Rollins held up a hand to stop him.

"I do not need to speak with you right now, Mr. Evans. It's in your best interest to keep things that way, as I imagine you wouldn't like the consequences of coming to my attention. You and Mr. Quintz need to return to your dormitory."

Rollins swept past them and into the hall, raising two fingers in a small wave to indicate Logan was to follow him.

Logan followed.

He had *known* it was a trap, that Martin was trying to hurt Jace and possibly Logan, and he'd gone into a red-hot rage and lost his shit anyway. Recalling Jace's white face, wide eyes, and obvious hurt, Logan still knew he'd do it again if Martin stood before him now. He rubbed his aching hands, flexing in and out of fists as though testing how much knuckles could hurt.

When they reached the director's office, Rollins gestured for Logan to sit, then settled himself heavily in the chair behind his desk. He stared at Logan over his steepled hands for a minute or two, silent and unhappy. Logan slumped in the low seat with its scratchy fabric, waiting for Rollins to deliver the bad news.

"You've had a rough time of it, haven't you, Mr. Cardot?"

That wasn't what Logan had expected to hear. His head shot up, and he fixed the man with a curious stare. "Um, I suppose so, sir. A lot of us have."

Rollins grunted and nodded. "True enough." He folded his hands over his ample gut, leaning back in his desk chair with a sigh. "You and Mr. Evans are hard cases. You're the sort of boys who give me heartburn. Your dean seems to think the two of you have great potential, though, and your good grades and positive influence on the younger students who look up to you outweigh the bad behavior you've displayed."

"Bad behavior, sir?" Logan said with wide, innocent eyes.

Rollins leveled a no-nonsense stare at Logan, then flicked his eyes down at Logan's knuckles. "You've been in two fights since you came to this school, that I know of, and you've seriously hurt boys on both occasions." His tone left the sentence open, though he didn't add any more transgressions to the list. Either he didn't know about the raids and the illicit activities with Jace, or he didn't have enough hard evidence to accuse Logan—or perhaps he simply didn't want to tip his hand.

When Logan didn't respond, Rollins sighed and continued, "The fact that you seem to have been encouraged by or jumping to the defense of Mr. Evans on both occasions makes me concerned Ms. Lowell's judgment may be flawed. I would hate to think her recommendations to me in regards to your futures at Childers Coast and beyond were ill considered."

"Jace had nothing to do with those fights," Logan protested. "That was all me."

Rollins's eyes wrinkled in a not-quite-smile. "Loyalty is admirable, Mr. Cardot, but I assure you that lying to protect your friend will do nothing to benefit either of you."

He hesitated before speaking again. "I…have heard some rumors regarding your friendship with Mr. Evans, and some of what your fellow students had to say in the cafeteria seems to confirm them." Logan went very still, his blood pumping like ice through his veins. "I'm not going to ask if they're true, and I would prefer you didn't tell me either.

"But I do want to remind you ChilCo is a government-run institution subject to the policies and oversight of the government and its officials. Regardless of how our faculty and staff may feel, relationships of…an unusual nature…are forbidden by Hallsburg law."

Logan swallowed hard, waiting for Rollins to say he would turn the boys over to the Black Lapels. Martin had been massively understating the case when he'd said the Lapels didn't like "his kind." Logan knew full well how foolish he and Jace had been, how cavalier they'd been with their own lives every time they touched, kissed, snuck away together.

As his breaths came shorter and faster, the weight of his fear pressed on his chest, crushing him. Director Rollins frowned, and then, in a surprising move, stood and rounded the desk, setting a hand on Logan's shoulder.

"I'm sorry if that sounded like a threat. I meant it as a warning. You and Mr. Evans seem to have made enemies at the school, and they now have dangerous information about you, if it is true. I'm not in the habit of turning my students over to the Hallsburg Special Police, but their recruiters will be on campus in the coming weeks as we move into placement season, and the right word in the right ear at the wrong time could be disastrous for you both."

"Jace and I are friends," Logan said, not meeting Rollins's eyes. His mouth was stuffed with cotton, thready and dry. "What's unusual about that?"

Rollins squeezed his shoulder. "Of course. Then I recommend the two of you stick to your schedules religiously. Do not be found out of bounds. Do not be found out of bed at night. Do not be found in faculty and staff areas. When this school has a Lapel presence, my hands are tied; leniency, turning a blind eye to misconduct—these are no longer options."

Rollins knew, maybe about everything. Had Ms. Lowell told him? Logan snuck a glance at the man through his lashes and saw him staring levelly back at him. "Yes, sir."

"Good lad." He clapped Logan on the shoulder, then sat again with a noisy exhale and a groaning complaint from the chair.

"Why are you talking to just me about this? Why not Jace?"

Rollins rubbed his temple with one hand. "Because your situation is more precarious than his. Your name has already made an appearance on certain lists of undesirables and individuals whose loyalty to Hallsburg is in question. Adding another mark to your name could be disastrous for you. You wouldn't appreciate being placed on the red-pen list."

Logan absorbed that in silence, sticking his blood-gummed fingertips together and pulling them apart over and over. Rollins spoke again. "I don't want to see that happen, Mr. Cardot. You're part of the Childers Coast family, and you're a smart, driven young man. I don't want to see you swept away into…" He trailed off, probably unable to find an ending to the sentence that fit the gentle tone he was trying to strike.

"You can go see the nurse about those hands. They need ice, and possibly more. You'll be off the rugby team for the foreseeable future as punishment for fighting. I'll consult with Ms. Lowell to decide if anything else needs to be done."

"Yes, sir," Logan said again, quietly. He stood and made it to the door before turning back. "Sir, can I ask a question?"

Rollins raised his brows, permission enough, and Logan said, "What Martin said… How many people at the school know what happened to Jace when he was a kid? Students, I mean?"

"I'm not sure what you mean," the director replied.

Logan didn't believe that for a second, but he flatly clarified, "How many people know you rehomed Jace with a monster and he came back hurt?"

The director cleared his throat and frowned, lines appearing around his mouth and between his brows. "We always strive to retain the privacy of residents," he said stiffly, but then he sighed heavily. "Any student who was at Childers Coast when Jace was rehomed would know he left and returned a few months later. That should be the extent of it, but Ms. Lowell and I had a…rather spirited conversation about Mr. Evans's difficulties and were forced to do some damage control when other students overheard. Very few residents still at Childers Coast would have been here during the incident, but Mr. Sneed was among them."

Another wave of hot anger rolled up in Logan at these people Jace trusted so much; they had exposed him to that nightmare experience, then further exposed his darkest moments to the cruelty and scorn of other kids. "You guys really fucked up with him, didn't you?"

Rollins inhaled sharply, but his face was inscrutable. "That will be all, Mr. Cardot."

Logan headed to his dorm room, walking slowly as he tried to sort through his thoughts. What would he and Jace do? Any hint of a scandal was likely to get Logan, at least, disappeared with a quickness, especially with the Black Lapels coming to campus.

The Lapels were his main concern, the most pressing matter, but he couldn't ignore the growing attention and hostility from the other boys at ChilCo either. Jace had been the shining defender—or the villainous enemy, depending on which hold you were in—of the school for years; both sides seemed to think his relationship with Logan was something to be ashamed of, and the latter would use it against him.

Did they have to break up? Agree not to interact in public? Should Logan petition Ms. Lowell to find him a placement quickly so he could leave Jace in peace? Logan didn't want to do that. More to the point, Jace wouldn't allow that, even to his own detriment.

In the Eagle common room, eyes followed him as he made his way to his room. Someone helpfully called, "Jace is waiting for you up there." He nodded in acknowledgement and ascended the stairs.

It wasn't just Jace waiting in the dorm room; the full crew was there. All heads swiveled toward Logan when he opened the door.

"What happened?" Jace demanded, shooting to his feet. "What did he say?"

"Are you booted?" Bails called from his bed.

Logan stood awkwardly in the doorway and rubbed his right hand, now swelling noticeably. "I'm not booted. I'm off the rugby team for now. And I'm…we're…" He glanced around the room at all the boys watching him. This was a conversation he really only wanted to have with Jace, but he could see from their faces that the rest of the crew wouldn't leave. "Rollins says we're in danger when the Black Lapel recruiters are here. He said he can't turn a blind eye to anything during placement season. We could be arrested."

"Why?" Bails piped up.

Jace crossed the room and wrapped Logan in a crushing hug. Logan hugged him back, letting some of the anxiety and tension from his meeting with Rollins drain out of him; Jace was so solid, so strong, so sure, so smart. His presence was an immediate reassurance. Nothing truly bad could happen to them with Jace on the case.

One of the Bens spoke up when neither Jace nor Logan answered Bails. "Because being gay is fucking illegal, numb nuts." Another Ben added, "And Lapels hate gays."

"I *know* that," Bails said. "I mean, why would you be in danger? How would they prove you were gay? They don't arrest people when some random kid says, 'Hey, go arrest them.' Don't do any gay shit while they're here. Boom, solved."

Squints shrugged. "He has a point."

Jace hadn't let Logan go, and Logan held on to him right back. Across the room, Bails mimed an exaggerated vomiting episode, complete with gruesome gagging. "This would be that gay shit I'm talking about," he said. Jace raised one arm toward Bails and extended his middle finger, then unwrapped himself from Logan.

"You're just off the team? That's it?" Jace asked quietly, pulling far enough back to see Logan's face and grabbing Logan's hands.

"Well, he said he was gonna talk to Lowell about whether I needed more punishment than that," Logan explained. "I think he knows more about us than we thought. Seems like maybe he just hasn't been looking too hard for proof."

As Jace nodded, a thoughtful expression overtook his face. "Lapel recruiters…"

"Yeah," Logan said. "Fuck, my hands hurt. Loosen up a little."

Jace's expression turned inward, as the gears spun in his head. He released Logan with one hand to tap his fingers against each other like he was counting thoughts. "This could be perfect."

Logan frowned. "I don't see how."

When Jace's eyes met Logan's, they were bright. "Government officials have the power to shut down our rehoming program."

A chorus of "Huh?" around the room told Logan the rest of the crew didn't know what he and Jace had been up to. Logan wasn't sure what Jace was planning, but he saw in his eyes that he'd dreamed up something. "How can I help you?"

"Not you, Homeschool," Jace said. "You're gonna stay the hell away from the Lapels while they're here. In fact, I don't want you even hearing the plan—plausible deniability. Martin's full of shit, but he had a point: I don't want you drawing their attention at all."

*Too late*, Logan thought. Whatever Rollins had meant when he'd said Logan was on "certain government lists," he was sure he'd already had their attention. He didn't say that to Jace, though. There was fear enough in the way Jace hadn't completely let go of him yet, how he was clinging to Logan's hand with strength that made his injured knuckles ache.

"What about us?" Randy said. "Whatever you're planning, we all want in."

Jace grinned at his crew. "This'll be our biggest adventure yet." With a last quick kiss, Jace said, "Go see the nurse about your hands. I need to tell everyone else the plan."

Squints hopped off his bed and headed for the door. "I can walk you there." He held the door open and waited for Logan to walk through before speed-walking past him down the stairs and toward the common room.

"How are your hands?" he asked.

As they pushed into the halls half filled with students, Logan examined his swelling hands. Now that the adrenaline was out of his system, they throbbed excruciatingly, long slow swells like passes of a lighthouse lamp. As he flexed them, the pain grew momentarily blinding before it ebbed again. "Uh…" he said, laughing tightly, "they probably don't hurt quite as much as Martin's face."

Squints exhaled a sound that wasn't quite a laugh, more of a release of tension. "You, uh, definitely would've killed him if Jace hadn't pulled you off him."

Shooting a glance at the smaller boy from the corner of his eye, Logan tried to dissect Squints's tone. Carefully neutral, it didn't indicate whether he approved or disapproved, so Logan wasn't sure how to respond. If anything, Squints might have sounded scared. "Yeah," he said uncomfortably. "The shit he said about Jace—I kind of lost my mind."

Squints nodded, staring ahead down the hall. "I heard that too," he said quietly.

Logan, still struggling to understand Squints's thoughts, said in the most lighthearted tone he could summon, "And you didn't turn into a big, red rage monster. I guess that means there's something wrong with me?"

Squints flicked a glance at him, a faint smile on his lips for the first time since they started talking. "It means I never, ever want to be on the other side of a fight with you. I'd definitely die." He chuckled darkly, shaking his head. "Glad you're on our side."

"I'd never hurt you, Squints," Logan said, feeling lighter. "You're good to the core. And besides, Jace would rip out my liver and force-feed it to me."

That made Squints laugh in earnest. "True. How *did* I come to be friends with the two scariest motherfuckers in Hallsburg?"

"Keep befriending scary motherfuckers, and eventually *you're* the scariest one in Hallsburg," Logan said. "How much farther is Ms. Timmons's office?" The pain from his hands was radiating up his arms now, making it hard to think about anything else. Even swinging his arms to walk sent surges of agony down through his fingers.

"It's in the next wing. You okay?"

"Yeah. I'll make it."

As they silently walked through the halls, Logan noticed the way other kids' eyes flicked toward them then quickly away, whispers racing up the passageways past them. *Fuck.* He couldn't have better drawn attention if he'd tried. If he had Martin in front of him, he'd beat him again just for starting this stupid shit.

"I never want to see that asshole again the rest of my life," he muttered. It was mostly to himself, but Squints heard and snickered.

"Well, don't look now."

Logan looked up, of course. A couple of white-uniformed nurses were escorting Martin out of the building, one pushing him in a wheelchair while the other crouched beside him, talking to him as they walked. "Fuck. He did walk out of the cafeteria, right?"

"Yeah." Squints shrugged. "Probably a precaution."

They swung into the nurse's office, an open room with a handful of chairs and beds separated by sheets on tracks, with Ms. Timmons's desk through a door at the back. The trim woman with her blunt blonde bob was at the sink, washing her hands. Her face hardened when she looked up and spotted Logan. "Ah," she said, no warmth in her voice. "I wondered whether I was going to see you."

Logan swallowed and shot a glance at Squints, who drew the corners of his mouth down toward his chin in a brief, uncomfortable frown. He vaguely recalled Ms. Timmons being much kinder when he and Jace had had the "stomach flu," so he had to assume she was less than pleased with him due to the state he'd put Martin in. "Yeah," he said awkwardly, "I need something for my hands. I think something's broken."

She sniffed then looked him over for a long moment before crossing the room. When she took his hand, she was rougher than she needed to be, and Logan bit down hard on the urge to cry out. She turned it over, pressing her thumb into his palm, his knuckles, the swelling along the back of his hand. All the while, he concentrated on breathing evenly, not shouting, not groaning, and not pushing her away.

"I can't do anything for you but give you some ice," she said at last, dropping his hand. "Rest them, ice them, and keep them elevated over your heart. Anything else?"

"I…" Logan supposed he had expected more anger from the school officials about his actions, so this shouldn't have been a surprise, but the director's conversation with him had given him a false sense of security. "Could you give me anything for the pain?"

Ms. Timmons sighed like she had never been more put-upon in her life. "Fine." She crossed the room to a small, locked cabinet of medicines and supplies and retrieved a small vial and a syringe. After a cursory wipe of his arm with an alcohol-dampened tissue, she injected whatever it was. Only then did she ask, "Have you ever had ketevenal before?"

"Uh, no," he said. "Not that I know of. Why?"

Through narrowed eyes, she studied his face for a moment before saying, "Just a moment. Take a seat, please. I'll be right back." She ambled into the tiny back room before shutting the door behind her. Logan was baffled.

A tug on his sleeve reminded him Squints was with him. "We need to go," Squints mouthed as soon as he had Logan's attention.

"Now?"

Squints nodded and waved toward the door for extra measure. He cast a glance back toward the room where Ms. Timmons had disappeared and put his hand on Logan's back, hurrying him out and back into the hall. They were ten speed-walking paces away before Logan could ask, "Why are we fleeing the school nurse?"

"Well, for starters, I think she hates you," Squints said dryly.

"Yeah, what's the deal with that?"

Squints shrugged. "She's always had kind of a soft spot for Tiger and Bear. Don't ask me why. So I imagine she's pissed about Martin. But also—" He threw Logan that uncomfortable look again. "She's, you know, *really* devout. So if any rumors got around…"

"Ah."

"I thought we should leave *just* in case you're one of the weirdos who gets ket mouth."

"Ket mouth?"

"Yeah," Squints said. They had to pay more attention to making their way through the halls now, crowded as they were. As they dodged people finding their way to their afternoon classes or chores, Logan held his hands clutched to his stomach so no one would bump them. Although, actually, now that he thought about it, they weren't hurting all that bad anymore. Whatever she'd given him must be doing the trick.

"Let's grab some ice from the cafeteria and head back. Ket mouth is a reaction some people have to ketevenal. Something like one in twenty people, I don't know—pretty rare. For most people it just relieves pain and knocks you out, but for some, it makes you real talkative, makes you say things you don't mean to say. And you, sir, have a lot of things you don't mean to say."

"True," Logan said. "Wouldn't wanna tell the whole world about my doings and goings and…so on." His head felt a little loose on his neck, no doubt the result of finally releasing the tension from the fight. He felt good. Great, actually. His hands didn't hurt at all.

Squints grabbed a sack of ice from one of the lunch ladies and turned back to Logan, and something about the way he frowned at

Logan was hilarious. Logan started to chuckle, then outright laugh. "What?" Squints said.

"Nothing. Jus' kinda funny, s'all." His tongue was too large in his mouth, getting in the way of shaping his words. "Whoa…what's going on? Feels weird."

"Fuck," Squints said under his breath. "Hey, Connor?" The boy he'd shouted to, a small, mousy-haired kid half their age, looked up with wide brown eyes that got even wider upon seeing Logan. "Can you run up to our room and tell Jace I need help? Quick."

The kid nodded and darted off through the growing crowd in the halls. "Help with what?" Logan asked. Or tried to ask. The words squeezed out bonelessly, slumped around their missing consonants.

"With you," Squints said impatiently, trying to rush him through the halls back toward their dorm. "I'm never getting you all the way back to Eagle and up those stairs by myself."

"I can walk!" Logan said, too loudly.

"Sure, for now." Squints chuckled, shaking his head. "You *would* be a ket mouth kid. Can't be normal for two fucking seconds."

"Thas' not very nice," Logan said. "Can't help it I'm not normal. I mean, *you* try living in a fuckin' basement for seventeen years then come to a school where everything's weird and everybody already knows everybody and nobody fucking likes you 'cept the one guy who's supposed to not…I mean, not supposed to…I mean, we're not supposed to—"

"You have to stop," Squints said sharply, though he was smiling. "Stop talking."

Logan tried. He really did. He squeezed his lips shut and followed Squints, but walking took an awful lot of concentration, and the more he focused on putting one foot directly in front of the other, the less concentration he had for keeping himself from muttering, "Step a foot, other foot, now your foot, let's go foot."

Squints was very obviously trying not to laugh. Someone shoulder-checked Logan, and he lost his balance completely, thumping into the wall. "Hey!" he said. "Can't jus' go 'round knocking people into walls. What if I'd…what if I was—"

"All right, up you go, Homeschool."

A very strong arm wrapped his shoulders and hefted him up, and a familiar smell, grass and sweat and musk, and that was Jace's voice talking. Logan swiveled his head, and Jace's face was close to his as he hoisted Logan back to his feet.

"Oh, hi," Logan said.

"Hi," Jace said back, suppressing a laugh.

"You're so pretty," Logan said, and then Jace did laugh.

"Thanks, but it's time for you to shut up now, Homeschool," he said. "Save the compliments for when we're all back in the room."

Logan let them half lead, half carry him to the dorm, but he frowned in confusion. "S'not a compliment. I mean, it *is*, but I'm not jus' making it up. You're…you're…you *are* pretty. Or do you not like being pretty 'cause you're a boy? M'not trynna be mean. Jus' wanna say I wanna kiss you."

"*Oh*, my God," Squints said loudly. "For fucks' sake, shut *up*."

Jace wasn't looking at Logan. He was looking around the hall, like someone might attack them. There weren't many people here, and everybody who looked at them seemed to be laughing. Happy people didn't attack anybody.

Logan's feet had gone numb, so he wasn't really sure what they were doing at the end of his long, unwieldy legs. His head was so fucking heavy.

When they'd made their way through the common room and onto the stairs, Logan made a low sound of trepidation. There were…so many stairs.

When he tried to look up them all, he nearly fell backward. "Maybe I'll jus' stay down'ere in the common room…" he said.

"Yeah, that's not happening," said Jace. He shifted his arm around Logan's waist and practically lifted him off his feet. "Squints, get his other side. You can *walk*, Logan. Use your feet. Did Timmons *know* he was a ket mouth kid?"

"I don't think she did, no," Squints said. "But thank fuck we left when we did."

"Was he talking like this before I showed up?"

"Yeah," Squints said. "Though not quite so…obvious. You gotta quit being so *pretty*."

"Fuck off," Jace said good-naturedly. "You okay, Logan?"

Logan picked his head up. "M'so tired."

"Yeah, that's ket for ya," Jace said. "Let's get you up to bed."

Logan chuckled. "*Your* bed."

"We can switch, sure. Yours is probably cozier," Jace said evenly. "Mine's right under the air vent. Plus you're across from the windows, so you get that nice sunrise wakeup call."

"No, I meant—" Logan's words were cut off by a sudden rough shake from Jace as they reached a landing.

"We're almost upstairs, Homeschool," Jace said, his tone pleading, though Logan couldn't think why.

They made it up the last two flights of steps, Logan's head swimming, and then they were in their dorm room, and all the boys were up asking questions Logan couldn't think fast enough to understand. "Back up. Back up!" Jace shouted. "Let me get him to bed!

What are you all still doing in here anyway? Get to your afternoon shit! I don't want a whole dorm room of write-ups. Get out."

Exasperated, Jace dropped Logan onto the bed, yanked his shoes off, and threw the blankets over him as the others filed out. Squints stayed back, leaning against his bedpost.

"M'sorry," Logan slurred. He could barely keep his eyes open.

"For what?"

"I do' know. You're mad a' me. You an' Squints."

"We're not mad at you, Homeschool." Jace bent down next to the bed so he could look Logan eye to eye and set a hand on his cheek. "You beat the piss out of the biggest asshole in the school then got ket-mouthed by the school nurse. You didn't do anything wrong as far as I'm concerned."

"She really hates me," Logan said.

"Probably. But I don't. And Squints doesn't. And the rest of the crew doesn't either. Even Director Rollins seems…neutral. And you're the one who said, you know, to focus on the people whose opinions you care about. Who cares what Ms. Timmons thinks of you or me or any of us? She's just a person who works here."

His thumb running over Logan's cheekbone was so comforting that Logan closed his eyes, giving in to the lassitude settling into his bones. "S'not fair," he said, barely a whisper.

"What's not?"

Logan was already half asleep, the dark behind his eyelids lit up with hallucinatory light and movement, but he fought to answer. "Should be able…to kiss my husban—" Something was wrong with that. He couldn't think. "My…"

"Your what?" Jace's tone was insistent, and the hand on Logan's cheek shook him a little, trying to wake him up gently.

"Sorry…you're not…yet—"

Logan felt Jace close to him, his breath on his skin and the curls tickling against him, like the other boy had leaned in to listen. The hand on his face tightened, then resumed its gentle stroking of his cheek.

"Yet?" The word was so quietly spoken that Logan wasn't sure he'd heard it.

He slipped away, pain free but always aware that it was lurking out of sight, following him through his nightmares, waiting for him to let his guard down enough for it to sneak back in.

# 10

## DRAWING ATTENTION

Logan sat, slightly nauseous and barely conscious, in Ms. Lowell's office chair later that afternoon, having struggled awake just in time for the part of his schedule that used to contain rugby practice. His hands ached again, though Jace had wrapped them in ice after the ketevenal had knocked him out, and the swelling wasn't as bad as he'd feared it would be. Logan couldn't bear to go back to Ms. Timmons, so he'd come here instead.

The Eagle Hold dean walked briskly back into the room, shutting the door behind her and holding out a pair of pills and a glass of water. "Here. This won't do nearly the same to dull the pain as ketevenal, but it also won't make you high as a kite until you pass out either." Her voice was crisp with irritation.

"Thanks," he muttered, swallowing them audibly. "I'm really sorry, Ms. Lowell."

"For what, exactly?" She sat in her chair, looking at her paperwork and not at him, shuffling things back and forth in a way that didn't seem to achieve anything.

Logan gently rubbed one hand against the other, feeling for the tender places. "I…know I wasn't supposed to draw attention. But if you'd heard the things Martin said about Jace—"

"I've heard all about the incident, Mr. Cardot."

With a sigh, Logan bowed his head. "Director Rollins said I was off the rugby team for the foreseeable future. What should I be doing when I'm supposed to be at practice?"

With a snap of paper, she straightened a stack and set it across another. "Do you have any idea how much danger you've put yourself in?" she said, her tone icily calm. "Never mind what you did to Mr. Sneed—he'll be fine, fortunately, although from what I hear, you had *no* intention of him walking away from that. Why would you endanger yourself *and* Mr. Evans this way? The Black Lapels will be on campus *tomorrow*, and I—" She sighed sharply and rubbed her forehead. "You cannot act this way, Mr. Cardot!"

"I know. I *know*. I'm sorry. I don't—I don't know how to handle being *hated* like that." Logan knocked the heel of his hand against his forehead and sighed. "It doesn't matter. I know I shouldn't have, and I know I'm in trouble. Can you tell me what I have to do during rugby practice? And if I have any other punishment coming?"

After a pause in which Ms. Lowell said nothing, he said, "You're not going to take back the applications for my placement, are you?"

She looked up sharply, her manicured brows drawing down in consternation. "Of course not. You and Mr. Evans will *both* be removed from the rugby team—permanently. The director seems to think this can be laid at your feet alone, but you and I know if you hadn't been the first to jump on Mr. Sneed, Mr. Evans would have." When Logan opened his mouth to protest, Ms. Lowell said, "*You* will come and work in my office as a second chore rotation every day until you're placed. Mr. Evans will be sorting some files for me in the basement. End of story."

"Jace will be miserable in the basement alone," Logan said.

"Yes, he will," Ms. Lowell said, "but *you* can't lift boxes with those hands. So you'll each have to deal with it. How are your hands, by the way?"

Logan flexed them, winced at the increasingly familiar lance of bright white pain, and shrugged as it faded into yellow and settled into a steady, background red. "They'll be okay."

She grunted noncommittally. "Well, if you can hold a pen to write, I could use your help filling out these name requisition forms."

"Name requisitions?" Logan took the offered stack from her and laid it out on his side of her desk. Two thin books sat on top, one labeled "Forenames" and the other "Surnames" and, beneath that, dozens of nearly identical forms. He flipped open the forenames book and saw row after row of names printed in three neat columns on each page, the first couple hundred struck through with black ink.

Ms. Lowell nodded. "I try to keep a pool of names already filed so that, as unnamed boys come in, we don't have to wait for the paperwork to know what to call them."

Logan let the book shut. "*You* name the boys? Out of a book?"

"If they come without one, yes. Some get a first name from their birth mother before they're surrendered; others don't—but all of them need surnames. You're a very rare case. I don't think I've taken in a boy in the last decade that we didn't give a new surname. But with you being so close to adulthood, and already on file with the Lapels by family name, it didn't make sense."

Drumming his fingers on the cover of the book, Logan said, "So if I flip back in here, I'll find the names 'Jace' and 'Evans' crossed out somewhere?"

"Evans, yes; Jace, no," she said, stapling a set of papers and flipping to the middle page. "Mr. Evans arrived with the name Jace."

"Is there a paper in here somewhere that says what his surname was before Evans?"

Ms. Lowell's look was knowing and stern and flatly unamused. "Drop that line of questioning right where you picked it up. First of all, no, I don't retain those records. And second, there is no world in which you chasing down Mr. Evans's birth mother results in anything but heartache. He was six hours old when he arrived at ChilCo. *We* are his family."

Logan laid out the first form on the table and picked up a pen, then flipped the book back open to the first page with unmarked names. "Gregory," "Hollis," "Isaac," "Jordan," the next names read. He wrote "Gregory" in the first line of the form, then crossed through it in the book and lifted the next available surname: "Stewart." There: the next baby boy to arrive at ChilCo's Eagle Hold would be Gregory Stewart.

Strange to think he knew the kid's name and fated childhood perhaps before he'd even been born. He checked a few boxes on the sheet and left the signature line blank for Ms. Lowell before continuing on to the next one.

His hands cramped and ached after five or so forms, and he set the pen down to flex and stretch them.

"Go back to your dorm room until dinner," Ms. Lowell said without looking up. "You'll help me with more forms tomorrow. For today, ice your hands and for *God's* sake, don't get into any more trouble. Send Mr. Evans my way when you see him."

"Are you going to tell me the plan now?" Logan said, standing thirty feet from his first morning class, trying to work up the courage to walk past the pair of Black Lapels chatting in the hall.

"Nope," Jace said. "You get to find out when everyone else does. I want your surprise to be genuine. No hint of a scandal."

Logan sighed. This morning, he'd taken more pills from Ms. Lowell, but they didn't do much to cut the ache in his hands. "They're not here for me," he reassured himself under his breath. Jace couldn't have heard him, but the curly-haired boy elbowed him—the most comforting gesture he'd make in front of the officers—and jerked his head toward the classroom.

"We'd better hurry," he said, then set off resolutely toward class. He even gave the Lapels a respectful nod as they passed, which the Lapels acknowledged with a glance. Logan slipped by like he was skirting a hissing alligator at the edge of a pond. His heart pounded in his throat as they slid into their seats.

The morning passed in a nightmare of anxiety. Lapels stuck their heads into classrooms at random, and each time, Logan's stomach tried to climb his esophagus and vomit itself out onto the desk. Jace bumped his shoulder as they walked to lunch.

"It'll be fine, but I want to warn you: the meal inspections will come from Lapels, not lunch ladies."

Logan tossed him a spooked, wide-eyed look, then tried to get his breathing under control.

*Don't draw attention. They're not here for you.* No matter how many times he repeated it, he couldn't relax.

They lined up as they had for the last few weeks; Logan's posture had never been so straight, his stare so steady on the opposite wall. From the corner of his eye, he saw a Lapel coming closer, and it took everything in him not to slither out of his skin to escape.

An outburst behind him made him jerk, and he saw Jace in his peripheral vision turn to look. He turned too. Two littles, maybe eight or nine, had their arms around a Lapel's waist and were shouting gibberish, laughing and trying to climb him like a tree. His half-amused consternation grew to annoyance when no amount of shaking or prying could dislodge the boys, and he had to get his partner to peel them off him.

"Ah, no," Jace said, wending his way through the rest of the boys to pick one of the littles up under the arms and set him aside. "Tim and Prentice don't mean any harm. They're just—damn, sorry about this. They haven't really been the same since they got sent back from their rehoming. It messes with kids' heads, you know?" One of the boys latched on to the second Lapel who'd been trying to help. "Oops, here—sorry. They can get pretty aggressive."

Jace patted each of the boys on the head, and they giggled and lined up with the rest of the students like nothing had happened. Jace shrugged apologetically, a what-can-you-do grin plastered on his mouth, and returned to his place next to Logan.

"What the fuck was that?" Logan asked under his breath, trying not to move his lips.

Jace shrugged innocently. "Couldn't say."

Well, that meant it had to be part of Jace's plan. But what the hell was he thinking, putting littles in the Black Lapels' path? No way would that end well. Jace didn't seem to have nearly enough fear of those officers—didn't seem to have any, in fact.

Logan couldn't say anything about the plan at lunch, and when they returned to the room, Jace refused to speak a word about it to Logan at all. None of the rest of the crew would talk about it either, and Logan was too tired and in too much pain to push it.

That afternoon, Logan trotted to Ms. Lowell's office, and Jace grudgingly stomped down to the basement with her instructions. As soon as Logan sat down, she handed him a stack of papers, barely looking up from her own work.

He was distracted, though, by the view through her open window. With the curtains bound back, he saw the rugby field. Two Lapels were out there, watching Randy and the others practice.

He stood up suddenly, ignoring Ms. Lowell's small sound of surprise, and made his way around the back of her desk to get a better view.

"They have clipboards," he said, barely realizing he was speaking aloud. "What are they writing down?"

"Notes," Ms. Lowell said, not turning. "On which of the grown boys show the traits they're always looking for in recruits."

Logan looked back at her. "What kind of traits?"

She continued writing, paying apparently little attention to their conversation, but her neck stiffened. "Strength, speed, dexterity. Leadership on the field and the ability to follow orders are in demand. Most things that make a good athlete are generally considered to make a good soldier."

A wave of cold prickled up his scalp, and he sat back down, picking up the paperwork again. After a long, long stretch of silence, he said, "Are Jace and I inside during rugby practice because we're being punished or because we're athletic?"

Ms. Lowell looked up, meeting his eyes over her glasses for a fraction of a second before turning back to her work. "You would prefer to be playing a game than sitting in an office filling out paperwork, yes? Sounds like a punishment to me."

Logan reached out and set his hand down on hers. He squeezed it, then released her before she had time to react and settled down to write neatly along the lines and boxes of the forms she'd given him. His hands throbbed, but he didn't complain once.

On the way to classes the next morning, Logan saw another little harassing a Black Lapel. At dinner the next night, two older boys, maybe twelve, danced around one of the Lapels who came in for inspection until the officer grabbed one by the face and physically threw him back. He didn't look amused, as the one the day before had; in fact, he looked furious.

Although Logan watched these things unfold with growing, sickening trepidation, Jace and his crew seemed amused and delighted by the Lapels' reactions. *Where is your fear?* he wanted to demand. *Why aren't you protecting those little boys from their attention? Those men are death.*

But no one else shared his dread. The more they talked about the Lapels, the more it seemed all the other boys perceived them as some sort of super-administration of the school, slightly better dressed and slightly more formal than the director and staff, but otherwise no different.

How could they not understand that the Black Lapels were something else entirely?

"Jace," he said, catching him before classes on the third morning of the Lapel presence before he could leave the dorm room. "Please, tell me what you're doing. I can't see how—I know I don't know the details, but the things I'm seeing—"

"No details, Homeschool," Jace said, grinning. "Plausible—"

"*Fuck* your plausible deniability," Logan said sharply. "Let me help you. Or at least help me understand how putting a bunch of little kids in harm's way will end the rehoming fairs. Because all I'm seeing is—"

Jace kissed him.

It was the first time they'd really touched since the Lapels appeared, and for all that it should have been comforting and pleasant, it sent a surge of fear through Logan so bone shaking he barely stopped himself from hitting Jace. "Don't. Not while—"

Jace looked wounded, but he shrugged then grinned again, erasing the hurt off his face. "I get that you're nervous, but it's really not that big of a deal. The Lapels come every year. They're not here to fuck with anybody; they recruit a bunch of boys who don't have a better placement to go to and they disappear again. We're not in danger up here in our room."

He tried to step forward again, but Logan grabbed his arm, both for the chance to touch him and to hold him at arm's length. "I don't think you understand the danger," he said.

He let Jace lead him to class. He watched littles provoke reactions from Lapels with more and more outrageous behavior, always explained away by "rehoming madness." He hid from Lapel recruiters in Ms. Lowell's office. And he quietly, constantly panicked.

The next day, four more Black Lapels arrived on campus, and they had a lot more stripes on their shoulders. First thing in the morning, they walked straight from the front doors into the director's office, and they still hadn't come out when Jace and Logan walked past toward the cafeteria.

"Forget lunch," Logan said. "Come to the room."

Jace followed, and as soon as they were back to the dorm, he tried to kiss Logan again.

"No," Logan protested. His hands were shaky, sweat plastered across his forehead and under his arms, but he felt cold. "What are you doing? All these boys you've involved in this scheme are gonna get in trouble. Did you see those senior officers? They're not here on a social call. They're here because they think something is seriously fucked at the school."

"Something *is* seriously fucked," Jace said. "The rehoming fairs. This is what we wanted! Senior officers can actually do something about them."

"Those boys are in danger! Do you seriously not care about them at all?"

Jace bristled. "Not care? I'm doing this for *them*. What the fuck are Black Lapels going to do to a nine-year-old that *they* fucked up with their policies?"

Logan took a deep breath, trying to get himself back under control. His hands were still swollen from the beating he'd given Martin, and flexing them cleared his mind slightly. "Whatever they want. They don't answer to anyone. The only people who are looking out for those kids answer to *them*."

In that moment, Logan missed his parents more than he had in months. Every one of these boys deserved people who cared, people who'd fight for them. Ms. Lowell, protecting the boys she could, wasn't enough. Parents would do anything to ensure their kids were safe. Now he had no one who would even care if the Black Lapels made him disappear, except Jace. Maybe Squints, maybe Lowell, but they'd forget him when the next boy in crisis appeared.

"These are children," Jace said, looking at Logan like he was the crazy one.

"Children you've told to act unnaturally around people whose job is to eliminate unnatural things. Children you've put in danger to right wrongs that were done to you a long time ago."

Jace reeled. "Why are you doing this? I'm *this* close to getting rid of this fucking system…this evil fucking—" He fought to reclaim control of himself. "Why are you against me?"

"I am *not* against you. I'm on your side and I always will be. I mean it. But you're being naive. You didn't involve me in your plans for this, and that's fine, but now that I see them in action, I want to help you. You have to think like a bureaucrat or a career military guy.

"For the Lapels to eliminate the rehoming fairs, they'd have to admit *their* system was a mistake. They'd have to own up to ruining the lives of a lot of children, and they'd have to admit something they've built our whole country on is flawed. It's a lot easier for them to blame that on ChilCo's staff or on the kids themselves. Is it harder to admit you keep placing children with unfit parents, or to say the kids got sent back because they're a bad batch?"

Jace took a deep breath, and for a moment, Logan thought he might take a swing at him. But the curly-haired boy swallowed hard and absorbed the words. "You think I made things worse for all those kids."

"I think you're putting too much faith in Hallsburg doing the right thing. These are the people who forced me to live in secret for seventeen years. They ripped me out of my home where I was *happy* and *loved*—" Jace flinched at the last word. "And they threw my parents in a work prison they'll *die* in, if they haven't already, for the goddamn crime of having a kid they—" Logan cut himself off because he was close to tears.

After a long moment, Jace said quietly, "Your parents made you live in a basement alone. Now you do whatever you want."

Logan inhaled sharply. "My parents loved me."

Again, Jace flinched. He turned his face away from Logan's and peeled every expression off it until he was blank as bone. "You really think this"—Logan threw a hand up to encompass all of Chil-Co—"is better than living in a family? A real, honest-to-God family with parents who give a shit about you and you have your own clothes and your own bed and people can *fucking say 'love'* without anyone flinching or calling it 'that gay shit'? It's not. This is a fucking nightmare. If I could go back in time and undo whatever it was that gave me away, do you think I'd be here? Hell no. *Fuck* no."

Logan stood, full of furious energy, and grabbed his book bag. "Think about the kids you say you're trying to protect. *Think* about what's actually going to happen to them."

Jace didn't say anything. Logan left.

Almost the second the door closed behind him, Logan tasted the bitter regret for what he'd said like metal on the back of his tongue. It was true, but he'd been wrong to say it like he had. If he walked away now, Jace would probably stew on it. But if he went back inside, they would both say more things they regretted.

Instead, he headed toward the lunch room, hoping to steal enough food to make it to dinner. Squints caught him in the hall and grinned, tossing him a roll already halved and stuffed with chicken. "Thought you'd be hungry, skipping and all. Where's Jace?"

"Dorm," Logan said.

Squints narrowed his eyes. "You two fight?"

"Goddamn, Squints, you're psychic," Logan said lightly. "Go talk to him. Take him this." He held the chicken roll back out.

Squints shook his head, not taking the food. "I got one for him too." He lowered his voice. "Don't let the Lapels win, Homeschool." He gave Logan a significant look, then trotted on toward the dorm and left Logan to laugh helplessly, Lapels lurking down every corridor ahead.

Logan stood in the bathroom, straightening the collar of his church shirt and staring into the mirror. His hair had gotten long, falling loose in his eyes, and it almost hid how haunted they looked with the deep, purple-black circles underneath them. He should've already been on his way to chapel, but he couldn't bear it.

"Get your shit together," he reprimanded himself, jabbing his finger against the glass. "So Lapels will be there? There're always Lapels there. They've never messed with you before. Today won't be any different."

The door behind him burst open, and he jerked, adrenaline dumping into him like he was about to fight for his life. But it was Jace, who didn't seem to notice Logan jolting back.

"You were right," he said, not even giving the door time to shut behind him before he was speaking. "I'm sorry, Logan. You were right. I don't know what the *fuck* I was thinking. I went to Rollins. I talked to him about the Lapels, about the fair, everything. I told him the kids were running a prank and he needed to tell the Lapels it was all a joke. He didn't say, exactly, but I got the sense the Lapels were talking about some seriously shit options."

Logan's mouth dropped open. "What's he gonna do?"

"He knows it was me, but he didn't really acknowledge it. I told him why. I think he gets it. He seems stressed out, but I don't think he's going to tell the Lapels it was me." Jace sat on the counter and dropped his head into his hands. "I didn't want anyone to get hurt. What if they're all on a list now? I'm a fucking idiot."

"It'll be okay," Logan said with more confidence than he felt, putting his hands on Jace's shoulders and squeezing comfortingly. "They're probably not—they're just kids. You headed it off. Rollins will put things right. It wasn't the best idea, but everyone's allowed a bad idea sometimes."

"No," Jace said. "They *trusted* me. All those kids trusted I was going to make things better. And I…"

"This is bigger than you. You have to accept that for now."

Jace grabbed the front of Logan's shirt and pulled him closer, staring at his chest with a dark, unhappy expression. "I'm sorry for what I said about your parents. I wasn't thinking."

"I'm sorry too," Logan said. Jace's closeness was almost overwhelming; his blue eyes, shaded dark by his long eyelashes, swallowed Logan up even when he was staring resolutely at Logan's chest. Logan desperately wanted to kiss him, but the Black Lapels felt ever present. He was afraid to even stand this close to him. They were alone in the bathroom, but all it would take was one person walking in. Jace seemed to feel the same way; he was pinching his lower lip ferociously again.

"Let's talk about something else," Logan said.

Jace gave him a grateful look. "Okay. What?"

"What was all that noise out on the grounds this morning?"

"Ah." Jace straightened. "Setup for the recruitment games."

Logan sighed. That wasn't really a change of subject, but it was, at least, not drawing Jace's face into deeper despair. "Have you played before?"

"Sure." Jace shrugged. "Never in the recruitment class, but I've won some of the games over the years. I wish I'd taken the grand prize last year; I'm always craving chocolate, and it's hard as hell to get Lowell to order any unless it's your birthday."

"You never worried about being in the spotlight with Lapels?"

Jace frowned. "Why would that matter?"

"Do you *want* them to recruit you?"

Jace blew his lips out noisily. "They mostly pull kids who can't get in anywhere else. Even if they did offer, it's not like they'd cart me off to Shalecrest for saying no. It's just an offer."

*Then why's Ms. Lowell hiding us?* Logan hadn't talked about that at all with Jace. Maybe he should have, but he hated starting arguments with him, and any time they talked about the Lapels, they seemed to argue.

"Oh, shit. We need to go," Jace said abruptly. "We'll be late. We'll have to run. Got everything?"

He bustled Logan out of the bathroom without waiting for an answer and herded him down the stairs, taking them so quickly Logan was sure they'd fall down a flight and break a limb or two. They did run once they got outside, not as gracefully as they might normally, given their tight, shiny Sunday shoes, but they still caught up with the tail end of the ChilCo chapel train easily enough.

They filtered in nearly last, every pew already packed to bursting. *Fuck*, there were so many Black Lapels.

Logan's nausea gave him a bullfrog's gullet of bile.

Jace bobbed his head, looking for an opening large enough—littles could squeeze in almost anywhere, but he and Logan weren't small—and Logan's heart dropped to his shoes when a Black Lapel spotted their predicament and waved them over, gesturing toward a gap in the dead center of his row.

Jace walked over with Logan following mechanically, every nerve in his body screaming for him to run. Half the row stood to let them in, and they edged past, wedging themselves into the center of a pew filled with Black Lapels. In front of them was another pew of Lapels, and when Logan chanced a glance back, the pew behind them was all officers as well. The only thing that kept him from vomiting all over his own lap was the knowledge that if he threw up, he'd draw the attention of every Black Lapel in the area.

He huddled in on himself, trying to be smaller, trying not to touch anyone. It was packed; Jace was as close as ever in church, and now Logan had the choice of pressing his shoulder to Jace's—unthinkable, terrifying…what if they *knew*—or pressing it against the neighboring Black Lapel's gray wool-uniformed arm. There wasn't enough air in this place. It wouldn't have been hotter if the hell described from the pulpit had opened up beneath their feet, releasing its sulfurous vapors into the crowd.

After weeks and weeks of chapel, Logan knew the chants and songs well enough. He should've been able to mimic everyone around them, but his mind and his tongue were numb. Everyone stood and sat twice over before the sermon began. When they seated themselves the second time, Logan was so stiff the Lapel to his right turned to ask, "Are you okay?"

Logan mutely nodded, then turned his eyes to the front. Jace tried to nudge him companionably, but Logan jerked at the contact.

He kept his hands folded in his lap, hiding the last of the tell-tale swelling from his fight with Martin.

The sermon was as it always was, with extra exhortations to "heed the call of service," which no doubt was meant to encourage the boys to sign up with the Hallsburg Special Police Force. Father Robinson asked the Lapel recruiters to stand to receive a special blessing; the man seated directly to Logan's right stood.

Then all that was left was the kneeling and the oil; it was the first time Logan had ever been eager for it. They stood, filed back, dropped to their knees as usual. One of the Black Lapels asked to be purified, and the rest accepted the oil without.

Then the priest reached Logan and smirked down at Logan's hands. "Looks like you've had too much of the rod, lately," he said, lifting one of Logan's hands to examine the damage to his knuckles. The Lapel next to him, the recruiter who'd stood, looked down at his knuckles too.

He tried to take his hand back without jerking it. "Just the usual scrapes," he said with an uneasy-sounding chuckle. He folded his hands together and let the priest drag the burning grease over his lips. When the priest finally, *finally* said his benediction and sent them on their way, Logan was the first to his feet, trying to flee without obviously running.

A hand closed on his shoulder.

"I'm surprised I haven't seen you around the school." It was the fucking Lapel recruiter. His hand was still clasped on him, so Logan couldn't exactly pretend he hadn't heard or make his escape. He turned and tried to smile without opening his lips so the oil wouldn't drip into his mouth. With his free hand, the Lapel held out a handkerchief.

Trying to seem grateful instead of petrified, Logan took the cloth and wiped his face with it before letting the man lift it back out of his hands and pocket it. He said nothing in answer to the man's observation, so the Lapel continued, "Maybe on the rugby field? Or playing basketball? You look like an athlete."

"Not much good at sports." Logan shrugged, then turned to leave, hoping the man would let it drop, but the Lapel walked alongside him toward the door.

"More of a boxer?" he said teasingly, nodding toward Logan's hands. "I've seen enough fights to know those hands."

"Just a friendly scrap."

"Did you win?"

"I…guess," Logan said. "Wasn't really a 'winners and losers' kind of thing."

The Lapel narrowed his eyes at Logan, his smirk losing some of its friendliness. "Are you okay? You seem nervous."

"Breakfast isn't agreeing with me," Logan said. "I'm hoping I can get back to the dorms before it decides to evacuate."

That made the Lapel laugh. He clapped Logan's shoulder, then gripped it again to keep him from walking through the door and out into the sunshine.

"I hope you're planning to join us this afternoon for the games, uh—what's your name?"

*Lie. Lie to him.* "Logan." When the man stared, eyebrows raised in silent prompting, he added, "Cardot."

"Nice to meet you, Logan Cardot. I'm Sergeant Spears. I'll see you on the grounds this afternoon!" He gave Logan's shoulder one last squeeze, then slipped out into the parking lot, leaving Logan stunned and frozen in the doorway.

Jace emerged from where he'd been waiting inside the chapel and swept Logan out with him. They were completely silent for half a mile as they walked back toward the school before Jace said, "So… what'd he say that's making you look like you're gonna barf?"

"He said he'll see me on the grounds for the games," Logan replied stiffly. "He'll be looking for me, specifically. By name. Because I told him my name."

"He's a recruiter and you're an ideal recruit." Jace shrugged. "It's not any deeper than that. He saw a big guy who looks athletic that he's never seen before, and he wants to try to woo you with uncomfortable wool uniforms and jackboots. That's it."

"That's it, huh?" Logan echoed faintly.

"That's it." Jace sounded resolute, confident. "And as good as you'd look in jackboots…" Logan shot him a look of pure annoyance that melted a little with the heat of the smirk Jace sent back at him. "…we both know you're not gonna join up. You're going to Durhoss with me. In a couple of months, we'll be out of this school, out of this country, far away in some coffee shop off campus, speaking Tychan and forgetting Black Lapels even exist."

Logan wanted that so badly it hurt to think about. He wanted to be gone *now*, this instant. He took a few deep breaths of the sun-soaked air, trying to relax, trying to imagine himself a thousand miles from this place. Jace's arm around his shoulders, sitting under an umbrella outside a café while people strolled by. Or, better yet, Jace's arms around him somewhere with no one else around.

"I don't know," he said quietly, glancing around to make sure no one was in range to hear. "If we were alone in another country, I don't think we'd be going out for coffee."

Jace cocked an eyebrow. "Oh? What would we be doing?"

"Knocking pictures off the wall in our bedroom," Logan said, whisper quiet.

Jace's eyes flashed pure, bone-melting lust with an intensity that almost stopped Logan's heart. It felt good for his pulse to race for any other reason than terror, even if only fleetingly.

Jace then made a face of mock outrage, pressing his hand to his chest. "Living together? How sinful. How scandalous. You're not my husband *yet*." He grinned at Logan's groan of embarrassment.

"That was the fucking ketevenal!"

"Yeah, yeah," Jace said, laughing. "Thing is, ket mouth makes you say *true* things you wouldn't have said otherwise. So admit it…" He looked up and down the path again and dropped his voice, though he didn't drop his teasing tone. "You want to marry me."

What was the point in pretending otherwise? He wanted Jace forever. "Of course I do."

Jace blinked like Logan had rung a bell in his ear or shouted him awake. The teasing dripped off his face; his brows turned up, his mouth opened, and he leaned toward Logan like he meant to grab him. It was a wrenchingly earnest face, and it was gone in a flash, buried over again with Jace acting friendly and normal and like he'd never longed for anything in his life. "Well," Jace said evenly, "we know what's on the agenda once we get out of here."

Logan laughed. It wasn't a *laugh* really. Nothing was funny. But he didn't know what else to do with that little bubble of happiness in the midst of everything else at ChilCo.

Jace grabbed his arm, jerking him off the path and into the trees. "Jace, what are—"

"Come to the treehouse with me."

Logan hesitated, dragging his feet enough to slow the other boy down. "We shouldn't do that. What if—"

"They don't know about it," Jace said. "We just built it out of nothing. Why would anyone come looking in the middle of the woods? I want time with you. We *deserve* time." That earnest face had returned, and as terrified as Logan was, he couldn't summon the will to deny that face anything it asked for.

"Okay."

They ran through the woods as though something were chasing them, with none of the whooping and howling of when they'd run with the crew. Just them, in silence, dodging trees and crashing through underbrush in their church clothes. When they reached the treehouse, not a soul was around, and even the birdsong was quiet and distant. Jace threw himself up the climbing holds as though a flood were rising beneath him, and Logan was quick behind.

Panting from the run, Jace sat on the floor under the window, the only place they could be sure no one from the ground could see them. He ripped off his church shoes and chucked them, then chased them with his shirt as fast as he could unbutton. Logan crouched to do the same, muttering, "This is a really bad idea."

"The best ideas are usually the worst ones," Jace said. Absolute nonsense, but he gave Logan no time to refute or respond. He grabbed Logan's head with both hands, kissing him ferociously, all the pent-up need trying to force itself out at once. The bottom fell out of Logan's stomach, this time out of pleasure, not fear. He had missed Jace like deserts missed rain, worse than he'd even realized. The first kiss was a cool glass of water after weeks of dehydration.

To keep them below the window line, Jace pulled Logan down on top of him, then let go of Logan's cheek with one hand so he could unbutton the boy's shirt.

Between kisses, he gasped out, "Where should we live? After we graduate."

Logan smiled against Jace's mouth, holding his weight on one forearm and sliding fingers over the smooth skin of Jace's abs. "By the sea." His mouth formed the shape of Jace's, the faint burn of the holy oil heating their lips and tongues. "Lots of books. One big bed."

After pulling Logan's shirt off him with a grunt of effort, Jace arched up to bite his neck, his shoulder, his chest. Then he rolled, putting Logan on the floor, leaning over him. "Dogs?"

"One dog," Logan agreed. It was so hard to catch his breath with the way Jace's lips were feathering down his body. "One cat. Friendly neighbor kids we can teach swear words."

When Jace laughed against Logan's belly, Logan wriggled from the tickle of his breath. Jace bit his hip, yanked his trousers down. "I want that. All of that." His eyes flicked up toward Logan's, arresting in their intense blueness. "All of you."

"I'm yours."

A noise in the trees somewhere below them made them freeze, hands unmoving on each other's bodies. In complete silence, they strained to hear, not even breathing.

Then the sound came again, like laughter but more animalistic, a chittering call. Not a bird, though. Jace peeked up over the edge of the window and scanned the ground, and then relaxed as he laughed. "It's a couple of foxes gekkering. Where were we?"

But the unexpected noises had broken the slim barrier in Logan's brain that held back the ever-present fear. He couldn't relax again. "I… Can we just…?" He pulled Jace down on top of him again, all the way down so they lay chest to chest. Then Jace slid his arms under Logan so they could fully wrap each other up. At first, their heartbeats were wildly syncopated, off beat from each other and frenzied. But as Jace's arms tightened around him and Logan nuzzled in closer, relaxing into Jace's hold, the rhythms melted together, synchronizing.

"I'm so afraid," Logan whispered.

Jace ran his fingers through the hair at the nape of Logan's neck, slowly drawing out the tension. "Afraid of what?"

"Everything," Logan said breathlessly. "I'm afraid we won't get to do those things. I'm afraid of the Lapels. I'm afraid of Hallsburg and everyone in it. I almost don't want to dream about our future together because it…it feels like they'll rip it away from us."

"Hey," Jace said, sitting up enough to look into Logan's face. Their arms stayed tight around each other, their breathing almost perfectly in sync. "I don't care if it's a house by the sea. I don't care if we have a dog or a library. I don't care if it's Durhoss or some other school or no school at all and we're picking out of garbage cans somewhere. It's you and me—that's the dream. I don't care what else anyone takes from us. You and me together, we can do anything. We can conquer the whole world." He smiled. "I believe that."

Logan pulled him back down and kissed his shoulder. "Enamored with you."

"Obsessed with you," Jace said back.

"We have to go back. They'll be looking for us. For me."

"Fine," Jace said, stealing another kiss before he grabbed Logan's shirt and pressed it into his hands. "We'll go together."

# 11

## CHOOSE

On every inch of the cleared grounds, boys chattered and bounced and lounged and laughed, some stretching or warming up if they were taking the games seriously, but most biding time until someone called them to order. The air held the energy of a festival, and when Logan and Jace walked up together, most of Eagle Hold greeted them jovially.

Ms. Lowell was there too, frowning at Logan. He gave her a small, low wave, and the line between her brows deepened. She didn't return the wave, but instead ushered boys away from a central field marked off with a staked line of small, brightly colored pennants. There was a rich, turned-earth smell to the grounds that put Logan uncomfortably in mind of a grave.

The Lapels lined up around the edges of the field, laughing among themselves with the same festival energy, some carrying clipboards and others whistles or flags.

Jarringly, Logan realized most of them weren't much older than him or Jace. Seeing them chatting idly to one another, he realized they were just…young men. It made him shudder; he'd seen what their faces looked like when they were pointing a gun at someone, when they were hauling people to their deaths, and those faces should not have been able to stretch into normal smiles and friendly placidity.

"Glad you could join us, Logan Cardot!" The recruiter from church wasn't as young as the others. Strands of gray glittered in his blond hair, and where the others were fit, Sergeant Spears's body was easing toward paunchiness. His green eyes crinkled when he smiled, making him seem warmer and friendlier than he could possibly be. When Logan didn't answer him, he turned his eyes to Jace. "And you…I recognize you, don't I? Evans?"

"Jace Evans, sir," Jace said, sticking out a hand to shake the sergeant's. "I'm afraid I dragged Logan here, even though he wasn't looking to compete. He's not much of an athlete, but I told him it would be fun."

Spears flicked an incredulous look at Logan, then smoothed into his overly friendly smile again. "It will be fun! We love to see you boys get out there and do your best. Reminds us all why we're investing so much in the future of Hallsburg here at ChilCo."

Logan summoned a nod as the recruiter walked off to greet other students. Jace tapped the back of his hand against Logan's. "See? It's fine."

"Yeah," Logan said, but it didn't loosen the knot of dread in his belly.

A small platform, just two steps up onto a wooden box at one end of the field, served as a stage for Sergeant Spears, who climbed up and whistled them to silence. Everyone gathered closer, squinting into the sun to see the crisply dressed officer spread his hands wide, welcoming them in.

"We're happy to see so many excited participants in the games," Spears called, his voice booming enough to be heard all over the grounds. "Welcome, and good luck to all of you! Some of you are old hands at these games, but for others, this'll be new. For each event, we'll select a winning participant or team who'll get one of these prizes." He gestured toward a small table with plastic trophies stuffed with candy and trinkets.

"Performing well in those events will also earn you points toward our grand prize. Our overall winner will receive something truly fantastic this year—something we've never offered before." The boys leaned in as he paused, grinning at their wide-eyed anticipation. "The Governor of North Hallsburg has agreed to grant one request to the winner of our games. A single request. You can ask for anything, but I'll warn you to keep it realistic: if it's *not* in the governor's power to give, your request will be void and there will be no grand prize. So think carefully!"

As voices rose among the crowd of boys, he folded his hands across his stomach patiently. At Logan's left elbow, one of the Bens popped his head into the loose semicircle of Eagle Hold boys and said, "Jace, the governor could end the fairs."

Jace lit up like a firework, a frisson of energy running visibly through his entire body. "The governor could end the fucking fairs," he repeated in a whisper, vibrating with excitement. "Holy shit! We could just *ask!*"

Just ask? They could just ask for whatever they want. Anything the governor could grant. The opposite of whatever energy had seized Jace burrowed into Logan, coring him and devouring his breath. The governor could also grant pardons.

He could get his parents back.

If he competed. If he won. If he was willing to steal Jace's dream from him. If…if his parents weren't already dead.

Everything around him became a buzz of noise, though he knew at least some of it was intended for him. If his parents were alive, he could get them back. He could free them. *If* they were alive. Which—his stomach wrenched horrifically—which they weren't. There was no chance. Not a fucking chance.

Right?

"Right, Logan?"

"What?" Logan blinked up at Jace, who was shaking him by the arm, face glowing, missing tooth showing, so full of life and joy and anticipation that Logan had to squint like he was looking straight into the sun.

"I said, you'll help us win? We didn't win last year, but we didn't have you then. And the biggest of the Bears got booted last year, so we have less competition. We can win! We can get rid of the fairs for good!" So much hope. So much light.

Jace had earned that. He *had* hope. Logan's parents…that was a lost cause, hopeless. They were long dead. But he could help Jace achieve his dream, at least. He struggled to pull his mouth into something approximating a smile. "Okay."

All the crew was buzzing, hyping one another up, bouncing and whooping. Logan was shaking. His parents…there wasn't anything to hope for there. But he could compete, even if it drew attention he didn't want; he could give Jace that.

"Hey, you don't have to go all out," Squints said quietly, gesturing for Logan to bend down. "Jace said you didn't really want to compete. He and Randy are so good at these games, you basically only need to be another fast pair of legs. You could half-ass it and still win. You don't have to, you know?" He flexed his arms like he was showing off.

"I know," Logan said, nodding.

Squints frowned. "Then what are you so upset about?"

"Nothing. It's too late for… It doesn't even—nothing."

"Too late for what?"

From the pedestal came another whistle, and Sergeant Spears spoke. "Will you ask for money? Extravagant meals? Special treatment? Hopefully you all know what you're playing for. All of you who want to compete, form teams of four. We'll begin with a relay."

Jace, Logan, Randy, and Ben Witemeyer formed a team. Looking around, Logan knew few other teams could stand against them, but two or three could give them trouble, outfitted with the tallest, strongest, and fastest of the hold elders.

When Logan glanced back toward the sidelines, he saw Squints staring hard at him, a grim set to his mouth. Shaking himself, he focused on the competition at hand.

The games were simple enough: races and obstacle courses, kicking goals and tossing eggs and leaping into hoops on the ground from one end of the field to the other; tests of strength, agility, and speed. In some they competed as a team, urging one another to greater speed, higher jumps, more fantastic catches. In others, they were individuals, each trying to outdo the others and claim the top few spots.

Logan's team of four won the first, and Jace alone won the second of the games. The next two games were claimed by a massive guy from Hawk. Their team took tug-of-war next, though it was close, and they wished they'd taken Teapot instead of Ben. A dozen games went to as many different winners, and then Jace won again.

By Logan's math, Jace was the points leader, but the Lapels kept no visible tally.

The boys took a water break, collapsing onto the sidelines and trying to catch their breath. Squints plunked himself down beside Logan, handing him a towel to dry the sweat pouring down his face. "What did you mean by 'too late'?"

"Forget it," Logan said breathlessly. "It doesn't matter."

"For your parents?"

Logan jerked, then shot a quick look at Jace, who wasn't paying attention. "Don't say anything. They're already dead. The right thing to ask for is the end of the fairs."

"It's only been a few months," Squints insisted.

"It's been almost a year! They're—" He cut himself off, dropping his voice again. Someone had scooped out his insides, leaving flaps of flesh to rattle in the hollowness when he breathed. "They didn't even bring my dad's wheelchair when they took my parents. They're gone. They never would've made it this long. I *know* what Shalecrest is supposed to be like. It's a waste of a wish."

"They're your family! We have to *try*. Say something to Jace— he'd want you to have your family back."

"Not a word, Squints," Logan answered, trying to moderate his tone as he clambered back to his feet, dropping the towel in the grass. Every syllable Squints spoke cut like a blade dipped in holy oil. "Don't say anything to him. I mean it. We stick with the plan."

He turned his back on the spectacled boy and focused on the sergeant explaining the rules of the next game. The final game, it seemed. They'd roped off the field in a grid, making squares about six feet on a side, and Spears was gesturing to the one in front of him, where two of the Lapels demonstrated the game as he spoke.

"You'll be paired up with an opponent," Spears explained. "The goal is to eliminate the other person by getting them outside the ropes. You can push, you can fight, you can do whatever you need to do, but stay *inside the ropes* or you'll be eliminated. Once the first round of eliminations is complete, we'll match you up again until we're down to one winner. Clear?"

"Clear!" the boys called, and soon they were all matched up and tossed into roped-off sections of the field.

Only so many could fight at a time, so Logan and Randy waited their turn, watching Ben and Jace compete in their first rounds. Ben was placed with a much smaller boy who couldn't have been older than twelve. The two circled each other, darting quick and jabbing at each other, neither able to force the other back by much.

Jace, on the other hand, was paired with another placement-aged boy, but Jace hoisted him up around the waist and set him gently on the other side of the ropes in seconds; it wasn't really even a competition.

He trotted over to the winners' side of the field, grinning, and high-fived Ben when he eventually flipped his opponent onto his back and dragged him past the ropes by the foot. Logan and Randy were paired up with their own competition, and Logan faced the beastly kid from Hawk who was close behind Jace in points. Logan would just have to eliminate him.

"You're going down," the guy said. He snapped his head left and right on his thick neck, a sneer pulling the mustache he'd proudly cultivated crooked.

Logan didn't say anything, lunging toward the boy as the whistle sounded. His shoulder hit the Hawk hard in the belly, and for a moment, he thought his momentum would be enough to make him stumble back and out, but the Hawk rallied. He slammed a fist down hard on Logan's back just inside his shoulder blade, and the sudden numbing jolt of it made Logan let go. They backed away, then circled each other.

When the Hawk lurched forward, Logan's elbow snapped up, cracking straight up under the boy's chin. As he staggered back, shouting in pain, Logan pressed his advantage, kicking him hard in the belly. The Hawk doubled over six inches from the ropes, and Logan, with a massive grunt of effort, lifted him around the waist and hurled him backward half a step.

It was just, just enough. The nearest Lapel called it, waving the Hawk to the losers' side and giving Logan an appreciative round of applause as he pointed him toward the side of the field where Jace and Ben waited.

"That was fucking brutal," Ben said, offering a congratulatory fist to Logan, who knocked his aching knuckles against Ben's. "For someone who didn't even want to compete, you're out here to win."

So he wouldn't have to answer, Logan looked for Randy. He spotted him on the other side, and Randy waved and smiled ruefully when Logan caught sight of him. *Damn*—one less ally trying to get Jace to the end.

They were paired up again; this time Logan went head to head with a speedy but scrawny boy he'd never seen before. The boy seemed to know him, though, or had at least seen his last fight. He cringed away as soon as he stepped into the ropes and said, "If I step out, promise not to break me in half?"

Logan shrugged. "If you step out, I won't need to."

"Fair enough!"

As soon as the whistle blew, the boy raised his foot high, visibly stepping backward—then lunged low, going for Logan's knees.

On instinct alone, Logan rotated so the kid ricocheted off his thighs, and then Logan kicked backward. He caught the boy in the ribs, and he curled up, rolling under the ropes with a groan. When the Lapel called the fight, Logan reached to help the kid up, but he wriggled away as if in fear for his life. With a sigh, Logan retreated to the winners' side instead next to Jace.

"How'd you—" he started to ask, but Jace wasn't looking at him. Logan followed his gaze to Squints on the sideline, trying to communicate something with gestures and pointing. His skin went cold. "Hey," he said, nudging Jace until he looked away from Squints, "how'd you do?"

"Uh, fine," Jace said, frowning past Logan's shoulder. "We're close to the end now. How'd you do?"

"Hit a kid harder than I meant to. Hate these fucking games."

"A means to an end," Jace said. "I'm sure he'll forgive you a bruise or two, given what we're protecting all these kids from. Ah, shit, looks like Ben's out."

They paired up again, and again, Jace and Logan each set their opponent out of the ropes. This time, Logan managed to be gentler.

Then there were only four pairs, and Jace and Logan faced off against each other. Jace grinned at him. "Shall we really give them a show?" he said, a sparkle in his eye.

"No," Logan said flatly. As soon as the whistle blew, he stepped backward over the rope, and then kept walking toward the losers' side. When he sat on the grass there, Jace stood in the roped-off section, watching him with a troubled frown.

The final four were all reasonably large, athletic young men. Jace was well matched, and the tussle that erupted once the whistle blew was riotous. Although he was taking this quite seriously, Jace seemed to be having a lot of fun. He and his opponent were laughing at the end, even when Jace crowed his victory over the other boy's prone form. Jace helped him up and clapped him on the back, his good nature written all over his face. He'd earned this. He'd earned the request. He'd earned his dream.

Logan was happy to give it to him. He was echoingly, desolately hollow on the inside, but a small corner of him was happy to help Jace get what mattered so much to him.

Everyone crowded around more tightly for the final match. Squints came up from the sidelines, elbowing in next to Logan. The whistle signaled a ferocious match as Jace and the last boy—Hudson, Logan thought, another rugger—locked in so low to the ground it looked like a ruck. Their feet dug into the ground, tearing up the grass, as each of them flexed and strained to push the other back.

Jace doubled down, pushing so hard his face was turning purple. But as Hudson did the same, Jace released him, dropping to the ground. Hudson lost his balance, grasping at Jace as he fell across him. Jace rolled, kicked with his knee; Hudson barely dodged the strike, but the effort put him an inch or two from the ropes, and on his side. Jace scrambled to his feet, grabbed Hudson's shirt with both hands as Hudson also rose. The other boy made it only to his knees before Jace wrenched him upward and threw him back. Hudson collapsed backward onto his elbow, everything above the waist across the line.

Jace threw his fists in the air, dropped his head back, and howled his victory.

The Eagle Hold boys swarmed the field, climbing onto Jace, thumping him with the flats of their hands, howling along with him. Logan was slower to rise, slower to join them. He saw Squints slither through gaps, trying to get close enough to Jace to talk to him.

*Fuck.*

Logan darted forward, but he was too slow. Jace was already bent down, listening intently to what Squints was whispering. Squints was pointing at Logan. Logan froze.

*Don't do this. They're already dead. Don't waste this. Don't…don't give me hope.*

"I believe I'm the winner, Sergeant?" Jace called to the Lapel recruiter, and the boys around him answered with resounding shouts.

"Yes. Jace Evans is our winner!" Spears announced. "I'm guessing by the eagerness on your face that you already know what you want to ask for."

"Yes, I—" His eyes flicked over to Logan, who frantically shook his head.

"The fairs, Jace," he said hoarsely, but he wasn't even sure if Jace could hear him over the cacophony.

"I want the governor to pardon Eleanor and Frank Cardot," Jace said in a clear voice.

The sergeant blinked, confused. He shook his head to clear his ears. "Eleanor and Frank Cardot?" he repeated. Then his eyebrows shot up, and his eyes found Logan in the crowd. "These wouldn't be kin to Mr. Logan Cardot there, would they?"

The boys fell silent, recognizing something unexpected was happening. Stares darted between Jace, Logan, and the Lapel recruiter. Logan pushed his way to stand next to Jace. "Take it back, Jace. Ask for your favor."

Jace looked at him like he was crazy. "I'm sorry I didn't think of your parents sooner. If I had, it would have been what I was winning for all along. We'll figure something else out for the fairs. I was already making plans anyway."

He turned his face back up to the sergeant and said, "They are. That's my request."

Sergeant Spears studied the two of them. Space bloomed around them as other boys drifted back, edging into the background to observe this strange scene. Speculative whispers raced up and down the lines of students.

At length Spears opened his mouth with a wet, smacking sound and said, "The prize is *one* request. One request, one pardon."

Jace made a strangled sound, and Logan exhaled like he'd been gut punched. "You want me to choose—" He choked out. He shook his head, took a staggered step forward. "You want me to *choose* which parent gets their freedom? Whether my mom lives or my dad does?"

Assuming, of course, they *were* alive. Which…

Despair threatened to overwhelm him, but breaking through the dark clouds was hope. Hope he hadn't dared to have. And anger. That they would make him *choose* was cruel beyond measure.

"One request, one pardon," Spears repeated.

There it was: the flat, cruel face he remembered from the Lapels who'd stormed his house nearly a year ago. All humanity switched off with a flick of the wrist, plunging the gathered Lapels into the darkness, capable of absolutely anything.

Everyone stared at Logan.

In his peripheral vision, he saw Jace start to reach for him, then check himself. Everything was so still, so quiet.

How the fuck did they expect him to choose? What the fuck were they all waiting on him to say? It wasn't like he could open his mouth and say, "Pardon my mother" or "Pardon my father." He'd as easily choose whether to have his left eye or his right stabbed out of his head.

He couldn't breathe.

They wouldn't have survived. It had been too long. It was too late. He knew that—he *knew* that—but fucking hope wriggled its way in like a climbing vine, choking him. At last, after more silence than anyone could bear, he croaked out, "Whichever one is alive."

Spears clicked his tongue, scrunching his mouth to one side as he thought. "Whichever is alive?" he repeated softly, considering. Then he nodded. "All right. If that's the request, I'll make the call."

He stepped down off the platform, striding toward the building, and Logan's knees buckled. Jace and Squints were there in a second, one on each side, holding him on his feet.

They didn't say a word. Somewhere in the gathering, people were whispering, but no one within ten feet of Logan spoke.

He still couldn't breathe, ribs woven too tightly shut with that god-awful vine. The silence pressed in on him; all he heard was his heartbeat, blood rushing in his ears.

Who would it be? Would he see his mom again? He could practically feel the way her arms wrapped around him when she hugged him, practically smelled her linen-and-lavender scent. She'd hum under her breath, not even noticing she was doing it, filling their house with gentle music.

Or his dad—the idea of eating Dad's pot roast, of sitting in companionable quiet, each reading their own books, nearly drowned him in longing. Could he really do that again? Was he going to—?

Movement rippled from the doors of the school. Logan turned, and Squints's and Jace's hands tightened on him, gripping so firmly they'd probably leave bruises.

Hope was a vicious, deadly thing. Nothing could crush a person like hope. And by the grim expression on the sergeant's face as he remounted the platform, Logan knew he would be crushed. He tried to summon words, a movement, anything to forestall what might come out of that man's mouth. He didn't want to know. He didn't want—

"I hate to cast a pall over our games and Mr. Evans's victory," Spears said, "but I'm afraid the request to have whichever Cardot is alive pardoned will have to be voided. Over the course of their penance for their actions against the laws of Hallsburg, they have both passed on. However, in the spirit of the award, the governor has offered to extend a posthumous pardon for both of them. He'll be sending a certificate by mail to the school, which can be claimed by you, Mr. Evans, or Mr. Cardot if he wishes."

"*A certificate?*" Logan hissed, low and laced with fury beyond anything he'd ever felt in his life. Squints and Jace grabbed him harder; Logan didn't realize he'd dragged them a step toward the sergeant until Squints slid in the grass, desperately readjusting his hold. He shook so hard he had to speak through clenched teeth so his voice would come out clear. "Fuck your certificate. What the *fuck* am I gonna do with a piece of paper that says my parents shouldn't be dead when they are? Give Jace another request. A *real* request. Not this joke."

Spears spread his hands, his smile frozen in a cold mask. "I *did* say the requests needed to be realistic or they would be voi—"

"How the *fuck* could he have known?" Logan shouted back. "*How the f—*"

Jace stepped in front of Logan, right in his face, hands on his shoulders to push him back. "You have to calm down," he said in a low voice. "I know, I understand, but we *have* to go. Come inside with me, Logan. Right now. Let's go."

It was only anger holding Logan up now; he couldn't let it go. But he couldn't fight a Black Lapel sergeant in front of the entire school either.

Shaking Squints off him, he turned on his heel and marched to the front doors without another look at Spears. Several people reached out to touch him, but he jerked away, not knowing who it was or what they intended. He made it through the doors, and then his knees gave out again and he stumbled to all fours in the hall.

Jace picked him up, but he couldn't bear the help, couldn't bear the hands on him. "Don't touch me," he snapped. He walked to the common room, upright by sheer force of will, and dragged himself upstairs hand over hand on the banister. He was taking the steps too quickly for his numb feet and kept tripping, but he held himself up and carried on. Jace and Squints followed him, but they didn't touch him and they didn't speak.

As soon as they were in their room, Logan started to collapse onto his bed, but the thought of being trapped there, thinking about his parents, compelled him to his feet again. Instead he paced. It was hard to inhale, and every exhale caught in his throat like a sob.

Jace leaned against the edge of his own bed and tried to gently catch Logan's arm. "Logan, I'm s—"

"*Don't touch me*," Logan repeated. He couldn't even see Jace, couldn't see anything except colors and shapes. His parents were dead. He'd known, he'd known—of course he'd known—but he hadn't *known*. And he would never, ever see them again. That stupid, evil fucking hope he'd had for just a few minutes would strangle him to death.

"I have to… I need… I need—" He couldn't find words, could barely find the interest in speaking words at all. "A shower. I need a shower." He turned and paced a short distance each way, hands flexing at his sides.

"Here," Jace said, reaching past him to the hook where Logan always hung his towel to dry. He plucked it off and held it out at arm's length toward him.

When Logan took it, it felt foreign in his hands. What the hell was he supposed to do with this? Jace stood and extended his hands like he might touch Logan again, but he only guided him toward the door. "The shower is this way."

Without touching him, Jace led him down the hall, started the water, and tested the temperature with his fingertips. He took the towel back from Logan's limp hands and hung it on the hook outside the shower stall. When Logan made no move to undress, he said, "Do you need help with your…"

He trailed off as Logan walked in fully clothed, pawing the curtain closed behind him.

The water pouring over his head was numbing, blocking out the silence without adding anything he needed to process. He closed his eyes, leaning against the tiles, and tried not to picture the soft waves of his mother's hair when she leaned over to kiss him good night, or the strong, calloused fingers of his father's hands, or the way they hadn't been able to even hold each other for comfort when the Lapels had broken into their house to steal him away, or the warm tent of blankets and sheets his mother had turned his bedroom into for his tenth birthday, or the flat, smug smile of the sergeant pronouncing them long dead, or—

Logan's breath dragged, wet, through his throat in and out, wracking sobs shaking him. He clung to the tile behind his back with both hands to hold himself up. There were so many pictures in his head, and over and over he heard Spears say, "They have both passed on," and he'd never wanted any of this and why the fuck were they doing this to him and why and *why* and WHY!

He was screaming.

His hands were bleeding.

The tile was smeared with it.

He tried to pound his fists against the wall again and found he didn't have the strength. Somehow he was sprawled on the floor of the shower.

"Logan," Jace said gently. A hand gripped his knee, and Logan looked up into blue eyes. Jace's hair was quickly plastered to his head as he knelt in the stall.

"Why are your eyes so red?" Logan said flatly, unable to summon the inflection that would make it a question. "Looks like you've been crying."

"Well," Jace said with a grim, mirthless chuckle, "I must've gotten some sweat in them. Certainly nothing upsetting has happened in the last hour or so."

"Help me." Logan's voice broke.

Jace straightened, nodded. "Yes. How? What do I do? I want to help."

"I don't know." Closing his eyes again, Logan lay back against the tile. He would just stay here. Everything outside this shower stall was too cruel to be borne. So he'd stay here.

Jace shook him a little, grabbed his arm, and hefted him to his feet. Logan wavered, wanting to lie back down again, but Jace's strong arm around his waist kept him vertical while the other boy shut off the water. It was too much; he didn't want to be held, didn't want to be forced to stand and deal with the world. Anger surged in him again, aimless and vicious.

"Please don't touch me."

Jace hesitated then let go. "Okay."

He handed Logan his towel, but Logan simply held it, stepping out of the shower stall and catching sight of the horror show that was his appearance. Soaking wet, clothes clinging to him, his hair dark and dripping in his eyes, Logan's face was red from crying, red from the streak of blood across his cheek he must have gotten from wiping his hand there. His hands bled freely, making a mess of everything, and they hurt so badly he wanted to scream. Again.

With a growl of disgust, he turned his back on his reflection and scrubbed the towel roughly over his head. Everything hurt, especially his hands.

Squints took a step forward, and Logan jolted; he hadn't realized the smaller boy was there at all. "Shit, your hands look wrecked. I'll get you some ice and pain pills."

"Why couldn't you leave well enough alone?" Logan said. "I *told you* it was too late. I fucking told you. But you wouldn't drop it!"

With each shout, Squints shook like a pennant in a high wind. His face was blotched red, his lashes clumped wetly together. "I'm so sorry. I just thought…if there was any chance—"

"But there wasn't a chance, was there?" Logan towered over him. Squints reached up, put a hand on his chest to hold him back a step, and Logan grabbed his arm hard, yanking it until Squints was inches from him. "And now Jace's dream is dead and so is my family! We gained nothing!"

"Let go of him," Jace said. A warning tone and a warning hand on Logan's wrist.

Logan blinked. He took a deep, shuddering breath. He looked at Jace next to him, eyes wary and sad, and then he looked back at Squints. Squints was so small. Squints was crying.

"Ah, fuck," Logan said, dropping the boy's arm and backing away a step. "What am I doing?" He rubbed his hands over his face, gritted his teeth, and tightened his lips around the scream that wanted to escape. The strangled, grating sound he released instead was animal. "I'm sorry… I—"

He fled. If he lost Squints, if he lost Jace, he had no one in the entire fucking world. Not even himself, since he was sure he'd lost his mind. He left, but where could he possibly go? He'd hurt Squints, and now he couldn't even hide in the dorm room, the only sanctuary he'd had for months. It was late afternoon; there was nowhere he could go where people wouldn't see him, where people wouldn't talk. There was nowhere to hide.

"Stop," Jace said, bursting out of the bathroom after him. "I know you don't want to be touched right now, and sorry, but—" He grabbed Logan's arm and dragged him into the dorm room, all the way to his bed. He yanked Logan's wet shirt off him, roughly toweled him off, then said, "All of you needs to be dry right now. Am I doing it or are you?"

"I can do it," Logan muttered, embarrassed. He peeled off the rest of his clothes before dropping them with a slap in sodden heaps on the floor. As soon as the now-damp towel had mostly dried him, Jace snatched it out of his hands and put fresh, dry clothes into them instead. When Logan started to dress, not meeting Jace's eyes, the other boy crossed the room to change out of his own wet clothes.

Dry and warm, Logan sat on the edge of his bed, drained.

"Lie down," Jace said. He didn't wait for Logan to obey—he reached down and pulled Logan's legs up and around into the bed and shoved his shoulders back. All business-like efficiency, he un-clipped the curtains around Logan's bed and drew them, enclosing him in a dark cocoon. "Just lie down and close your eyes and don't go anywhere. Squints went to get you something for your hands. I'm gonna see about something to eat. Don't move! Okay?"

Cheek pressed to the cool pillow, Logan nodded. With his eyes closed, he listened to Jace cross the room again, fiddle with something paper, then tear it. He heard Jace walk briskly out of the room then shut the door behind him with such care that it barely made a sound. There was a scraping sound on the other side of the door, a faint thud of pressure, and the sound of Jace's footsteps disappearing down the stairs. And then there was nothing.

He didn't seem able to feel anything. It was a relief, after the raging inferno even the cold shower hadn't been able to put out.

Logan dozed.

After a while, he heard footsteps, multiple sets, making their way toward the room, and he braced for the other boys to come in, to want to talk, or worse, to whisper around the periphery of the room and leave him alone in the midst of them.

But the footsteps stopped, and there were a few murmured words, and then they retreated to the stairs and down.

When silence returned, the hollow feeling in his chest felt un-bearable. He sat up, dumping the blankets off himself in the process, drew his knees up, and set his chin atop them.

Strange that Jace hadn't come back, or Squints. When Logan wiggled his fingers, pain shot up from each knuckle to his wrist. He wouldn't have minded having that ice now.

Maybe he should go get some himself. He wasn't an invalid; he was just so tired.

Footsteps pounded up the stairs again, and this time they didn't pause at the door. All seven of his roommates filed in, led by Jace. "We've returned with reinforcements," he said.

First, Squints, bearing pills, which he dropped into Logan's palm before claiming the other hand and beginning to wrap a bag of ice around it. Then Randy and one of the Bens, who each dumped a bagful of candy, crackers, snack cakes, and various fruits onto Logan's bed. The other two Bens produced books Logan hadn't read, stacking them neatly on Logan's trunk. Jace and Bails stood back and watched, Bails looking vaguely uncomfortable.

Logan looked at the offerings, and looked at the other boys, and struggled to comprehend what was happening. Squints finished doctoring his other hand and stepped back, nodding in satisfaction.

"I talked to Ms. Lowell," Jace said. "I asked her to do whatever she could to accelerate our placements. She's gonna call the schools tomorrow. So we can get out of here. As far away as we can get, as soon as possible. Me and you, and Squints is coming with us too."

"If…that's okay," Squints broke in.

It made the hollowness in his chest ache to see Squints so wary of him. "I'm not mad at you, Squints." Logan's voice rasped out raw. "I'm so sorry for yelling and for hurting you."

Squints shrugged, but the transformation on his face as the anxiety cleared was immense. "I'm not hurt," he said casually.

"In the meantime," Bails broke in, "we're all set to do another raid. If you want to get your revenge on some Lapels, we'll help."

Logan frowned at Bails, skepticism coloring his voice. "Bails, you'd rather see the Lapels beat me to a pulp for being gay than help me get revenge on them. Why pretend?"

"That's not true!" Bails said, going pink in the face. "Look, I know I was kind of—I know I had a harder time with, you know, the two of you, but you and Jace are good in my book. I thought about it, and I shouldn't have said that stuff, and I *haven't*, right? Not for weeks. And let's be honest, that shit outside was *fucked* up. That was real villain shit, telling you your parents were dead in front of everybody and not even giving you another request. I—"

"*Bails*," Jace hissed, elbowing the boy hard to shut him up.

Logan waited for the surge of rage or queasiness to hit him, but somehow Bails's blunt restatement of the situation actually made him feel slightly better.

"It *was* fucked up," he said. He reached for the heap of food, the clumsy wrappings around the sacks of ice on his hands catching on the puckered quilting of his blanket.

From the stack, he scooped up a snack cake that looked just like the ones Jace had stolen for his birthday. "I'm surprised this much food made it all the way to me."

"It's all for you," Randy said.

Logan actually laughed at that, a surprised, mirthless bark. For all that he felt hollow, he wouldn't be able to eat even a quarter of that pile. "I don't have much of an appetite. Better if we share." He lay his hands on top of each other in his lap, balancing the cake atop the ice. "And…thank you all, for being willing to help. I don't want to fight any Lapels. I don't want to do anything, really. Just…sleep. And not wake up for a long time. Take some food. Eat it. Please."

They waited long enough to cast questioning looks at Jace and get his nod before they grabbed food, unwrapping and munching, seated all around Logan on his bed but not touching him.

He was so fucking lonely right then. He'd told Jace not to touch him, of course, and Jace seemed to have coached them all before they returned to the room. It was a kindness, something Jace was doing to try to help. But even though it made his skin crawl to think of being touched, without contact, he felt untethered, more isolated than ever.

Logan looked at his cake. His fingers were too bulkily wrapped to open its thin plastic wrapping, so all he could do was stare at it.

Jace's tanned hand reached into his view, gingerly picking up the cake. He hadn't realized how often Jace had touched him in passing, the brush of fingers or a shoulder or an elbow, until Jace was actively trying not to. God, they weren't subtle at all, were they? With a plastic crackle, Jace ripped open the package and held the cake out at mouth level for Logan to take a bite, if he wanted.

Logan looked up past the cake into Jace's face instead. "I'm sorry. We should have asked for the fairs to stop."

"I don't need a handout from the Governor to make that happen," Jace said with a tight-lipped grin. He brushed the cake against Logan's lips. "I was always planning to do it myself. Nothing's changed about that. Eat something, Homeschool." He grimaced suddenly; the nickname was old habit now, but based on the way he flicked a sideways look at Logan, brows upturned and mouth already parted to apologize, he thought it might be out of bounds now.

"Nothing has really changed about my parents either." Logan's shoulders collapsed toward each other, accordioning his chest. It took all his strength not to fold in on himself. "I...don't know why I reacted like that. I already knew. I *knew*. It shouldn't have been so hard to hear."

Jace sat beside him, brushing some food back into the pile and out of his way. He held the cake in the palm of his hand, staring at it. "You've been putting off reacting to it. And you couldn't hold it in anymore. Eat something."

Obediently, Logan took a bite when Jace offered the cake to him again. Although it turned to glue in his mouth, he chewed and swallowed. The skin of his hands ached from the cold.

"I want to go back to sleep," he softly said.

Jace nodded, but he shoved the rest of the cake in Logan's mouth. "Finish this. Then drink some water." He turned to the others. "Everybody take what you want and put the rest in his trunk." A flurry of scoops and grabs, but at least a third of the treats remained in the small pile on Logan's bed. Jace scooped those into the trunk alongside the books they'd brought him.

"Thank you," Logan said to the room. "You didn't have to do any of this."

All the boys muttered something different, so Logan couldn't pick out any of it, but he saw the indignation on their faces at the idea that they wouldn't have done it. Squints, especially, seemed incensed, like Logan was questioning their *right* to do it.

Uncomfortable, Logan tried to work loose the knots Squints had tied and free his hands from the ice. Gently, Jace pushed his fingers aside and untied them. He tossed the ice to Squints. "We'll have more for you when you wake up," he told Logan.

Logan nodded and lay back down, exhaustion crushing him into the mattress.

He blinked, he thought. Just a slow blink, but when he opened his eyes again, it was pitch-black in the room, and the faint rustles and heavy breathing of sleeping boys surrounded him. His bed shook, dipping on one side where someone's weight pressed down next to him.

"What…?" he mumbled, but Jace shushed him quietly.

The curly-haired boy lay next to him, arms and legs wrapping him up completely. He pressed his forehead to Logan's cheek, nuzzling in so his nose dragged a ticklish line along Logan's jaw. "You were making noise. Thought you might be having a bad dream."

Logan didn't remember any dreams, but he felt tracks of cold on his face, one across the bridge of his nose and the other across his temple and into his hair, where tears must have run.

"I told you," Jace continued, "you're not alone. You don't have to figure any of this out alone. I'm with you. We're all with you."

A rush of warmth and, with it, a rush of fear. If he still had people, if he was *not* alone, then he still had more to lose.

"We'll leave this week," Jace whispered. "You and me and Squints. Tycha will be warm. The sun's always out, not like here. We'll get tan. Classes will be easy, so most of the time we'll just explore. Eat something new every day. See if the stars are different that far away."

Logan closed his eyes, letting Jace take him somewhere else, relaxing into the almost unbearably tight grip Jace had on him.

Jace kept whispering, "We'll find Squints a girlfriend, someone sweet, and the four of us will move somewhere by the ocean when we graduate. They'll live right next door to us. Our dogs will be friends. And me and you, we'll sleep late every day and lie in bed like this. We'll get rings made that have each other's names inside and never take them off."

Logan was crying again, silent because he didn't want Jace to stop. It was too idyllic, this fantasy of his. But it was a beautiful,

beautiful dream, so Logan lay there, holding on to Jace's arm with both hands, squeezing in against him more tightly, and letting Jace fill his head with dangerous, insidious, deadly hope.

# 12

## WHAT MUST BE DONE

Logan sat silently through his classes the next morning and through lunch. He didn't say a word during his library chore rotation, and when he headed to Ms. Lowell's office to serve his time there, he didn't expect to speak to her either.

She was on the phone when he came in.

"...starting until the spring? But I spoke to your registrar about—yes, I understand. Mm-hmm. I was told a slot had opened for the fall semester." There was silence on Lowell's end as she listened, and then, "Have you *looked* at his scores? If anyone is deserving of—" She sighed sharply. "Yes, I'll hold."

Impatiently, the Eagle dean tapped her nails on her walnut desk, and her teeth worried her lower lip. Logan sat in his usual seat and fiddled with the straps of his backpack, trying not to seem like he was listening. He heard the tinny voice on the other end when someone picked back up, though he couldn't make out the words.

Ms. Lowell listened in for a moment, then said, "Yes, I know that. I asked if—" She laughed a little abruptly. "Well, you know how boys are. Once they're ready to go, they can't wait. Mm-hmm. Yes. What if—ah, yes." After a pause in which the other person spoke very rapidly, Ms. Lowell gasped. "Yes? Are you sure? That's… that's wonderful! Yes, of course!" She half stood, then sat back down. "Yes, immediately. You'll send the confirmation to—wonderful!"

She threw an absolutely delighted look in Logan's direction, the smile huge on her face, and he found himself smiling faintly back at her in echo, though he didn't understand what was happening. Then she focused back on her call. "All right, if that's settled, I need you to confirm the other two registrations. Quintz—that's a T-Z at the end—and Cardot, C-A-R-D-O-T."

Logan jerked, and then realization dawned on him. Jace had gotten in. The best, most exclusive engineering program on the continent, and he'd gotten in. Some emotion he didn't expect swelled in his chest, and it took him a moment to recognize it as joy. Jace was right—his hopes weren't crazy; they were coming true.

"Yes, slated for anthropology. Perfect. And the other—"

Her smile dropped a little as someone spoke on the other end of the line, and the edges of Logan's joy prickled, then burned. Something was wrong.

"What do you *mean* rejected? I *just* spoke to the registrar last week, and his acceptance was a nonissue." She paused, listened. "On *our* side? I didn't put any—" She cut off abruptly, a tremor running through her that wiped all trace of happiness off her face. "On whose authority?" she asked flatly. "Yes, I *will* be following up. I have to make a call on my end, but please don't give that spot away. *Please.* This is a mistake. Thank you. Goodbye."

She didn't even put the handset down, just pressed the switch hook down and started dialing. Logan tried to ask her what was going on, but she held up a hand. "Yes, hello. This is Miranda Lowell from Childers Coast. I need to check the placement status of a student here. Logan Cardot. Yes, that's correct. Of course, I'll hold."

Ms. Lowell turned to look at him with the handset clutched to her face, and whatever she saw in his face made her reach across the desk and grab his arm, squeeze it. He wasn't sure any gesture could've frightened him more. Something was very, very wrong. All the hope Jace had filled him with began to sour, to stew. He wasn't going to Tycha. He wasn't going to live in the sun with the love of his life, eating pastries and speaking new languages. He knew it, like he had known his parents were dead. He knew it to his core, but he still watched Ms. Lowell with dread and a sliver—a shred—of hope.

"I'm here," Ms. Lowell said into the phone. Whatever the person on the other end of the line said, it drew…a sound out of Ms. Lowell. Not a gasp, not a groan, but something awful in between, a breaking sound. "Why? *Why?* Does it give a reason?"

There were tears in her hazel eyes, thunderclouds on her face. Her lips ground against each other as she held her silence, listening. The pressure built until she burst out with, "He's a *fucking child!*" She exhaled sharply, shakily. "I'm sorry, I know. This isn't your fault. Thank you for…for checking for me." She listened again, then bleakly said, "Yeah," and dropped the receiver into its cradle with a slam.

Her hands pressed into her face hard, like she was trying to crush the tears back out of sight. Logan knew he was crying already. His entire body was numb, but it buzzed like a colony of bees had taken up residence inside him. He didn't seem to be sitting on a surface anymore; he floated, somehow too heavy to move and untethered from the earth entirely.

Ms. Lowell took a deep breath and dropped her hands. She squeezed Logan's arm again, but he only knew that because he saw her do it; he couldn't feel her at all. "Logan," she said thickly.

"I know." He was surprised by how level, how even his voice came out, though he couldn't seem to speak much more loudly than a whisper. "I'm not going to Tycha. I assume I'm on the…the red-pen list? I think that's what Director Rollins called it."

"Yes," she said.

He nodded. A tear rolled off his chin and splashed against the arm he had clutched to his stomach. "Tell me what the red-pen list means, please."

Ms. Lowell cleared her throat, but her voice came out froggy nonetheless. "Someone on the red-pen list can't cross borders. They aren't permitted to attend university or apply for jobs. They can't rent apartments and can't apply for credit or financial assistance. They're restricted from holding any public office and aren't permitted to have or home children. They are…enemies of the state."

Every word drove Logan deeper into the chair. It was so much worse than he'd imagined. He tried to picture *any* life where he wouldn't need to make money, to *live* somewhere.

Maybe if he was completely dependent on someone else? But if he lived with Jace here, someone would report them. Someone would catch Jace kissing him on the cheek or Logan being too domestic around the house, and then Jace would be red-penned too—or worse.

"I don't understand," he said. "Why a list? Why not just arrest me? Or kill me? From that list, it's clear they want me dead. No one could survive under those restrictions."

Anger rippled over Ms. Lowell's face, so raw and intense that Logan nearly felt the heat from it. "Because," she all but spat, "there is a way *off* the red-pen list. Five years of service in the Hallsburg Special Police Force."

"Oh." Logan stood and turned away from her, pressing his folded hands against his mouth. "Oh." An unhinged laugh bubbled out of him. "I understand."

He turned back around, laughing again. "I understand now. This is why you didn't want me playing rugby or drawing attention. So they wouldn't want me. Because if we don't sign up, they can just say, 'sign up or die in the streets.' I see. Well, I did fuck up *everything* yesterday, didn't I?" Vomit lurched up his throat, but he caught it in his mouth, swallowed it down.

"Let's just," Ms. Lowell said, raising a calming hand, "sit down and talk about this, Mr. Cardot. I'll call Mr. Evans up here and we can talk through the op—"

"No!" Logan snapped. "Don't say a *word* to Jace."

Her eyes widened in surprise. "He has a right to know—"

"*No*," Logan said, more intensely. "You won't say a thing to him. Because you and I both know *exactly* what would happen next. Jace would give up his spot at Durhoss. He'd find a place to live and a thousand ways to keep me alive while he worked and paid rent and did absolutely everything, and I'd be back in hiding, like I have been my entire life. He'd resent me in a week. I'd hate everything about my life, and I'd take it out on him.

"I heard the fucking fights my parents had every night of my life, and they *chose* their circumstances. And what happens when I pull Jace onto the red-pen list too? You think I'd survive putting him on the streets, making him a fugitive? Ruining *both* our lives? I'd fucking kill myself."

Ms. Lowell stood, putting out a hand toward him, but he stumbled out of her reach.

He was shouting, but he couldn't stop himself. "Jace doesn't understand how fucking bleak this world is. And he shouldn't have to. He should go to Tycha and be with his best friend and find out what the fucking stars look like there. And if you tell him what happened to me, he won't. Because he doesn't understand what he's choosing. Because he really thinks there's hope. Yesterday he actually fucking thought he could get my parents back for me. He doesn't understand—" Logan shook, but he wasn't crying anymore; he was a guttering torch of rage.

"But I *do* understand," he said, pounding his chest with a fist. "I know what's gonna happen. I know I'll walk downstairs and sign my fucking life away because I *know* there's no other choice. And if you tell Jace, I *know* he would sign his name right under mine, and he'd become the worst version of himself, and he *can't fucking do that!* I won't let him do that!"

"Logan, please listen," Lowell said, taking his hand between hers. "We will fight this. I will help you. There's no reason for—"

"Stop." Logan pulled his hands out of hers. His fingers shook, but it was hard to tell when he balled them into fists. "You can't help me. You can't save me. But I know what has to be done, and I'm gonna do it. I'm gonna go downstairs and save Jace. And I need you to promise me that you *won't* tell him where I've gone or why."

"That isn't fair to either of you."

"Yeah," Logan said, that deranged laugh breaking through again. "But he won't let me go if he knows. Jace has already proven he won't make the choice that *must* be made. So I'm not gonna give him the choice. Promise me you won't tell him."

Beneath the heartbreak, Ms. Lowell looked mulish. Logan pressed. "Do I not have a right to privacy? These are the details of *my* life, and no one else is owed them."

Her jaw flexed, eyes narrowing, and he knew he'd struck a chord. "You…do have that right, Mr. Cardot," she said tightly.

"Thank you." He yanked open the door and stormed out.

He knew what he had to do, but every step toward his fate felt like walking naked into the fires of hell. Jace first or the Lapels?

It had to be the Black Lapels first. He had to do something he couldn't take back; he knew once he looked Jace in the face, he'd lose his resolve. Swallowing hard, every line of him vibrating with suppressed fury, he made his way to the office next to Director Rollins's where the recruiters had set up shop.

Sergeant Spears was there, seated behind a folding table beside a younger Lapel, and the smile he turned up to Logan was too knowing, almost smug. "Ah, Mr. Cardot. Good to see you again. What can I help you with? Come for that certificate after all?"

Anger almost burned Logan to ash. His body tightened as half of him tried to step farther into the room, half to turn and leave instantly. He swallowed, loosened his hands, fought himself forward.

"I've come," he dragged past strained vocal cords and clenched teeth, "to sign up."

"Very good!" Spears said, his predatory smile widening. "Come, have a look at your options." He spread a brochure out on the table and pointed to one of the panels. "Our interior forces do the fine work of keeping our children and communities safe within Hallsburg. They support CRS and also do the day-to-day police field work. You'll be familiar with them."

Logan clenched the edge of the table until blades of pain stabbed up through his wrist. "Not that," he managed to say flatly.

Spears paused, licked his finger, and turned to another panel, pointing at the exotic-looking illustrations there. "In that case, you may be more interested in our peacekeeping arm. Peacekeepers se-cure our borders and work across the continent ensuring Hallsburg-ian interests are represented in every nation."

"I'm a PK," the younger officer said, leaning in with an enthu-siasm so guileless that Logan knew he had no idea of the currents between Logan and Spears, and must not be able to read the waves of rage coming off of Logan either. "It's pretty neat. You get to see a lot of different places. Nobody speaks Hallsburgian, which gets kind of annoying, but you get a lot of freedom to take care of problems the way you want, you know?"

Spears shot the younger officer a look, and he flushed pink and cleared his throat. "I just mean, it's a pretty good station."

"What are you good at, Cardot?" Spears asked. "What are you interested in?"

*Nothing you could possibly offer me.* "Languages," he spat out. "I speak a lot. Freelan, Thoglin, Old Dunisian, Tychan."

"Damn," the younger Lapel said. "The PKs are perfect for you then. We're always looking for silvertongues—you know, translators. You could probably advance pretty fast."

Logan closed his eyes, took a deep breath. A translator. That didn't sound *so* bad. When he opened his eyes again, Spears held out a pen to him. "How do I sign up to be a translator then," Logan said, too flat to be a question despite the words.

"You fill this out right here." Spears placed the tip of the pen on the first line of the form and tilted it toward Logan so all he had to do was put his fingers around it. "The aptitude test will help us find the right place for you, along with the preferences you list here."

When Logan didn't take the pen, didn't move, Spears shifted the paper and placed the pen on the bottom line. "If you'd like, I can fill this out for you. I've already got all your information." It sounded like a threat. "All I need is your signature, right here."

*I know what has to be done,* Logan thought. *This has to be done.*

He took the pen, cool and heavy as a knife handle in his palm.

He signed.

They tried to congratulate him, tried to shake his hand, but he recoiled from them. "Can I go tonight?" he asked.

Spears raised an eyebrow and chuckled. "An eager beaver, huh? We've got a truck heading back to Norford later this afternoon. If you can meet us out front in about an hour, you can catch a ride and start immediately."

Logan nodded and left without another word.

He'd done it: he'd made the first irreparable tear in the pretty tapestry of dreams Jace had woven for them. Now to cut the rest of the ties that bound them.

There was no way to convince Jace to leave him behind. No way to leave their relationship intact across the distance. And he wouldn't condemn Jace to a lifetime of hiding their true natures, to starvation in the streets if they misstepped. Not for anything.

He found Jace emerging from the basement, brushing dust from his hands and hair. Jace lit up when he saw Logan walking with purpose, but his brows drew down again when Logan grabbed his arm, pulling him toward an exit. "Walk with me."

"Okay," Jace said. "Is everything…I mean, did something—?" He clammed up as younger kids trotted by, then kept his silence until they were outside past the locker room, standing in the long grass between the practice fields and the trees of the outer grounds.

Logan released him, trying to control his breathing, trying to find the words to say.

"Okay, talk," Jace said. "What the hell's going on?"

The wind was strong out here, tossing Jace's curls wildly around his face as he studied Logan.

Logan looked down at his hands as if they could offer assistance. The bile he'd fought down earlier clawed and burned at his throat. "I…think…"

He couldn't bring himself to say it. It wasn't too late yet. If he told Jace what had happened, he wouldn't have to serve those five years alone. A selfish, horrible part of him reared its head, tried to stop him from saying what he'd come here to say. But then Jace would be trapped with him; Jace would be changed; and all that potential and opportunity would be wasted. *Jace* would be wasted.

He took a deep breath, preparing for the plunge, then said everything in a rush. "I think we should break up. Sorry. It's been great, but—I think we should break up."

At once, he turned to leave, hoping Jace wouldn't follow. But Jace didn't even let him get a step away before he'd grabbed him back. "Whoa, what? What the hell are you talking about?"

The curly-haired boy spun Logan around, one hand on his shoulder and the other on his wrist. "Where is this coming from? Are you…are you mad about yesterday? I'm sorry. I didn't think what it would—I just wanted a chance for you to see your family again. That's all."

"Let go of me," Logan said, his voice low and level. "People might be watching."

Jace blinked, then drew his hands back. "Is that what this is about? Are you afraid we haven't been careful enough? Or…did something happen? We can fight it, whatever it is. We'll fight it, you and me, together."

He was drowning, lungs burning as they filled with water, able to see the light above him but swimming deeper. "Nothing happened," he choked out. "It's…I'm done with this. With us. Those things you talked about last night…hearing them made me realize I don't want this anymore. I'm tired of being in your shadow. I don't want to follow along in your wake like Squints. I'm not good enough for you, and I'm done with being your pity fuck."

Again, he turned to walk away—*please, just let me walk away, Jace, don't chase*—but Jace ran around in front of him to intercept him. "Wait, please. Stop trying to walk away. What do you mean, you're not *good enough* for me? You're amazing. I'm crazy about you. Pity doesn't begin to factor into it."

"You're the king of the school. You're gonna go off and do incredible, brilliant things. I'm holding you back, okay? You could've made all your dreams come true yesterday, but instead I dragged you to hell with me. I'm not worth it. Please, let's just end this."

"I decide if you're worth it," Jace said. There was cold command in his voice, but Logan knew it was a veneer. Jace was shaken and trying not to show it. "*I* decide that. And you're worth *everything*, Logan. Please look at me. Look at me! You're not holding anything back. I want you. Just you, forever. Please."

This wasn't working. Logan felt his control of the situation slipping. He had to commit; he had to end it. He had to lie.

"Fine," he said. His voice was rough with the effort of not giving in, not crying, not apologizing. He closed his eyes so he wouldn't have to see Jace's face. "I didn't want to have to say this, but…fine. It's you. You're not enough for me."

Jace half laughed, an incredulous noise. "What?"

Logan opened his eyes again so he could assess the effect his next words had. "I need someone who can be honest with me. I need someone who can let me have a say in my own life, my own relation-ship—someone who doesn't *have* to control everything."

The pure, awful shock on Jace's face was gutting to watch. Gone was his surety, his confidence; in an instant, he became some-one Logan didn't recognize.

"I…I can be honest. I've *been* honest with you. But I'll be… and I don't have to—I'll back off, okay? I'll be what you need me to be. Please don't walk away from me. *Stop*, Logan, please!" He grabbed Logan's arm again, his fingers shaking as hard as his voice. "I'll be whatever you need me to be."

"You can't," Logan said. He tried to harden his voice, but the catch in his throat betrayed him. He pried Jace's hand off him, then stepped back out of range.

"I *can!* I'll do whatever I—"

Logan raised his voice over him, unable to bear Jace begging. "Tell me you love me."

Utter silence dropped between them like the deaf moments after an explosion. There were tears in Jace's blue eyes. *I made him cry. Again. I made the person I love most in the world beg me to stay and cry.* Logan was tearing apart. But he *had* to do this. He was saving Jace.

"You know what—" Jace's eyes begged Logan to back down, to ask anything else of him, but Logan ground his teeth until he heard his jaw crack and stared unblinkingly back.

Hesitantly, Jace said, "You know that I do. I like you, I want you, I *need* you. Please don't make me—no! Wait, please! Please don't leave me. Don't leave me, Logan. I can—I…love—"

Logan cut him off with a raised hand, a sharp motion Jace actually flinched from. "This shouldn't be a struggle, Jace. I love you. I really thought there was nothing wrong with you. But now I see you're damaged goods. All those pretty dreams you made up were just fantasies, lies. You can't love me. You're broken, and it's not fair to me to have to fix you."

Jace's mouth hung slack with true speechlessness, and Logan hated it. He couldn't bear to look at Jace *believing* him.

*It's all lies!* He wanted to shriek. *You know better than this! You know you're not broken! You know I'd follow you off the face of the earth if I could!*

To stop himself from saying it, to escape Jace's desperate shock and horror, he turned and finally walked away, faster with each step until he was almost running back into the school. In his wake, he left shouts and irritated grunts as he shoved people aside.

He had to get away.

Away, away, away from this place and those things he'd said and the face Jace had made when he'd said them.

He plowed through the front doors before sitting on the steps to wait for the Black Lapel truck. At least with them, everything could be a lie. It would have to be: they'd hate him if they knew anything about him at all.

He'd have to stay secret, stay nobody. But at least he wouldn't get to know anyone, see their heart and show them his own in return, then break it. He could simply be a shadow.

By the time Spears met him out front, he had pressed everything down into a compact ball inside. He didn't cry. He didn't emote. His hands didn't shake. They didn't even hurt really.

He was a shell, a shadow. He was nothing.

"Not bringing anything with you?" Spears asked, gesturing to Logan's empty hands.

Logan shook his head. What did he even have? Nothing worth bringing to the next five years. Nothing worth going back to the dorm and risking a meeting with Jace or his boys.

Numbly, he climbed into the truck and watched the buildings of ChilCo grow smaller, the grounds crowding in on them, boys becoming small and then specks and then invisible through the trees.

For the second time in his life, Logan was carried away from home by Black Lapels, leaving behind anything he'd ever considered family, leaving behind everything he'd hoped for his future, leaving behind his heart and his lungs and all the pieces and parts of him love had carved out for someone else.

How much could he lose before he wasn't a person anymore, before the pieces strewn across Hallsburg made up more of him than the walking shell did? He had nothing left to give.

He had nothing left but a seed of hate and the burning, all-consuming commitment to do what had to be done.

# Epilogue

## JACE, WASTED

Jace paced slowly behind the leather chair he was meant to occupy across from Dr. Roselle, swinging his legs in wide arcs as he put one foot in front of the other since there was too little room for long strides, concentrating on his shoelaces so he wouldn't have to look at the therapist's knowing face.

She waited patiently for him to get bored enough to answer the question, and eventually, with a sigh, he did.

"*Purpose.* I suppose you're not looking for the dictionary definition of the word," he said, shooting her a wry glance.

"Oh, I suspect you could define it in at least three languages," Roselle said, eyes sparkling with suppressed amusement. "But I'm not sure that would help you understand what *you* are in need of." Her Tychan accent softened the hard edges of the words, but her tone was firm. She wouldn't let Jace wriggle free.

"Maybe it would," Jace said, pursuing any conversational avenue that led away from the things he'd felt he was meant to do but no longer could—that way lay Logan, and he'd rather die than discuss Logan with this woman, or anyone else, for that matter. "Let's see: in Hallsburgian, purpose means 'the particular use for which something was designed.' So far, I've proven myself a deft hand at emptying liquor bottles. Maybe the best anyone's ever seen at it. So that could be my purpose." He smirked at her, wondering if she'd let that lie.

Not a chance. With exceptional dryness, she said, "The hospital visit suggests your mind, at least, is not designed for the party life. Try again. Think of your strengths."

"God, Doc, I'm good at everything, haven't you heard?" Jace said bitterly. "How's a man supposed to narrow it down?"

"You do have many strengths," she said mildly, not rising to the bait of debating his imposter syndrome again. "If you're not called in a particular direction by a skill, then perhaps consider your passions, the things you feel strongly about."

What did he feel strongly about? Protecting Squints and his new friends. Being someone new, stripped of all his ChilCo baggage. Missing Lo—no, *no*, not missing him. *Forgetting* Logan. As if that were possible.

And then, of course, there was the thing he felt strongest about, after that horrific run-in with the soldiers: *hating* the monstrous fucking Black Lapels.

"I want to graduate top of my class and be a great engineer, building things that make people happy," Jace said. A perfect answer.

"Nice try," Dr. Roselle said. "You were already on that path before the attempt. It was not enough to keep you here. It may be your future job, but it is not your *purpose*. Stop searching for the answer you want me to hear and tell me what you actually think. Like we've practiced: blurt out your first instinct."

"See, if I tell you my actual first instinct, you're going to write down in that little notebook there that I'm still suicidal, and then I'll never be free of these *delightful* little sessions," Jace said with a vicious grin, more of a mirthless baring of teeth.

"The goal of therapy is not to escape therapy," Dr. Roselle repeated for perhaps the dozenth time, her constant script. "If you're still suicidal, Jace, we need to address that."

"I was never suicidal," Jace said, repeating *his* script for the dozenth time too, knowing she didn't believe a word and maintaining the lie smirkingly anyway. "It was an accident."

"Purpose, Jace," Roselle said firmly, steering them back. "What drives you forward? What keeps you focused on the future, on maintaining your own health and safety so you can achieve your goals? What change do you want to make in the world?"

*I want Logan back. I want to be where he is, where I'm* supposed *to be. I want to stop feeling so wrong all the goddamn time.* He couldn't say that. He would never let her put Logan Cardot's name in that notebook. So, fine, he'd say the suicidal thing.

"I want every Black Lapel occupying Tycha gone."

Dr. Roselle's brows twitched upward, but she kept her voice even as she prompted, "Gone?"

Jace raised a brow at her. "You think I'm going to tell you what I actually want to do to them, so you can write down *danger to himself and others?* I want them gone. I want their boots off the necks of the people here. Let's just imagine together that I want them all to retire peacefully to their little homes in Hallsburg, never to darken Tycha's doorway again."

"If you truly wanted them to retire peacefully, after what you've told me they did to your friend, I would find that more concerning than thoughts of violence," Roselle said dryly. "You want to fight them? You're only one man—going toe-to-toe with armed soldiers seems unwise. But you're bright, charismatic. You could become a politician with the goal of negotiating their exit from the country. That would be more likely to actually remove them from Tycha in a meaningful way, don't you think?"

Jace glanced down at the floor, smirking. He *was* going to fight Lapels, but he certainly wouldn't go toe-to-toe with them in the streets. He was going to do what he did best: build something that destroyed them all.

He could do it. He'd designed bombs before.

"Sure, Doc. A politician. Sounds like a purpose to me."

# Acknowledgements

It takes a special kind of community to write books that make people deeply care about characters and then make those characters miserable until their eventual happy ending. It requires the sort of people who will talk to you like your imaginary friends are real, flesh-and-blood humans you both know.

My fantastic editor, Angela Brown, is one of those people, and her faith in this series and help in polishing it to a shine were absolutely indespensable.

My sister is another. Our text messages are packed with years worth of crying selfies she sent me so I could fully understand the weight of what I'd done to her with the narrative, and there is no one fonder or more protective of my wanted boys.

My husband and his lifelong friends both showed me what men caring about each other could look like and extended that care to me and to my stories, and I will always be grateful.

Thank you to my friends and beta readers who hoped and feared and gasped and cried and rejoiced with Jace and Logan, who asked the sort of questions and made the sort of demands that shaped a world where these boys could fall in love and fight back.

semcpherson.com
For more of the wanted boys, Jace and Logan,
and for other series from S. E. McPherson

**The Wanted Boys Series**
Wanted Boys
*Wasted Boys (Nov 2026)*
*War Boys (June 2027)*
*Wicked Boys (Nov 2027)*
*Worthy Boys (June 2028)*

**The Heart-Mage Trilogy**
A King's Trust
A Villain's Hope
*A Queen's Lament (Mar 2027)*

## About the Author

S. E. McPherson has been a writer of speculative fiction since they were eight years old, binding books with a hole punch and tied yarn. While they took a brief two-decade detour into the career of a marketing executive and won many boring business writing awards, they've found their way back to storytelling and illustration. Their debut novel *A King's Trust* was named to Kirkus Reviews' Top 100 Best Indie Books of 2025 and Best LGBTQ+ Indies of 2025.

*semcpherson.com | @semcpherson_writes | @semcpherson.bsky.social*